Peter Longley was brought up in southeast England and educated at Tonbridge School in the 1950s before reading theology at Cambridge. In 1965, he spent the summer as a kibbutznik in Israel. From 1967–1977, he was the estate manager of Tullamaine Castle in Ireland, which was then American-owned, and it took him to Georgia, USA, where in 1978 he went to sea as a ship's artist. Later, he became a cruise director with Royal Viking Line, and in 1989, he joined Cunard as the cruise director of *Queen Elizabeth 2*, where he met his Bavarian-born German wife. Cruise ships took him all over the world in the 1980s and 1990s until he retired and became the horticultural interpreter of the Springfeld Botanical Garden in Missouri, USA. He started writing novels in 1978, and he returned to England in 2017.

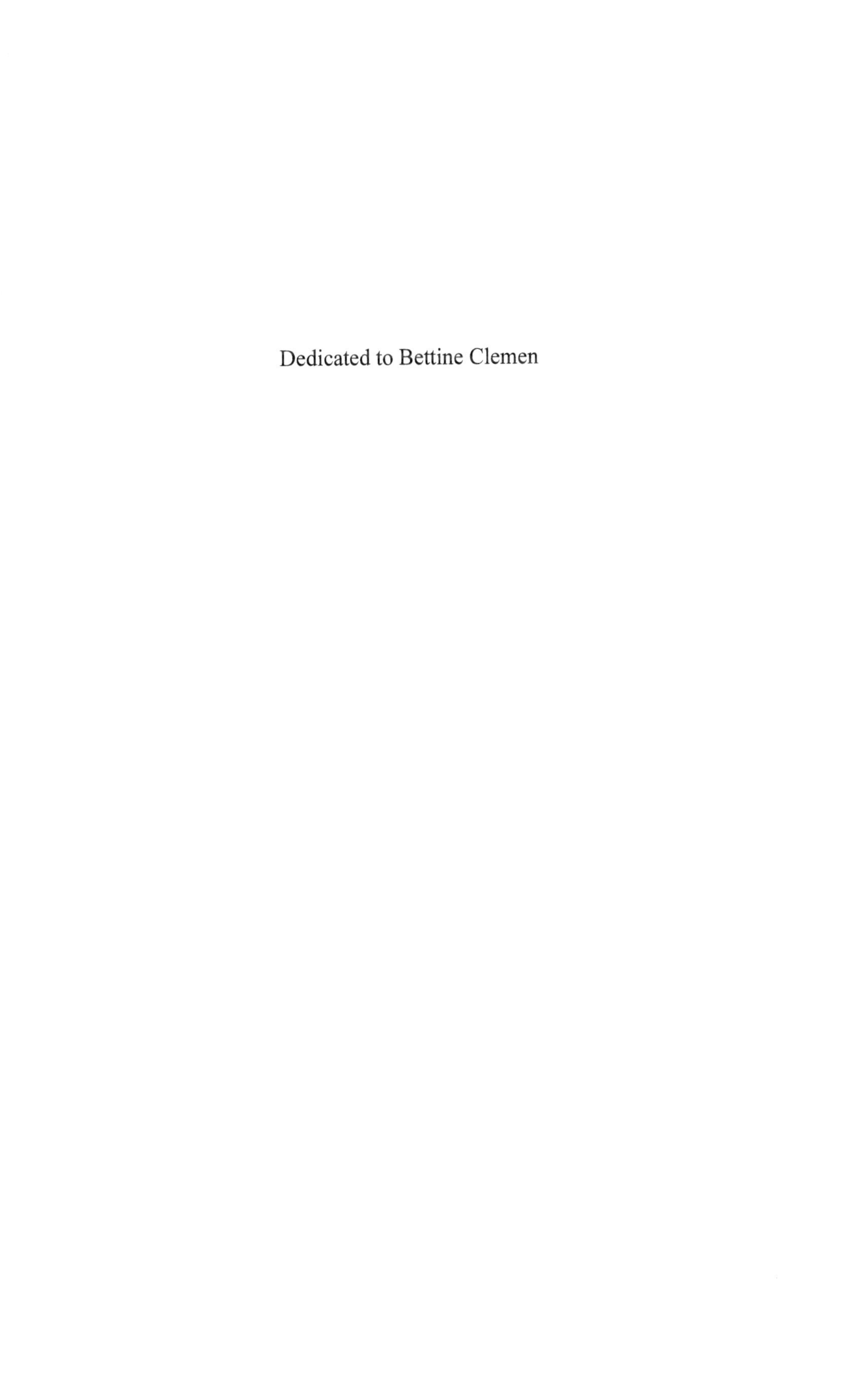

Dedicated to Bettine Clemen

Peter Longley

WHEN THE COWS COME HOME

AUSTIN MACAULEY PUBLISHERS™

LONDON * CAMBRIDGE * NEW YORK * SHARJAH

A CIP catalogue record for this title is available from the British Library.

ISBN 9781035859825 (Paperback)
ISBN 9781035859832 (Hardback)
ISBN 9781035859849 (ePub e-book)

www.austinmacauley.com

First Published 2024
Austin Macauley Publishers Ltd®
1 Canada Square
Canary Wharf
London
E14 5AA

I am indebted to Julia Boyd for her amazing research into the lives of ordinary German people during the years of the Third Reich as recorded in her two books, *Travellers in the Third Reich* and *A Village in the Third Reich*. That village is Oberstdorf, in Swabia, close to the borders of Austria and Switzerland.

My principal characters are fictitious in this historical saga, but part of the background to life in Oberstdorf that I portray, I owe to the detailed historical research made by Julia Boyd and Angelika Patel.

I was fortunate enough to meet Julia Boyd shortly after the publication of *Travellers in the Third Reich* at an Historical Association branch dinner in London in 2019.

I am also indebted to my ex-wife, Bettine Clemen, a Bavarian by birth, who has introduced me to her amazing corner of Upper Bavaria—Berchtesgadenland. Berchtesgaden has become my second home. My frequent visits to Bettine living on the Obersalzberg above Berchtesgaden, became the inspiration for this story.

Finally, I am indebted to have been privileged to see the sun rise and set in the mountains of Bavaria, to hear the sound of the cowbells and the beauty of the first snows. When I am there I see mighty Watzmann every day. In the forests, woods and meadows I smell the pine and see the alpine flowers, and in the lakes I see the reflections in the still glacial waters. In the valley below, I hear the church bells of Berchtesgaden. I am inspired by it all in my love for these people.

Table of Contents

The Families

THE MOELLER FAMILY

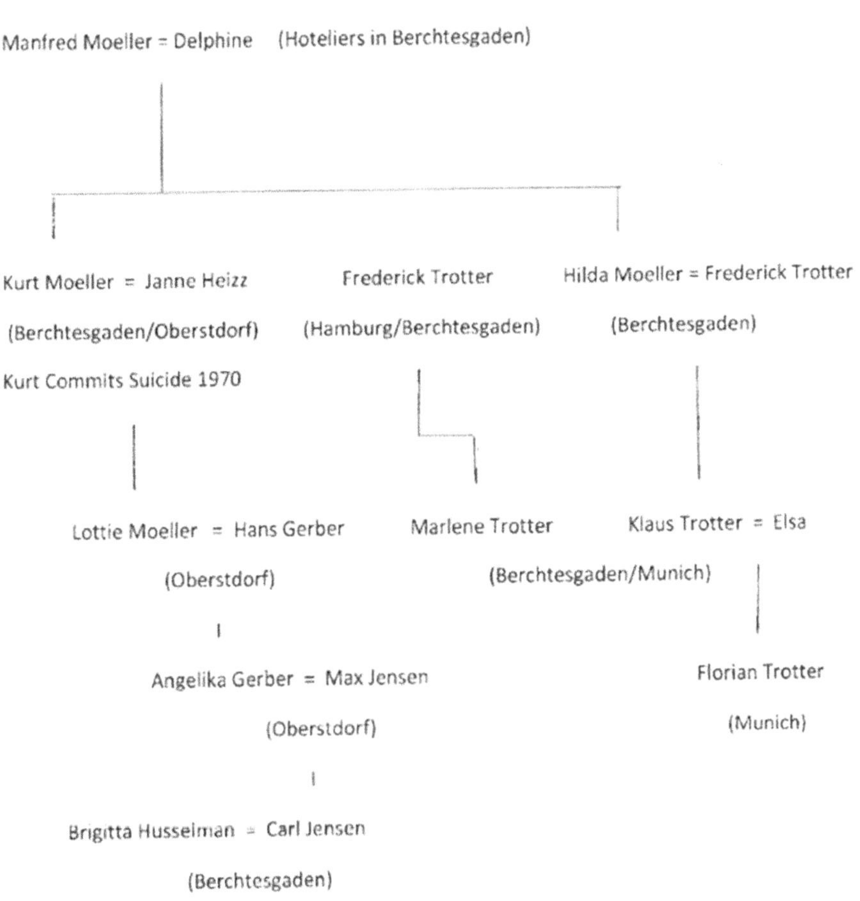

THE FINKELSTEIN FAMILY

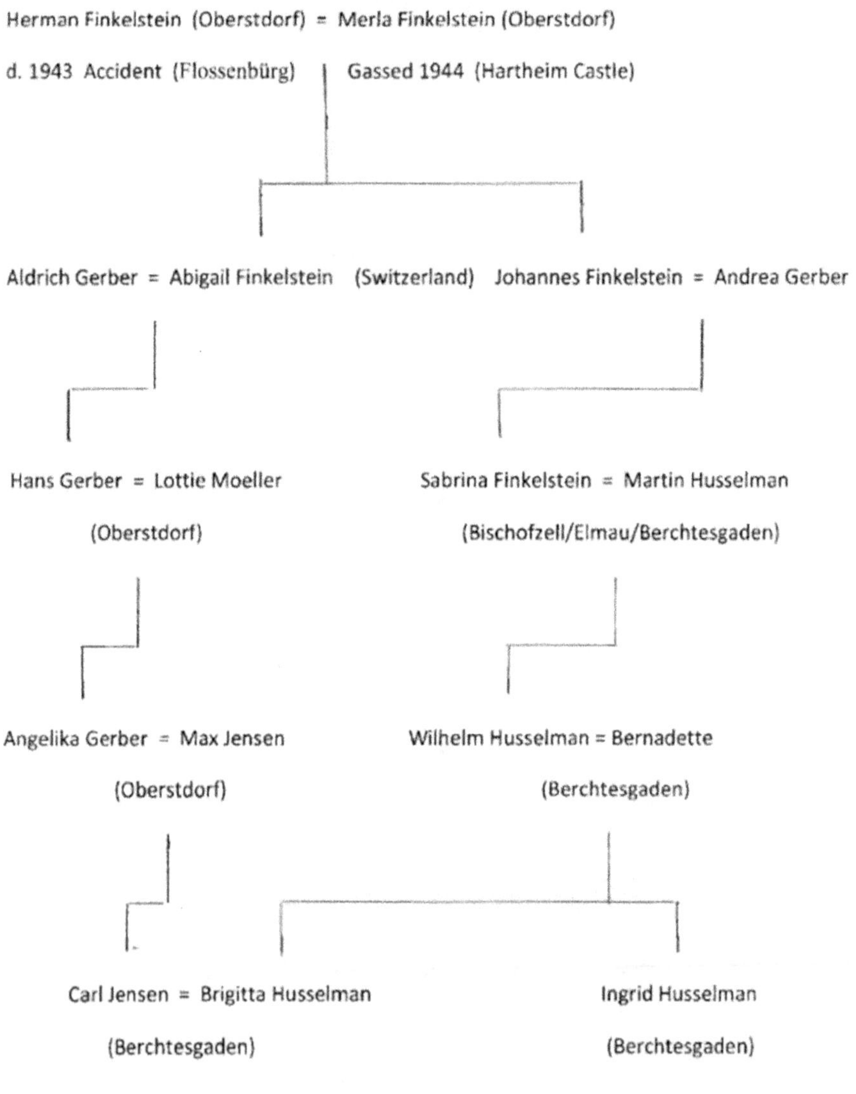

THE TROTTER FAMILY

Alfred Trotter = Ursula Trotter

(Hamburg)

Killed at work in 1945 Firebombing | Killed in 1943 Firebombing of Hamburg

(Hamburg) Eugenie = Frederick Trotter = Hilda Moeller (Berchtesgaden)

Killed in 1943 Firebombing

Marlene Trotter

(Hamburg/Berchtesgaden/Munich)

Klaus Trotter = Elsa Homberg

(Berchtesgaden/Munich)

Florian Trotter

(Munich)

THE GERBER FAMILY

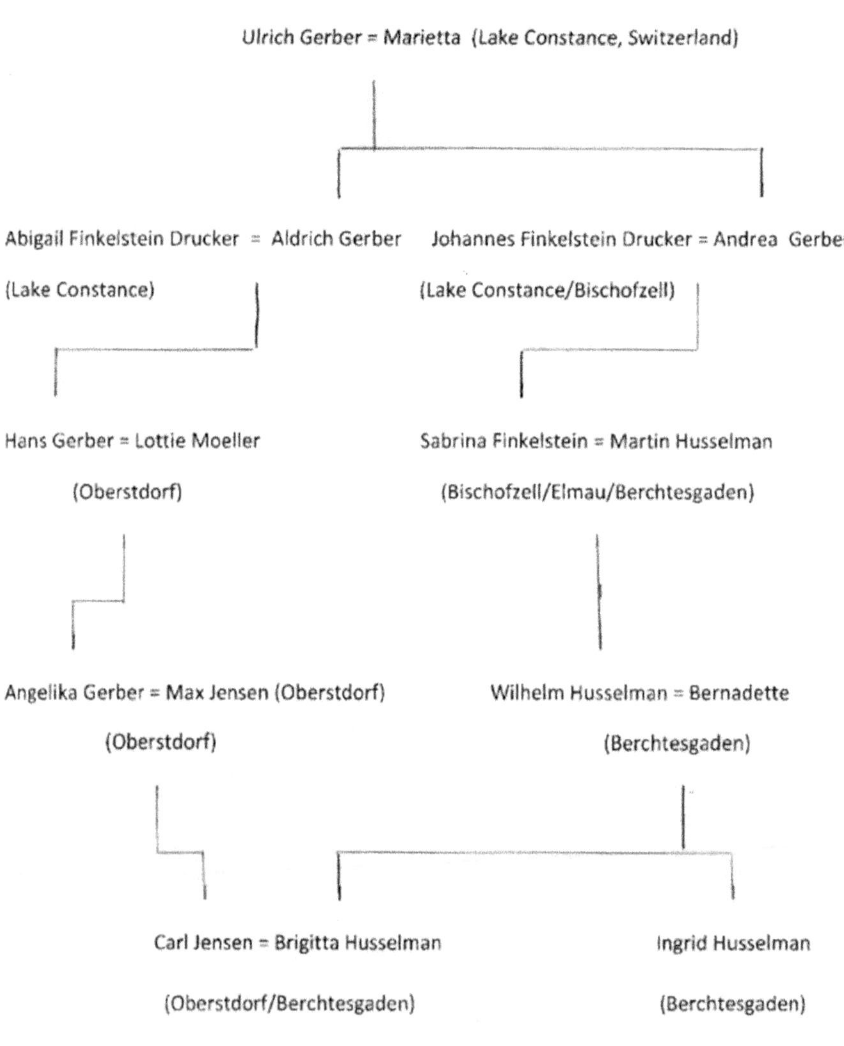

Chapter One
The Cows Come Home 2019

Brigitta Husselman pulled her arms through the fleeced sleeves of her anorak and wrapped the garment around her. Her rosy cheeks reflected the damp cold as she leaned back against the flat ferry's rail that separated the cowherds from their livestock. *Nice,* she thought as she felt the warmth of her cow's breath on the back of her neck as it nuzzled her. The lake was shrouded in mist as she stared ahead, the pontoon parting the smooth waters in long low ripples to either side. The engine chugged and the cow bells clanged, their sounds echoing off the grey cliffs of the Königssee.

Brigitta's boots were muddy from the slurry outside the Alpine hut where she, her sister Ingrid and her father had spent the night. The lower skirts of her Dirndl were splattered. Her younger sister looked up at Brigitta with wide eyes— it was Ingrid's first time rounding up the cows. A ray of autumnal sun filtered through the mist and lit the straw colour of the young girl's plaits. "Our crown's going to be the best," Ingrid said. "Purple, white and gold, it's much prettier than Carl's pink and black."

Brigitta smiled. She knew Ingrid was teasing her. She reflected on the long summer with Carl—making hay, picking berries and swimming in the moonlight at Hintersee. *My, was that cold, but Carl kept me warm.*

Increasing sunlight broke through the mist as they passed the great waterfall tumbling down the steep mountainside on their right. Ingrid looked up at her sister. "You know what my friend said in school, 'Hitler and Eva Braun went skinny-dipping there'."

Brigitta blushed, enhancing her rosy cheeks even more.

The mist then parted ahead to reveal a blue sky and caused the autumnal trees on Christlieger Island to sparkle in different stages of yellow, green and brown.

The cows bellowed as if they knew they were coming home. The brass of their bells glinted in the sudden brightness.

"You take Arabella off with you first," her father said. "Mutter will be ready to belt and headdress her, but you will have to lead her."

"What about me?" Ingrid asked with appealing eyes.

"You can help Briggita…Mutter and I will bring the other two."

As the cow ferry eased towards the Königssee slipway, the other farm girls in their Dirndls and the lads in Lederhosen joined with the seasoned Bavarian farmers to greet the awaiting tourists crowding the foreshore. They all knew this time-honoured Alpine ceremony was a popular annual event, and the cold discomfort of the Alpine meadows in the mist that had greeted them earlier had given way to a warm autumnal sun. The cobbled square was full of people waiting in anticipation, eating crêpes and drinking beer. Ever so slowly, the ferry eased its forward flap into the slipway. Brigitta's and Ingrid's mother was there, already holding Arabella's crown and belt. The gold glittered above the bands of purple and white.

As soon as Brigitta had Arabella ashore, her mother approached, holding the ungainly crown. Brigitta's mother's face was leathery and bronzed compared with her oldest daughter's rosy-cheeked porcelain skin. Her uncle took the lead rope and held Arabella's horns, as mother and daughter strapped the crown to the cow's halter. Every time Arabella shook her head in resistance, the great cow bell rang out as it jangled beneath her neck.

Task accomplished, Brigitta turned to the crowd of onlookers. A smile crossed her face as she looked up at the crown now rising upwards from its engraved leather mount blazoned between Arabella's horns. Hours had been spent sewing those ribboned flowers in white and purple—the family colours of their small herd of Hinterwälders. These cows were a fast-disappearing breed, but Brigitta's family had proudly kept them going for three generations. The warm rays had also now dried the mud from the fringes of Brigitta's skirt. The tourists took their photographs. Ingrid joined her sister and tried to reach for the crown. Arabella shook her head and pawed one foot at the cobble stones.

"Be careful, Ingrid!" Brigitta said. "She doesn't like that."

Their mother was now busy with her father crowning the other three Hinterwälders. The pen where they were waiting was filling up as different farming families proudly dressed their cows, marking the end of the long summer months grazing up in the Alpine meadows above the Obersee.

Brigitta watched as Carl Jensen struggled with his cow's horns. She laughed, but Carl was too fixed on his task to respond. Soon, the cows would race through the village in a stampede until they reached the road beyond. Leading through the Schönau Valley, it would take them home to their winter meadows and sheds.

Arabella was the first cow out of the gate with Brigitta holding onto her lead for all she was worth, but Carl and his cow, in that pink and black headdress, were close behind. Ingrid looked back at him shouting, "We were first out of the gate! I bet we get home first."

Moments later, there was a crash. Brigitta turned around. Carl's cow had hurtled into a stand of tourist trinkets outside the Königssee Dirndl Shop. The rather prim lady, Frau Forster, who kept the shop, was frantically waving her arms, hoping that the cow wouldn't come through the doorway itself. The sound of clattering hooves behind Arabella, however, drowned out the commotion. More of Brigitta's attention was taken by the wolf whistles of some of her Berchtesgaden teenage school friends cheering her on. Ingrid laughed as Arabella pooped a large cowpat that splattered on the cobbles right in front of the lads. The cows clattered on to the cheers of the tourists.

Once the cows had made their way out of the village, they settled down, ambling along the Schönau road and sniffing the air knowing that they were home. People ran to watch them until the cows separated to follow the paths to their various farms and winter pastures.

Brigitta and Ingrid led Arabella down the track leading to the Husselman farmstead—a wooden chalet building with balconies still overflowing with late petunias and geraniums. Their parents were close behind them with the other two cows, and in the farmyard, to the obvious joy of the cows, those awkward crowns and belts were removed. The Hinterwälders were let loose into their pasture to return to their customary life of chewing the cud.

"You did well," Brigitta Husselman's mother Bernadette said, "but now, both of you, into the bath. You have mass tonight at the Stiftkirche. We can't have you smelling like a cattle byre."

Brigitta and Ingrid were the incense bearers for Father Johannes at the Stiftskirche church attached to the old ducal palace in Berchtesgaden. The palace was still owned by the Wittelsbach family, Bavaria's secular rulers, and since Napoleonic times, its kings until 1918. It was rumoured locally that they had never signed abdication to the Bavarian throne at the end of the First World War, but that wasn't taken very seriously. Now known as the Duke of Bavaria, Franz

Bonaventura Wittelsbach spent a brief period of the summer every year in Berchtesgaden when his roses were at their best.

* * *

Wilhelm Husselman drove his daughters into Berchtesgaden where they ran into the Stiftkirche vestry to get robed up for their ceremonial role. Wilhelm and Bernadette took their place inside the large, cold and rather dark church. It was the evening of the autumnal harvest festival. One of the ladies of the altar guild was still lighting the candles and adjusting the piles of fruit and vegetables among the flowers in front of a statue of the Virgin Mary to the right of the lower altar. A priest checked the large open bible on the lectern to the altar's left before adjusting the host in its gilded tabernacle on the high altar. All was ready. People started to fill up the pews in the chancel and the main body of the church as the coming dusk took light away from the tall clear windows. Sharp at 6:00 p.m., a bell rang, and the lights came on illuminating the sanctuary area, enriching the gilding and coloured marbles of the high altar. The clergy, altar boys, and Brigitta and Ingrid dressed in rich red cassocks and white embroidered surplices and ruffs, appeared from behind the reredos. Brigitta was swinging the large silver censer from which wafts of incense arose, while her sister carried the pot beside her in which the precious aromatic substance was stored. As the acolytes took their seats in front of the high altar, the sisters presented themselves in front of Father Johannes. He spooned the precious material into the censer, strengthening the aromatic smoke, before taking the censer from Brigitta and waving it around the lower altar. Slowly, the rings of smoke drifted into the upper spaces of the sanctuary. The mass was offered up to Almighty God and the service began, interspersed with music from flute and organ drifting down from the elaborately-carved loft at the back of the vast church.

Dressed in these impressive robes, and with her long brown hair flowing over the white ruff and surplice, Brigitta looked older than her seventeen years, and Ingrid appeared like a little angel beside her. The altar boys, like cherubs, were only about ten years old, but they all knew their tasks. Well-rehearsed, they handed the priest what he needed, rang the Angelus bells with vigour, and bowed and genuflected with reverence.

* * *

Carl Jensen's family had originally been from Berchtesgaden. They had been innkeepers before the Second World War, keeping a pretty little Gästehaus on a meadow above the town, but Carl's great-grandfather, Kurt Moeller, had married a girl from Swabia in the far west of Bavaria—Janne Heizz. They set themselves up as farmers in an Alpine valley near Oberstdorf where Janne's family had a small herd of those same hinterwälder cattle. Carl was aware that there was something dark in his family that might have partly precedented this move, but it was all in the past.

After the cows had come home, Carl spent his evening drinking with his neighbour's son, at one of the Schönau beer gardens—a pretty inn with fine mountain views where the last of the autumnal sun lit up the crags in streaks of pink as darkness descended.

"Are you still going out with that young Brigitta?" his friend asked. "I understand she's quite religious."

"None of your business," Carl replied, as they clinked their bottles of Lowenbrau. "I'll have to admit, though, she handled her cow pretty well."

"Better than you at the Dirndl Shop. Did you see Frau Forster's face when your cow came running at her in the doorway? I thought you and your cow would end up inside. What a laugh that would have been."

Carl put down his bottle with a thump and leaned in towards his friend. "Well, we didn't, did we—my skill at controlling the beast. At least it showed that my cow had spirit, and we still got home long before yours."

"Well, you were just showing off, it's Brigitta, isn't it?"

"Perhaps," was all Carl replied, and they clinked their beer bottles again.

Chapter Two
Berchtesgaden 1938–1939

Kurt Moeller adjusted his brown shirt as he looked in the mirror. The shiny black epaulettes revealed his number and the badge on his left sleeve his school emblazoned below the red band with the black Third Reich swastika. He was proud to be serving in the Hitler Youth. His older sister Hilda even worked in the dairy at the Fuhrer's Berghof, and she had befriended the Fuhrer's companion and often hostess at the chalet—Eva Braun.

Hilda had first been to the Obersalzberg estate in 1936 with other children from her school in Berchtesgaden. As he often did, Fuhrer Hitler had invited them to a children's tea party. It was there that she had met Eva Braun who was able to later get her the position in the dairy. Kurt remembered the day proudly when his older sister had come home shouting for joy, "I got the job. They hired me. I'm working for Mein Fuhrer at the Berghof!"

Kurt raised his right arm in front of the mirror. "Heil Hitler," he said with pride as he made the Nazi salute. His father called up to his room. "Coming," the youth shouted back, and he joined his father, who drove him to the Hitler Youth Camp on the outskirts of Berchtesgaden. It was exciting, and he had a purpose.

* * *

Security was very strict working on the Berghof estate, so Kurt's sister had to live in the assigned dormitory for the dairy workers in a converted hayloft. Nobody was allowed in or out of the Berghof estate guarded by the Schutzstaffel—the black-uniformed elite corps and self-described political soldiers of the Nazi Party. Hitler was often not there, but this Nazi headquarters on the Obersalzberg was top secret. Although Hilda missed living at home in her father's Gästehaus and helping out in the kitchen and dining room, she was immensely proud to be a part of the Berghof entourage. To her, it seemed that she was at the centre of the world. Staff still talked about the visit of the 'King of England' who had come with his American wife in October the previous year, although Hilda had been corrected by her supervisor at the dairy.

"He wasn't king by then," the man had said. "He abdicated the British throne in order to marry that divorced American lady, but it might be better if he was still king. He likes our Fuhrer."

Now, in September of 1938, the prime minister of Great Britain, Neville Chamberlain, was visiting the Berghof. Important people came and went when the Fuhrer was in residence. Eva Braun, however, never usually told Hilda anything about these people. When she visited the dairy, they talked about the cows and exciting things like the next performance being planned for everyone working on the estate at the new Theatre Halle that had been built for their enjoyment.

* * *

There was a house in Berchtesgaden that Kurt and his friends called "the Jews' house." It belonged to Herman Finkelstein, a very precise and fussy man, who had been a professor of engineering at the prestigious Ludwig Maximilian University of Munich. It was reported that with the rise of the Nazis, in 1933 he was stripped of his position, disgraced at the Munich University, his library seized and his books burnt in the square. He had fled with his wife Merla to the Bavarian Alps. They had settled in Berchtesgaden where they had an apartment looking out across the old town towards the great mountain of the Watzmann. Their two children—Johannes and his little sister Abigail—went to the same school as Kurt Moeller and his younger brother Harald, but nobody talked to them much. Kurt observed his brother and some of the other younger children taunting them in the playground, laughing at them and shouting, "Finkelstein! Finkelstein!"

* * *

News of Kristallnacht in early November 1938 was greeted with indifference by most people in Berchtesgaden, but it did have the effect of increasing rhetoric within the Hitler Youth. Kurt listened intently as his instructors became ever more vociferous in their condemnation of 'those evil Jews undermining the Third Reich'. The riots of Kristallnacht were applauded, and Jews living in what they had considered safe terrain in the mountains of Bavaria became increasingly nervous.

At eighteen, Kurt was drafted into the Nazi divisions marching into Poland. He was now proudly fighting for the fatherland. Resistance to the well-trained German troops with their Panzer tanks was minimal. Villages were reduced to ruins and their inhabitants were rounded up. The Polish Jews in particular were targets.

Kurt's unit found themselves on the mopping-up operation after attacking a largely Jewish village. His commander ordered them to send the Jewish villagers to their synagogue where they were to be sorted out for transport to 'the work camps'.

"Lock them in!" the commander briskly ordered, and the doors were barred.

"Sergeant Moeller," he bellowed, "fetch the petrol cans!"

Kurt's unit was then ordered to saturate the wooden synagogue and set the building ablaze.

Very quickly the dry old timbers burst into flames, the windows cracked and the pathetic cries of the terrified villagers, unable to leave, drifted into the air. Eventually, the walls and the roof caved in on the last Jewish peasants still alive, and the reek of burnt flesh rose up from the ashes. Only then did Kurt's commander give the order to leave.

At first, Kurt was excited by the great bonfire that they had created—the darting flames leaping up the timbers, the sparks flying. But then he heard the cries from within, and his stomach churned—this was different from firing shells at the enemy, this was mass murder. He listened to the camaraderie of his comrades shouting, "They were only Jews!" He found it hard to join in, but they felt that their actions were justified. They were orders after all. It was their duty to exterminate Jews from the rapidly expanding Third Reich, and Poland was quickly falling to the Nazi swastika, and that at least gave Kurt pride.

This blitzkrieg was a remarkable success. In no time, Kurt's division was on the move again, thrusting deeper and deeper into the vast plains. Warsaw fell, and they turned to the south. One of their main tasks there was to arrange the transport of Polish Jews, many to the Bavarian work camps of Flossenbürg and Dachau.

Chapter Three
The Finkelsteins 1940s

Merla Finkelstein found Abigail crying in her room. "What is it, my dear?" she asked.

"School," the little girl whimpered. "They hate us at school, Mutter. They make fun of us, laughing at us. They dance around us calling us names."

"Who?"

Abigail ran into her mother's arms. "Mostly the boys…there's this mean boy, Harald Moeller. I hate him, Mutter. He's older, but he gets the others to gang up on us."

"So what do they call you?"

"Sometimes 'Jude', but usually they just laugh at our name, shouting, 'Finkelstein! Finkelstein'!"

Merla held her daughter until she stopped sobbing. She dabbed her eyes. "I'm very sorry that they're so mean to you," she said, "we'll have to do something about that, but let's go to the kitchen and get some cake."

She called out to her son who was playing in the garden. "Johannes, come and join us for cake."

When the school closed for the spring holiday, Herman and Merla arranged for their children to stay with their Auntie Francine, Merla's sister in Swabia. Aunt Francine was married to a Lutheran farmer and they lived near Oberstdorf—a small Alpine town close to the Austrian and Swiss border. "It will be safer for you there," Merla said. "We don't think Berchtesgaden is really a safe place for us anymore. We want you to make new friends…real friends. You'll like it at Auntie Francine's…they have a lovely farm."

Francine and Uncle Helmut Drucker drove to Berchtesgaden to pick up their nephew and niece. Merla and the professor watched as their children left in the touring car. They could see Abigail's face pressed against the back window. A tear formed and rolled down Merla's cheek and a lump formed in her throat. Silently, hand-in-hand, she and the professor walked back into the house that they now rarely left.

Merla was arranging a vase of spring flowers to cheer herself up in their silent world without the children. It was a sunny day that made the still-white tops of the Wartzmann glisten, but here in the valley, the fresh green leaves of spring were opening as they always did. Cherry and apple blossoms covered the boughs of trees in Berchtesgaden gardens, and the roar of snowmelt rushed in the rivers, but an unexpected knock at the front door brought panic and fear.

"Who's that?" Merla called out to her husband as she trembled. "Can you see?"

Professor Finkelstein peered through the lace curtains. "Oh my God! It looks like a group of uniformed men, some in brown and some in black—the Schutzstaffel. It's hard to make out which group they are, but I think one of the youths with them might be Manfred Moeller's youngest boy, that Harald who so upset Abigail. I don't recognise any of the others."

"No surely not…not us!" Merla screamed. She ran to her husband. "Herman, surely not us!"

Herman held her as the knocking increased. They trembled together, silently looking into each other's eyes. There was a loud noise as if their visitors were trying to break down the door. Merla and Herman froze, clinging to each other even tighter.

There was a mighty crash.

Merla and Herman could hear the authoritarian shouts of Schutzstaffel guards in the entrance hall. There was no escape. The front door must have given way. The guards burst into their living room.

"Herr Professor Finkelstein?" the leader asked.

Herman nodded.

"You are to come with us."

Two of the guards seized the professor and two more grasped Merla. They took them out and bundled them into a car. They were driven to the military barracks where they were locked in a cell.

Herman sat on the iron bedstead with his wife staring at the floor. "Thank God the children are safe," was all he said.

Hours ticked past before they were taken to the commandant's office. There, they saw the Mayor of Berchtesgaden seated at the commandant's desk.

Remaining seated, the mayor said, "You have been selected to do great work for our fatherland. Transport will be arranged for you tomorrow." Then, he stood and stretched out his arm. "Heil Hitler," he shouted, and he left the office. The guards returned the Finkelsteins to their cell.

Once alone, Herman and Merla looked fearfully at each other. Merla was the first to speak. "Do you think this means that they'll keep us together?"

"Well, at least they haven't taken us out into the yard and shot us," was all Herman replied.

Merla shuddered and spluttered, "Why?"

"Because we're Jews," and he took her into his arms.

The next morning, soldiers painted an 'R' on Merla's forehead and an 'F' on Herman's, before escorting them to a waiting truck already filled with other Jews and misfits from Berchtesgaden with painted foreheads. Forced to stand like cows in transport, the truck drove them to Freilassing where they were escorted into the Bahnhof. Those with letters other than 'F' were sent to Platform 3 and those with an 'F' to Platform 4. Soldiers forced Merla and Herman apart and sent them off in their separate groups. Merla looked back, but the last time she could see her husband was as he was being shunted over the footbridge to Platform 4. He disappeared into the shuffling herd of distressed humanity heading for the train of cattle cars awaiting their transport. A moment later, an engine puffed in, pulling a train of box cars alongside Platform 3, obliterating her view. Merla was herded into a similar cattle car that reeked of urine. The smell made her gag, and as others were pushed into the car she was shuffled into the middle, her only support being all those people around her.

The car jolted and then began to trail the engine, black and white smoke and steam finding its way through the boards, mingling with that smell of urine to almost asphyxiate them. Uncomfortably jostled against each other, with no room to move other than to hold onto each other, this human cargo, reeking of body odour, was moved onward for two or three hours.

"Where have they taken my husband?" Merla kept sobbing. At first, nobody responded to her among those jammed in around her. Finally, a once fairly well-dressed man in a now crumpled three-piece suit asked if her husband was 'F' or 'D'.

"F," Merla answered shaking with fury, "that's the problem, we were separated."

"What's your name?" the man asked.

"Merla Finkelstein... My husband is the great professor, Herman Finkelstein," she answered through her tears.

The man proffered a handkerchief from his pocket, "Professor Finkelstein... the Munich professor?" Merla dabbed her eyes, "Yes."

"I remember him. I was a student at the Ludwig Maximilian myself...a medic...Dr David Baumgardner." They tried to shake hands, but the crush made it impossible and the wagon jolted, making them all lose their balance.

Moments later, when it settled down again, the kindly doctor continued, "They're probably sending him to Flossenbürg. They've been sending engineers there. That's where they build those Messerschmitt planes."

"So, where are we going, then?" Merla asked.

He looked up at her forehead. "'R' for Ravensbrück, I'd say."

An hour or two later, the train pulled into Munich. There, men and women were separated again. Merla noticed that most of the women were branded 'R' like her, but most of the men, including Dr Baumgardner, were branded 'D'. The men were crammed back into the cattle box cars before the train shunted off again. After what seemed an eternity with the women herded together on the platform, another train pulled in, stopping in a cloud of smoke and steam. These cattle cars were slightly larger than on the first train, and the women were forced aboard. In these box cars, there were triple wooden bunks, and Merla took possession of one in the hope of some rest for her aching feet. There was also a little room to move around and a primitive commode in one corner with a hanging curtain for privacy. A whistle blew and slowly the train began to move. It was many hours later that it finally came to a stop. The box cars were opened to the shouts of SS guards. Glad for their release and the end of this uncomfortable ride, the 'Rs' clambered onto the platform. Guards kept them bunched together before marching them alongside the track and under a large iron arch displaying the slogan, 'Arbeit macht frei'.

"Work makes you free," Merla muttered as she looked up. "What work?"

* * *

Professor Herman Finkelstein's train took him in the opposite direction as it pulled out of Freilassing, clanging its way northeast until it arrived at a siding outside Flossenbürg in the Fichtel Mountains, near the Bavarian border with the German Protectorate of Bohemia and Moravia. Mostly men, the prisoners were offloaded and driven in crowded trucks to the work camp where they were divided between carpenters and engineers.

"Name?" the SS officer shouted at Herman.

"Herman Finkelstein," the professor replied.

The guard looked down his list and pointed to the left. Herman was with the Messerschmitt factory workers. Those on the right were led off to some other area where it seemed they were to use their building skills to increase the number of dreary dormitory huts that made up the camp. Daily, Polish Jews and other sundry prisoners were swelling numbers at the camp as the Wehrmacht—the Third Reich war machine—secured the vast area that now encompassed Greater Germany.

Hitler's efforts then turned to the west. A blitzkrieg through Denmark and on into neutral Norway with lightning speed gave the great Nazi war machine encouragement to attack the French and British. Messerschmitts and ships would now be as important as the Panzer tanks if these tasks were to be completed. The very next day, Herman Finkelstein found himself at his bench in the Messerschmitt factory hastening the task.

* * *

Sergeant Kurt Moeller was given leave in the early summer of 1940. The Polish operation was winding down and it was felt necessary for some soldiers to return home to help with farming the land along with the Hitler Youth and the German League of Girls. The uniformed Kurt, carrying his kit bag, walked from the Berchtesgaden Bahnhof up through the old town. It felt strange to be back in the Alps after the long months in the flat plains of Poland. On all sides, the mountains rose up from the Berchtesgaden Valley. The meadows on their lower slopes were full of the wild flowers of late May, and the first of the hay was being cut for next winter's forage, its sweet fresh fragrance drifting on the air. Cows were being led up to the higher alms for their summer grazing. War seemed a long way from this agrarian scene.

At the Moeller Gästehaus, Kurt was surprised to see his sister Hilda helping out at the inn, looking sweet in a fresh Dirndl skirt. She was quick to explain to her hero soldier that it was only temporary. "Fraulein Braun has arranged for my promotion from the dairy to the Berghof itself," she explained. "I'll start there next week. This is a huge honour for me. I will be in the personal service of Mein

Fuhrer." Kurt hugged her as if she was his younger sister rather than two years his senior. He had himself grown up while in combat, and he felt himself to be more important than in the past—the man about the house, especially now that his younger brother Harald was also growing up.

Kurt and Harald walked together above the inn and lay back in a meadow in the warm sun regaling each other with their stories. Still only a 'soldier' of the Hitler Youth, Harald was the first to bring up the subject of the Jews.

"I've been working with the Schutzstaffel," he said with anti-Semitic pride. "I was there when we cleared out that stuck-up Frau Finkelstein. Sent her off to the camps I believe. She looked terrified, Kurt." A satisfied smile crossed his face. "She never did fit in here, did she? One of those Munich people—that professor's wife—I'm glad they're gone."

For some reason, it bothered Kurt. He felt uneasy as he reflected on his own part in rooting out the Jews, especially burning all those innocents in their own synagogue in Poland. He'd played his part, followed the orders, herded Jews onto the transports and sent them off to 'the camps'. In fact, that had been a major part of his war effort in Poland after the fall of Warsaw. But his stomach churned as he saw his brother's satisfaction. *Maybe he will think differently when* he's *conscripted,* he thought, *when he comes face to face with the brutality of war and the stench of death.* He thought back on his own naïve enthusiasm for the Nazi principles when he had been a 'soldier' in the Hitler Youth, and he became quietly silent, lying back and embracing the warm sun that splashed on his face.

The following day, Kurt and his brother were sent to the farm of their neighbour, Hannes Stack, to help with the haymaking.

News filtered through on exciting bulletins of how the mighty German army had routed the French and the British in Belgium and had them on the run at Dunkirk. Belgium had fallen, the Maginot had been skirted, and the march on Paris had begun. On 14 June, the news was all about how the French capital had capitulated. Upper France was won. Il Duce Benito Mussolini, in Italy officially declared war on France and Great Britain. The Third Reich and Fascist Italy now held all of Europe except for Spain, that country, in neutrality, still reeling from its own civil war. Adolf Hitler was indeed, the great Fuhrer, who had made the fatherland rise again.

* * *

Hilda Moeller returned to the Berghof estate. She was now at the beck and call of the Fuhrer himself and was trained in all of his domestic foibles from how he liked his tea brewed to how he liked his shirts to be ironed. In all of this, Eva Braun was a great help to her, and in appreciation, Hilda was often entrusted with the double honour of caring for both Eva's Scottish terriers and the Fuhrer's Alsatian dogs.

Hilda hadn't been in service at the Berghof for long, when after his declaration of war on Great Britain and France; Il Duce Benito Mussolini arrived in Munich with his foreign minister, Count Ciano, to discuss immediate plans with the Fuhrer. It was expected that the Italian leader would be invited to the Berghof as in the past. Hilda prepared their rooms.

But Adolf Hitler didn't appear pleased with Il Duce, and he came back from Munich to the Berghof alone. Eva rarely ever said anything political, but she loosened her tongue as together she and Hilda Moeller fed the dogs.

"Apparently, Mussolini was embarrassed over the late entry of Italy into the war," Eva said. "Mussolini met with Hitler determined to convince him to exploit the advantage he had in France by demanding total surrender and occupying the southern portion that's apparently still free. The Italian leader clearly wanted 'in' on the spoils, and this was a way of reaping rewards with a minimum of risk."

Eva smiled as she gave her terriers, Negus and Stasi, 'Leckerli' treats.

"Our Fuehrer was in no mood to risk things, and was determined to put forward rather mild terms for peace with France," she continued. "He needs to ensure that the French fleet remains neutral and that a government-in-exile is not formed in North Africa or London. He also denied Mussolini's request that Italian troops occupy the Rhone Valley and that Corsica, Tunisia and Djibouti should be disarmed. Apparently, Mussolini left the meeting frustrated and very much embarrassed, stating 'that his role is only secondary'."

Hilda was only half listening. Places like Corsica, Tunisia and Djibouti meant nothing to her, and besides, the dogs were barking as they always did at meal times. It was enough for Hilda to just know that Eva was looking out for her and had noted her disappointment.

* * *

With France secured, as the summer of 1940 drew on Hitler turned his attention to Great Britain. Following the collapse of France, the Luftwaffe had spent most of the latter half of June and early July preparing for a coming battle with the British.

Kurt Moeller was initially drafted into 'Operation Sea Lion' as part of the infantry invasion force ready to cross the Channel, but Hitler bowed to Göring's confidence in the Luftwaffe to bring Britain to surrender without the infantry, so Kurt found his division sent down into southern France instead, to reduce the last of the French resistance. The level of German confidence had gone from strength to strength, and Kurt continued to feel the pride.

Göring's propaganda fed out to the victorious land troops as they heard of the Luftwaffe bringing Britain's Fighter Command to its knees. In September, German bombers moved in on London. The 'Blitzkrieg' had now reached the British capital. Assuredly, the British would now succumb. The humiliation of 1918 had been redeemed—'Heil Hitler'.

* * *

In October, the cows on the high Alpen meadows above the Swabian Bavarian town of Oberstdorf were being rounded up for their annual descent down to the valley. Abigail and Johannes Finkelstein were helping their Aunt Francine and Uncle Helmut. They had repaired the last year's crowns stored in the hayloft, replacing the fabric of some of the red and orange cloth flowers— the colours of Aunt Francine's herd. This happy event took their minds off the possibility that something must have happened to their parents. There had been no letters all summer, but Aunt Francine had comforted them by suggesting that it was better not to write as 'it could lead to difficulties if anyone in Berchtesgaden found out that they were here in Oberstdorf'.

Being married to a Christian farmer, Aunt Francine only paid lip service to being Jewish. She hid her nephew and niece as Lutherans, registering them with her husband's name, 'Drucker'. They even started attending the small Lutheran church in Oberstdorf. Abigail and Johannes also hid their identity at school, where they were considered to be orphans living with their aunt and uncle. It was all very secretive to the young teenagers, but in some ways exciting.

Today, Helmut Drucker and Johannes would lead their cows once Francine had affixed the crowns, and Abigail, dressed in her prettiest Dirndl, would just hang out with them when they finally brought the cows down into Oberstdorf. In the town square, the brass band was already tuning up to welcome the cavalcade, and the beer was flowing at the tables of the Hirsch Tavern. Mayor Ludwig Fink and his family were on the podium at the town hall opposite the great Catholic Church of St John the Baptist, ready to welcome the annual spectacle.

At about noon, the sound of clanging cow bells announced their arrival, and soon the cows could be seen. With their crowns by now slightly tilted, they were led past cheering children and lederhosen-clad lads. There was little to distinguish between the racial mix as the whole village came as one to honour the means of most of their livelihoods. These people were Bavarian, they were Alpine and they were Oberstdorfers, and the war that as yet had barely reached these folk was not much of a topic of conversation. The October sun still shone with surprising warmth, and the beer frothed, as the cows moved through the town to disperse in their separate groups to their outlying farms.

Later that evening, Johannes and his younger sister hung out with new school friends at the Park Hotel. Abigail was concerned that her brother was drinking beer. They laughed together as they watched the great and the good of their little town dancing around in its only ballroom. Among their new friends were two protestant Dutch boys from the Hohes Licht children's home, run by two old-fashioned aristocratic spinsters, Hetty Laman and Elisabeth Dabelstein.

* * *

When Merla Finkelstein first arrived at Ravensbrück after that horrendous train journey, she was agreeably surprised. She looked across the great square. It was surrounded by manicured lawns, with flower beds on which bloomed bright red flowers. A wide street, which led to a large open area, was flanked by two rows of wooden barracks. On both sides, were planted young trees, and along the roadside ran those flower beds as far as the eye could see. The square and the streets seemed freshly raked. When taken to her hut, she was impressed to see iron bedsteads and clean sheets and blankets, more like a hospital ward than a prison. *Perhaps this work might make me free,* she thought.

The work was in the Siemans and Halske factory making field telephones, and although long hours and rather repetitive, it wasn't that bad except for the constant surveillance. Even the food was tolerable. Merla's first meal in Ravensbrück exceeded her expectations when she was served sweet porridge with dried fruit, plus a generous portion of bread, margarine, and sausage. It irked her, however, that sewn into her striped prison dress was the dreaded 'Jude'

31

star—two inverted triangles of yellow cloth that somehow she had been able to avoid in Berchtesgaden. If the tales were true, she was now a marked Jew, who at best might end up in a ghetto, but at worst could be taken out and summarily shot.

As the first year went by, more and more huts were built, and more and more females were incarcerated many of whom were not Jews and whose badges denoted other categories—civilian criminals from the Reich justice system sporting green triangles or political prisoners—social democrats, liberals, socialists, communists and anarchists—sporting red triangles. Increasingly, there were also prisoners marked with blue triangles, designating that they were foreign forced-labourers, many of whom did not speak German. The lawns and the flower beds were neglected now, and the food rations became much more basic.

By the time 1941 morphed into 1942, the place was becoming grossly overcrowded and the iron bedsteads were replaced with triple wooden bunks. Sanitary conditions deteriorated, and life was becoming intolerable. Merla fell ill and was not able to work the long hours at the factory. Instead, she was forced to labour in the camp laundry, but she was becoming weaker and weaker.

The guards appointed to her block pulled her from roll call one morning and told her that she was being sent away for medical treatment. If so, there were many others also awaiting transport for medical treatment. They were bundled back into the box cars of a recent transport that had unloaded hundreds more prisoners. The train then pulled out of Ravensbrück, and several hours later they found themselves offloaded at Linz in Austria, where they were bused to Hartheim Castle—a hospital outside the village of Alkoven. The place certainly had the appearance of a hospital with doctors and nurses. Merla was personally checked out by a Dr Rudolph Lonauer, and in her weakened state was happy to be back in a real bed, with considerate care from ward nurses and an improved diet. After two or three days, however, she was taken down to the showers on the ground floor. The nurse said that she would wait for her outside as Merla joined others in the shower room. The guard then left them alone to their ablutions, locking the door behind them. Suddenly, the showers stopped, and the room went dark. There was an eerie silence and the air began to smell funny. Merla started to choke. She felt lightheaded and fell to the floor. She struggled and gasped, and then, all went blank.

Herman Finkelstein gave up enquiring as to where his wife might have been sent. Nobody ever gave him an honest answer, and in order to survive at Flossenbürg you had to cooperate. Herman was aware that he was in a privileged position as a supervisor at the Messerschmitt works, even though he had to wear the dreaded yellow star. His engineering skills were in demand as he worked on better and better designs for the Luftwaffe's Bf109 fighter planes.

The professor was working on his drawing board when there was a loud noise down on the factory floor. A ball of flame engulfed his office and the floor gave way. He landed in rubble, blacked out and never regained his consciousness.

Chapter Four
Kurt Moeller on the Eastern Front
1941–1943

After failing to bring Great Britain to its knees and suffering large Luftwaffe losses, Hitler broke his uneasy alliance with the Soviets and attacked along the new German state's Eastern Front. The Wehrmacht was now marching southwest through the rich Soviet lands of 'the Ukraine' and holding a line from outside Leningrad in the north through Belarus. But it was in 'the Ukraine' that the best prize was to be gained in securing the rich grain lands of the Soviets and cutting the Russians from using their Black Sea ports.

* * *

Kurt Moeller was a good mountain climber and also a competent skier. When he was reassigned to fight the Russians in 'Operation Barbarossa', he was attached to the 1st Mountain Division and sent for training at the high-altitude school at Sonthofen in Swabia. There, he met the famous Oberstdorf mountaineer Lieutenant Gerd Aurich. Before joining the 99th Regiment of the Mountain Division, they were both given a brief leave, and Kurt travelled with Gerd Aurich down the road to Oberstdorf. The pretty valley surrounded by the Allgau Alps reminded Kurt of the Berchtesgaden Valley and home, and he immediately took a liking to the place. *When this war is over, I would like to come back here,* he thought. *I would like to explore these mountains.*

Their leave was short, however, just enough time for Gerd Aurich to visit his wife and little son Christian, while Kurt hung out at the Park Hotel. In just two days, they had to start their long journey east to Warsaw to join up with the 99th.

In Warsaw, Kurt shared with Gerd where he had fought in 1939, and the Oberstdorfer mountaineer was impressed by the old city's walls, towers and fortifications, but somewhat shocked at the terrible poverty and dirt. Food seemed in very short supply and all they could find to eat in the marketplace was a bag of six walnuts.

The lieutenant picked one out and rolled it between his fingers. He shook his head, "This is what we are fighting for?"

"Yes, and it won't get much better," Sergeant Kurt Moeller informed him.

So it was, as they moved onward southeast to Kasatin in the autumn of 1941. There, a lieutenant from Dresden joined them and spoke of the appalling atrocities he had witnessed in the slaughtering of Jewish peasants. Kurt felt his stomach sour as the memories returned, but he kept silent. On 10 October, they reached Kirovograd. They learned that just ten days before several hundred Jews had been taken to nearby anti-tank ditches and shot. Kurt remembered what his brother had said about the arrest of the Finkelsteins, and it gnawed at his own conscience.

Billeted in a shelled-out farmhouse, Kurt looked anguished. "Are the Jews really that bad?" he asked.

"We don't think too much about them in Oberstdorf," Gerd answered. "They've been coming to the mountains from the northern cities for years. We welcome them…they're good for our business."

They shared a cigarette.

In the morning, all around them, they saw destruction. The land had been savaged by both the retreating Russians and their own German soldiers.

A few days later, they reached the mighty Dneiper River and they knew that they were in the heart of 'the Ukraine'. They crossed on a pontoon at Kremenchuk, where the river was about half a mile across, and they were taken onwards in trucks. There was mud and desolation everywhere. The dead were still lying in the ooze, along with numerous rotting horses. The smell of death was appalling, and yet in the distance, they could see huge fields of corn, maize and sunflowers—part of the reason for this putsch of the Nazi Third Reich. At Poltava, they knew they were near to the front lines. The area had only recently fallen in the German advance and obviously, the fighting had been fierce. There were burnt-out tanks on the streets, and many of the shelled buildings were still smouldering.

It had taken a full two weeks to travel from Bavaria to the front, but on 18 October, they reached their division command post and were finally able to report for duty. They were sent onwards to Artemovsk where the 99th were in the thick of the fighting. Most of the wheat fields én route had been torched by the Russians, and when they reached Konstantinovka, an industrial city where there had been important ironworks, almost everything had been destroyed. The people were miserable and starving.

"How will they survive the winter?" Lieutenant Aurich said. "What misery…Good God, four weeks ago, I was at home in Oberstdorf. What happy hours those were." He paused and stared at the ground, probably thinking of his small son. He smiled at Kurt, "Never mind…tomorrow we will join our regiment."

The Orberstorfers and Kurt were then split up into their respective units to face this hell that had become the Eastern Front after such a swift and positive advance. Kurt and Gerd were separated. The winter became bitterly cold, and the skies were eternally red with the flames of destruction.

Kurt reflected on those orders in Poland back in 1939 when now, his new commanding officer reminded his troops of their present role. Quoting from *The Guidelines for the Conduct of Troops in Russia,* he said loudly, "This struggle demands a ruthless and strenuous crackdown on Bolshevist agitators, irregulars, saboteurs and Jews. Anyone who has ever looked into the face of a Red commissar knows what Bolsheviks are. There is no need here for theoretical reflections. It would be an insult to animals if one were to call all the features of these largely Jewish, tormentors of people, beasts. They are the embodiment of the infernal, the personification of an insane hatred of everything that is noble in humanity. In the shape of these commissars, we witness the revolt of the subhuman against noble blood. The masses whom they are driving to their deaths with every means of icy terror and lunatic incitement would have brought all meaningful life to an end had the communist invasion of our fatherland not been prevented at the last moment."

Kurt heard his neighbour whisper, "Heil Hitler," but Kurt's mind was still in Poland watching those Jews being incinerated in their own synagogue—the flames of total destruction—and there, he had been carrying out these same orders. He put his hand to his chest. His heart felt like it had been stabbed, but the feeling soon passed.

Little by little, the German regiments advanced, securing 'the Ukraine' and setting their sights on the rich oil fields in the Caucasus Mountains of the southern Soviet Union.

In December, Kurt's unit heard of the attack on the United States by the Japanese in Hawaii. A cheer went up from the men of his platoon as they heard the bulletin on the field wireless. There was little love lost between the German Third Reich and the United States because of the way that the Americans had dominated German humiliation after the first Great War. Nor was there much fear of the United States when they declared war on both Japan and Germany on 8 December—Hitler and Mussolini controlled all of Europe, except neutral Spain and Switzerland. *There's not much chance of the Americans ever gaining a foothold*, Kurt thought. *War between Japan and the USA is too far away to be of any immediate consequence.* The 1st Mountain Division dug in along the Mius River in south-eastern Ukraine until they could advance in the spring.

It was with great sadness, however, that Kurt heard in the early New Year of 1942, that his friend, Lieutenant Gerd Aurich, had been severely wounded and had later died at Kramatorskaya. His eyes watered as he thought of Gerd's young wife and her little boy in Oberstdorf. *I think Gerd said his name was Christian.*

The Ukrainian winter was horrendous with bitter winds bringing temperatures as low as fifty below. Men simply froze to death, their clothing being grossly inadequate. Kurt dug a dead Russian soldier out of a snow bank. "The bolshies have better," he observed. "Look at this poor bugger's warm quilted jacket. They're used to this cold."

When spring finally came, the division went on the offensive again. Fighting was intense, but in July they achieved a major breakthrough. The southern Russian city of Rostov-on-Don fell to the Third Reich. It was 'the gateway to the Caucasus'.

* * *

Hilda Moeller was excited when she was asked again to make rooms available for Il Duce Mussolini and his entourage at the Berghof. Mussolini was due to meet with Fuhrer Hitler on May Day. This was apparently going to be a very important meeting, and Hilda felt proud to be on the world stage.

The Obersalzberg was looking at its best. The fresh green leaves were out, contrasting with the dark conifers. Snow still clung to clefts in the mountains, and the first wildflowers were blooming in the meadows. Geraniums and petunias were already spilling out from the Berghof balcony boxes, and blue skies held the puffy clouds of late spring. Goats bleated, and cows with their newborn calves grazed in the fresh green paddocks.

Il Duce and his party arrived at the Berghof on the afternoon of the last day of April 1942. Hilda could see them arrive with their escorts as she looked out from the room where she had just placed a welcome dish of Bavarian chocolates. Everything looked right, so now she must leave. It was never her role to be a party to these great meetings of state, but it was exciting. *He is rather short and round*, she thought as she closed the lace curtain. *He probably eats too much spaghetti*. She laughed to herself, pleased with her assumption.

* * *

The next day, the leaders all met in the Berghof's Great Hall—Adolf Hitler, Albert Kesselring and Il Duce Benito Mussolini with his Chief of the Italian Defence Staff. At this meeting, the gossip was that a General Rommel should start 'Operation Venice'. An offensive that at the end of May they expected would finally capture Tobruk. If successful, Rommel was to go no further east in North Africa than the Egyptian border, to give time for the invasion of Malta in mid-July. The capture of Malta from the British would secure the Axis supply lines to North Africa before the invasion of Egypt with the Suez Canal as their final objective. It was reported that the North African campaign had not been going very well for the British, and Rommel had proved himself with his tactical skills. Now was the time to get the British out of Egypt and to cut them off from the canal that was 'the lifeline of their empire'. This meeting concluded and the Italians left with heavy SS escorts the next day.

Hilda later heard that before leaving Obersalzberg, the Italian leader visited the mountain-top Kehlsteinhaus or 'Eagle's Nest' to see the red Italian marble fireplace that he had donated to the project for the Fuhrer's 50th birthday back in 1939.

In June, German troops were universally buoyed by the reports that they received of how the now Generalfeldmarschall Erwin Rommel, known as 'the desert fox', was successful in recapturing Tobruk and pushing on towards Egypt. Hopes were high that it would not be long before the British would be forced out of Egypt giving the Third Reich control over the valuable Suez Canal. But they became dashed at the First Battle of El Alamein in July which stalled the advance.

For Kurt, the 1st Mountain Division in southern Russia had a new mission now—'Operation Edelweiss' under the command of General Hubert Lanz. Captain Heinz Groth of the 99th was to recruit a high-altitude combat unit to secure the passes around Mount Elbrus, the tallest peak of the Caucasus, before moving rapidly north-east to capture those all-important oil fields. Kurt and his Oberstdorf friends were recruited. Groth himself was from Sonthofen in Western Bavaria, and along with Kurt, and possibly in memory of their good friend Gerd Aurich, they decided what an honour it would be to climb Mount Elbrus in the name of the Third Reich.

On 7 August, the 99th mountaineers reached the foothills of the snow-capped mountain, and Groth, Kurt Moeller and the Oberstdorfers were determined to claim the peak. They set out as if on a peacetime expedition to test all their climbing skills. They crossed the River Kuban over the one bridge that the Russians had not blown up when retreating into the mountains. After a demanding march through the foothills, they arrived at the mountain proper and set up their base camp. Here, they learned about Hut 11, an extraordinary building locally called Elbrus House, built up the mountain at about 4,000 metres. Apparently, it looked like a Zeppelin airship and stood about three storeys high. It had been built by the Russian travel agency, Intourist, and it had opened just before the war started in 1939—a hotel that could accommodate a hundred tourists. Groth was determined that it should be secured by the Oberstdorfers, its position now being of strategic importance, commanding the view of all the surrounding mountain passes. Groth took some of the men to reconnoitre the building.

As they approached the extraordinary structure, a shot rang out, echoing in the hills.

"Duck and take cover," Kurt commanded his unit. "Russians!"

Kurt's unit was only minimally armed as their objective was to climb the mountain. Silence fell across the still landscape again. Groth with his unit appeared on the left, approaching the building. There were a few men outside now, and Groth confidently walked up to them as if he thought that they were part of his climbing team. Kurt and the Oberstdorf climbers watched as Groth was taken inside.

After a few minutes, about twelve Russians left the building with their hands up.

"Looks like they've surrendered," Kurt whispered as he watched the frightened men scurry off into the conifers.

There were no more shots. Kurt then led his men into the building. Groth and about four Russians were laughing and sharing tots of vodka.

"Sergeant Moeller, meet our new recruits," Groth gestured. "I told them 'the Zeppelin' was surrounded by German soldiers and most of them left, but these four decided to stay and help us climb the mountain. They're all Russian mountaineers and meteorologists."

The building had all the amenities of a luxury hotel, with showers, storage rooms and a fully equipped kitchen with pantries of food. Best of all, there were quantities of modern mountain equipment and clothing far superior to their own.

The Russians poured Kurt a vodka. Groth stood up. "Welcome to Edelweiss Hut," he said as they knocked them back. Later, Kurt had the luxury of sleeping in a hotel room with a made-up bed—*What joy*.

On 19 August, they made their first attempt at the ascent. When they set out, the weather wasn't too bad, but later, conditions became appalling. There was a violent blizzard and thickening fog. The driving snow was so intense that the men were blown off the ice steps that they had hacked out with their pickaxes. After so long away from the Alps and climbing, altitude sickness also affected some of them, but determined, they cracked on. Crawling on all fours, the flagman reached the summit. The Reich war flag was tattered, ripped to pieces in the storm, but somehow in the snow they secured it to their metal post together with the regimental pendant. The flags' toggles rattled in the near gale-force wind.

Groth's words blew from him as he proclaimed as best he could, "We salute the Fuhrer, our Bavarian homeland and Germany. We salute this storm-torn peak, the highest in the Caucasus, and the men in our Mountain Divisions who are fighting in the valleys and passes. We salute the mountain."

The descent was even more difficult than the ascent, but miraculously nobody was killed or seriously injured.

A few days later, when the weather had cleared, Groth ordered them up again so that they could replace the damaged Nazi flag.

"Good grief, it was a good thing we did come back," Kurt noted when they reached the perceived summit. "Look! This isn't the summit."

They were standing on a snowy ledge and to their right the summit rose up a further few metres. Plucking the regimental pendant from the snow, they set about cutting a series of steps up in the ice to take them to the top. There, they re-planted both the pendant and the replacement Nazi flag.

Kurt stood with his men. "Heil Hitler!" he snapped. "We now rename this mountain Mount Hitler."

* * *

Hilda Moeller wasn't in Hitler's study at the Berghof, but from the hall, she could hear the Fuhrer's rage. He was locked in there with Albert Speer. "Those crazy mountaineers," the Fuhrer yelled, "they should be court-martialled! They pursued their idiotic hobbies in the middle of the war—to occupy a ridiculous peak—Dummkopf!"

Speer appeared to say something, but Hitler just raged on. "I don't care to give my name to some Bolshevik mountain…We are at war!"

Hilda tiptoed away. Staff sometimes spoke of the Fuhrer's raging, but this was the first time she had heard it for herself.

* * *

It seemed that the war was no longer going quite the way that the Fuhrer had planned. Rommel's quick successes in North Africa had met with a stalemate at El Alamein. The British had been on the run, but somehow, propped up by their 'bloody empire' with Indian and New Zealand forces, they had foiled Rommel in a bold last stand. By now, Generalfeldmaschall Rommel should have been at the gates of Alexandria and Cairo, but no…he was now holed up in the desert in a standoff. He hadn't lost territory, but he had been thwarted.

Meanwhile, in early August 1942, Britain's Winston Churchill and General Sir Alan Brooke—the British Chief of the Imperial General Staff—visited Cairo on their way to meet Joseph Stalin in Moscow. Apparently, they had decided to replace the British General Auchinleck, who had stood against Rommel at El Alamein, appointing their XIII Corps commander, William Gott, to their Eighth Army command, and General Sir Harold Alexander as commander-in-chief of their Middle East Command. Intelligence revealed that Persia and Iraq were to be split from the Middle East Command as a separate Persia and Iraq Command and Auchinleck had been offered the post there of commander-in-chief, but he had apparently refused it. Gott was killed on

41

the way to take up his command when his aircraft was successfully shot down by the Luftwaffe. And now, a Lieutenant-General Sir Bernard Montgomery had been appointed in his place, to take command on 13 August. Rommel would have to get the measure of someone new before he could march into Egypt.

* * *

Kurt Moeller's platoon along with the 99th Regiment pushed on through the Caucasus clearing Soviet resistance from the mountain passes. The road to the oil fields looked secure. There were only minor skirmishes with the Russians. Kurt's unit was then suddenly sent north to assist the German 6th Army in the Battle for Stalingrad.

Stalingrad was strategically important to both sides as a major industrial and transport hub on the Volga River. Whoever controlled Stalingrad would have access to those Caucasus oil fields and would gain control of the Volga. On 4 August, the Germans launched an offensive. The attack was supported by intense Luftwaffe bombing that reduced much of the city to rubble. The battle degenerated into house-to-house fighting as both sides poured reinforcements into the city.

Now a lieutenant, Kurt and his men found themselves on a street leading into Stalingrad's ruined centre, defending the skeleton of a once Soviet department store. A pocket of Russians was still holding out between them and the Volga River. Daily sorties into the ruins across the street proved to be highly dangerous. There was a crack of rifle fire. Kurt heard a Russian bullet whistle past his left ear. He ducked into a stairway leading into a basement and held his breath. *A narrow escape,* he thought. There was a further exchange of fire, and then a period of silence. When Kurt emerged, he saw that the platoon sergeant who had been behind him, one of the Oberstdorfers, had fallen and was bleeding profusely. The bullet had hit the man's chest but missed his heart. The soldier was struggling to draw a breath. They carried him into the basement, but by the time they reached the concrete floor, the sergeant had passed away—blood oozed from his mouth and his eyes lolled in their sockets. Kurt made the sign-of-the-cross and took the Obersdorfer's tags. "We'll have to leave him," he said. "Follow me...we need to get back to our shelter."

By mid-November, the Germans, at great cost, had pushed the Soviet defenders back into narrow zones along the west bank of the river. It looked like a Third Reich victory. But on 19 November, the Russian Red Army launched a two-pronged attack, targeting the Romanian armies protecting the German 6th Army's flanks. The Axis flanks were overrun and the 6th Army was cut off and surrounded in the Stalingrad area. Hitler was determined to hold the city at all costs and forbade the 6th Army from attempting a breakout; instead, attempts were made to supply it by air and to break the encirclement from the outside. The Soviets were successful in denying the Germans the ability to resupply through the air which strained the Wehrmacht to breaking point. Nevertheless, the Germans were determined to continue their advance and heavy fighting was waged for another two months.

Two more of Kurt's Oberstdorfers died of frostbite. *What a waste, and they were mountaineers,* he thought.

On 2 February 1943, the German 6th Army, having exhausted their ammunition and food, finally capitulated after over five months of fighting.

"Like Napoleon all over again," Kurt said dishearteningly as what was left of his frozen, starving unit shuffled through the snow and ice, still free, not yet prisoners-of-war, but desperately moving west towards the European sunsets as best they could.

* * *

Kurt's brother Harald was finally fighting for the fatherland. He was now a real soldier, having graduated from the Hitler Youth. He was to join the 15th Panzer Division in North Africa.

Two brilliant tacticians now faced each other in the North African desert at El Alamein—Generalfeldmaschall Erwin Rommel and the British General, Sir Bernard Montgomery. Germans heard that Rommel knew that the British and their imperial forces would soon be strong enough to attack. Harald heard among his fellow soldiers in training that the only hope was for the Wehrmacht forces fighting in the battle for Stalingrad to quickly defeat the Red Army and then to move south through the Caucasus and threaten Persia and the Middle East. If successful, large numbers of British and imperial forces would have to be sent from the Egyptian front to reinforce the Ninth Army in Persia, leading to the postponement of any offensive against the German army. It was rumoured that Rommel had certainly hoped to convince the German High Command to reinforce his forces for the eventual link-up between Panzerarmee Afrika and the

German 6th Army fighting in southern Russia, enabling them finally to defeat the British and their imperial armies in North Africa and the Middle East.

But Rommel fell ill and had to return to Germany, leaving General George Stumme in charge. In the meantime, the Panzerarmee dug in and waited for the attack by the British Eighth Army or the defeat of the Red Army at Stalingrad. The news from the Russian front wasn't good, and before the grand scheme could begin, the British General Montgomery was able to strike.

After his brief Panzer tank training, Harald Moeller would now be joining the Panzerarmee Afrika with reinforcements for the Afrika Korps. Harald looked from the troop carrier at the sandy shore, dotted here and there with little palm trees and olives in a yellow haze beneath clear blue skies. This was different to any terrain that he had ever known—flat, mostly barren but with rocky outcrops, a far cry from Berchtesgaden. The carrier entered the harbour of Derna. In no time, Harald was assigned to his tank crew in the 15th Panzer Division, and before they knew it they were heading out over the desert sands.

Harald's Panzer unit was set to face the British forces that were trying to break through Rommel's minefields. At first, all seemed to be going well. The British tanks bogged down as they approached and were repressed.

"Easy this time," the tank commander said, "but don't get complacent. The word is that the British are now importing American Sherman tanks into the desert. Apparently, they will have a superior range to us. It's not going to be easy."

"The Americans," Harald muttered to his neighbouring gunner, "are we now fighting the Americans?"

"So, it seems…at least their armour," the gunner replied.

The morning of Saturday 24 October brought disaster for the German headquarters. The Axis forces were stunned by a British attack and their messages became confused and hysterical, with one Italian unit apparently communicating to the Germans that it had been wiped out by 'drunken negroes with tanks'—such was the contempt that the Axis forces felt for the British imperial troops. 'Without bringing in their bloody empire they would have been toast' was the cry through the ranks. The reports that Stumme had received that morning showed the attacks had been on a broad front, but that such penetration as had occurred should be containable by local units. Stumme went forward to see for himself, and under fire, he suffered a heart attack and died. The Fuhrer was forced to request Rommel's return to Africa.

Rommel's arrival boosted German morale, although there was little he could do to change the course of the battle. At dusk, with the sun at their backs, Axis tanks from the 15th Panzer Division and the Italian Littorio swung out from a hill, to engage the British. The first big tank engagement began.

Harald's unit cheered as they gained a hit on a British Crusader tank. The vehicle exploded in a ball of fire. Adrenalin ran high and they sought out their next target. Over a hundred tanks were involved in the battle that day, and half were destroyed before nightfall. It was a standoff, and neither position was altered.

The main battle in late October was concentrated around Tel el Aqqaqir and the 'Kidney' feature at the end of the British and Australian Divisions' path through the minefield. Both battalions had difficulty finding their way in the dark and dust. At dawn, they hadn't reached their objective—an outcrop named Woodcock—and had to find cover and dig in some distance away.

The next day, some hours of confused fighting ensued, involving tanks from the Italian Littorio and troops and anti-tank guns from the 15th Panzer, which managed to keep the British armour at bay. Rommel decided to make two counter-attacks using his fresh troops. At a place known as Snipe, mortar and shellfire were constant all day. Rommel launched his major attack. German and Italian tanks moved forward.

The desert was quivering with heat. There was a terrible stench. The flies swarmed in black clouds upon the dead bodies and tormented the wounded. The place was strewn with burning tanks and carriers, wrecked guns and vehicles, and over all, there drifted the smoke and the dust from bursting high explosives and from the blasts of guns.

On 28 October, the 15th and 21st Panzer Divisions made a determined attack on the British but were halted by artillery, tank and anti-tank gun fire. A shell struck Harald's tank and they were engulfed in their own ball of fire. Incredible pain, intensive white light, and Harald knew no more, his corpse crushed in the wreck of the turret.

* * *

In the afternoon, the Germans paused to regroup to attack again, but they were bombed for two-and-a-half hours and were prevented from even forming up. This proved to be Rommel's last attempt to take the initiative, and as such his defeat here represented a turning point in the battle.

By late morning on 4 November, Rommel obviously realised his situation was desperate. The Generalfeldmarschall telegraphed Hitler for permission to fall back to Fuka, near the Egyptian border. As further British blows landed, Thoma, Rommel's Second-in-Command was captured, and reports came in from the Ariete and Trento Italian Divisions that they were encircled. At 5:30 p.m., unable to wait any longer for a reply from Hitler, Rommel gave orders to retreat.

On 8 November, to the surprise of many, American troops started to make amphibious landings in Morocco and on the North African coast.

Chapter Five
The Beginning of the End 1943–1944

On 27 January, towards the end of the first month of 1943, bombs rained down on the U Boat submarine bases at Wilhelmshaven in Lower Saxony. Wave after wave of bombers flew over the base wreaking havoc below. Three were shot down by the German defences. They showed that the bombers were American and not British.

A few days later, the shattering news of Germany's defeat at Stalingrad sent shock waves through the whole nation. The people of rural Germany now woke up to the reality of the Fuhrer's war—the Third Reich might be defeated. On 18 February, Berchtesgaden hotelier Manfred Moeller listened to the radio and heard Goebbels speak to them from Berlin.

'Stalingrad was and is fate's alarm call to the German nation…My task is to give you an unvarnished picture of the situation…We want no false hopes and illusions. We want bravely to look the facts in the face, however hard and dreadful they may be.

'We know that the German people are defending their holiest possessions… their families, women and children, the beautiful and untouched countryside, their cities and villages, their two-thousand-year-old culture, everything indeed that makes life worth living…Total war is the demand of the hour…Everyone knows that if we lose, all will be destroyed.'

Manfred called his wife Delphine. "You need to listen to this," he said pulling up a chair near the large standing radio in the parlour as he puffed on a pipe.

'We can no longer make only partial and careless use of the war potential at home and in the significant parts of Europe that we control. We must use our full

resources, as quickly and as thoroughly as it is organisationally and practically possible...Therefore, a series of measures must be implemented...We have ordered, for example, the closing of bars and nightclubs...Countless luxury stores have also been closed.'

"What about us?" Delphine said looking at her husband. "The Gästehaus… will we lose our home?"

"Of course not, Delphine…now listen!"

Goebbels' voice continued. *'What good do shops do that no longer have anything to sell, but only use electricity, heating and human labour that is lacking everywhere else, particularly in the armaments industry? What German woman would want to ignore my appeal on behalf of those fighting at the front? Who would want to put personal comfort above national duty? Who, in view of the serious threat we face would want to consider his private needs above the requirements of the war? I am firmly convinced that the German people have been deeply moved by fate's blow at Stalingrad.'*

"Do you think Kurt is still alive?" Delphine said, tears welling in her eyes as she remembered the horror of the news just three months ago of the death of her youngest son Harald, killed in action in North Africa. "Kurt might have been killed too or been taken prisoner."

"We must have faith," Manfred said. "We have not been informed of his death."

Goebbels went on to demand that the nation step up the war effort. He left no one in any doubt that only a superhuman effort on the part of the entire population could save the Reich, and indeed the whole of Europe, from 'Bolshevist Jewish enslavement'.

'The German people now know the awful truth, and are resolved to follow the Fuhrer through thick and thin...Now, people, rise up and let the storm break!'

* * *

When Kurt finally arrived back in Berchtesgaden after his long trek from the retreat at Stalingrad, he was greeted by his father with the news that his young brother Harald had been killed. Hilda, who was on a rare visit home from the Berghof, sobbed in Kurt's arms.

"It's not going well, is it?" she spluttered. "The Fuhrer is furious."

They sat on an old bench in front of the Gästehaus in silence as they stared at the mighty Watzmann.

The Gästehaus was closed.

Kurt told his family of the appalling suffering he had witnessed in 'the Ukraine' and southern Russia. "We were no better than them," he said. "Whole villages were burnt, livelihoods ruined, and all for nothing, and now…" He burst into tears, "Now my brother has been killed…for what purpose…nothing." His heart ached. He left them and wandered off into the hills where at least there was some solace.

Delphine and Hilda did their best to console. They fed him as best they could so that he could regain his strength. In the spring, he was called up again, this time to serve with the 10th Army in Italy. Once again, he donned the uniform of a lieutenant in the Wehrmacht of the Third Reich.

* * *

On 16 May, Germans heard of a horrendous attack on three vital dams that powered the vast Ruhr Valley steel works—the industrial hub of the Third Reich, with coke plants, steelworks, armaments factories and ten synthetic oil plants. The raids were British, following their RAF bombing raids on the Ruhr through March and April, but culminating in the surprising destruction of those heavily protected but vital dams, and the resultant flooding of large areas of the Ruhr Valley. They had apparently used some strange bouncing bombs that had allowed time for their pilots to climb their bombers above the range of fire before the bombs breached the dam walls.

In July in Italy, where Kurt now found himself in the German 10th Army, American soldiers and airmen were also now supporting the British, who after their success in North Africa had overrun Sicily. The Mediterranean sea-lanes were opened for enemy merchant ships for the first time since 1941. Things moved fast. These events led to the Italian leader, Benito Mussolini, being toppled from power in Italy on 25 July, and to the Allied invasion of Italy in September. British and American troops landed at Salerno on the western coast, while two supporting operations took place in Calabria and Taranto at the toe of the mainland. There was no question now to the German populace that the Americans were in this war.

The confused Italians now offered little resistance as the Allied forces moved up Italy towards Rome. The German 10th Army dug in to make a stand at the strategic pass of Monte Cassino in the Apennines. The landscape was dominated by a Benedictine monastery of great historicity, and units, including Lieutenant Kurt Moeller's, were told not to disturb the monastery itself but to dig in below the monastery and along the Gari River.

* * *

Seventeen-year-old Janne Heizz was looking forward to bringing their cows down from the Allgau meadows. It had been such a wonderful day for her the year before—a sort of rite of passage. It was the first time she had really had a good evening out with the boys of Oberstdorf away from the prying eyes of her parents. She remembered how they had danced at the Park Hotel, all in their best Dirndls and Lederhosen, and the beer had flowed and sausages sizzled. It was the first time she had really been kissed…well a proper kiss. It was Albert, from the neighbouring farm, after they had listened to the brass band before the cows came home. This year, on St Matthew's Day, she would be with her father to round up their herd of red and white, horned Hinterwälders and lead them into town. But things were very different now. There was no brass band in the market square, and so many of the boys were now conscripted or had returned from the Eastern Front or North Africa, wounded and weary. The cows were crowned and they ran into town, but the applause was mute.

All joy seemed to have gone out of the lives of these once happy people living on the edge of western Bavaria close to the Austrian, Liechtenstein and Swiss borders. A new wave of anti-Semitism was also raising its head, spurred on by Goebbels' comments on 'Bolshevist Jewish enslavement'.

At the Hohes Licht children's home, Hetty Laman called Abigail and Johannes Finkelstein's school friends, Pieter and Hendrick, into her study.

"I am sending you away," she said. "You will be travelling with your friends Abigail and Johannes Drucker and their mother, Francine. It's not really safe for you here anymore. Frau Drucker will take you somewhere where you will be safe and you can finish your schooling and be apprenticed to work."

"Because we are Jews?" Pieter asked. "We aren't Jews now, we're Lutherans."

"That's true…but some people don't see it that way," the kindly old owner of the children's home said. "It's the same for Abigail and Johannes. They were adopted. Their real name isn't Drucker, but Finkelstein. Sooner or later, that will come out. It's better that the four of you should stay together with Frau Drucker in a safer place."

The two boys looked at each other, suspicious frowns on their faces. "But we like it here," Pieter said.

"When it is safe, you can come back," Helen Laman assured them.

The next day, with no more than backpacks containing a change of clothes, Frau Laman took the boys to the Drucker farm. They shook hands with the elderly lady and she leaned into them, kissing them both on their cheeks. Herr Helmut Drucker then bundled them all into his car, the four children squashed into the backseat their backpacks on their knees. Pieter looked back at Frau Laman as they drove away into the dusk. Ahead, were the high peaks of the Allgau.

They drove along what seemed a series of dirt mountain roads taking them through valleys and over passes in the forests of the western extremities of Austria. Periodically, they stopped to relieve themselves in the woods as the large harvest moon rose above the Alps. Pieter and Johannes laughed as they sought competition as to who could shoot their pee the furthest. As dawn broke, Helmut Drucker stopped the car.

"You must walk from here," he said. "It'll take you a while, but with my car, we can't go further without arousing suspicion. You should make it this afternoon. When you see the big lake, you'll be very close to Switzerland."

He kissed his wife. "Good luck! I'll soon be joining you."

"I know," she said, slowly letting go of him, "soon". Her fearful eyes looked up at him appealingly.

"Soon," Helmut assured her.

Helmut watched as the four children walked away with Francine on the grassy path that would take them to the border.

* * *

On 15 February 1944, it was bitterly cold in the foxholes below the stately Benedictine monastery defending the ridge of Monte Cassino in Italy. Lieutenant

Kurt Moeller blew warm air into his hands. Repeated artillery attacks on assaulting Allied troops had denuded the forestation below the monastery. Fears escalated that they might not be able to hold the Gustav defences as their area of the Senger Line, more popularly known to the soldiers as the 'Winter Line'. Kurt looked into the sun as he heard the sound of aircraft in the glow. Out of the sunburst came wave upon wave of glinting silver bombers. They were not British. As they passed high above him, he realised that they could be American. Terrific explosions followed, and bombs rained down on the sacred monastery shaking the foxholes. Wave upon wave of bombers kept pummelling the convent. Dust filled the air. Some of the bombing was inaccurate, and along the mountain to Kurt's left above the small town of Cassino, many of his men were blown to smithereens. The carnage was awful and there was simply nothing that Kurt could do.

When finally the last wave came through and the dust settled, the great monastery above them was simply a pile of rubble.

Later, Fallschirmjäger paratroopers were dropped down to occupy the area and established defensive positions amid the ruins.

On 16 May, Polish soldiers launched one of the final assaults on the German defensive position as part of a twenty-division assault along a twenty-mile front. Two days later, a Polish flag followed by a British flag, was raised over the ruins. With this Allied victory, the German Senger Line collapsed, and the German defenders were driven from their positions.

Kurt's unit found themselves now holding the line at the new Allied bridgehead at Anzio, halfway between Monte Cassino and Rome. It was brutal and bloody but he survived without a scratch. The 10th Army was now in retreat. It seemed inevitable that Rome would fall. The southern half of Italy was now in the enemy's hands.

* * *

Francine Drucker and her charges settled in Switzerland at Bischofszell. They had met their contact at Rorschach on the south shore of Lake Constance. He had driven them to the small farm that he had found for them to live at in the fertile rolling hills just outside the mediaeval town straddling the banks of the River Sitter. The farmhouse was very old, with thick, stone walls and a steep, Dutch-style roof with stepped gable ends. The Druckers and the Dutch boys

Pieter and Hendrick were given three rooms on the third floor with dormer windows that looked out along the river to the distant Rhatikon Mountains of Liechtenstein. There was a dairy and a small herd of brown Swiss cattle. The property was owned by a rather dour cheese maker, Daniel Schwegler, who soon put Francine and the children to work in the dairy, where he taught them the process of making a soft, rich and creamy cheese encased in a waxy cover.

"Do you think we will ever see Mutter and Vater again?" Abigail asked her aunt.

Francine put her arms around the eleven-year-old girl. "It depends on this war," she answered. "They've probably been taken to the camps. They may not even be alive, Sweetie."

The girl looked up at her aunt. "You mean they could be dead?"

"We might never know…but we're safe now. Switzerland is not part of this dreadful war."

Tears welled in Abigail's eyes and she pressed against her aunt, who patted her back gently. Finally, the girl looked up at Francine, a faint smile forming across her face. "They'll be in heaven now, then?"

"For sure…and they might be a lot better off there. We have to be very brave, Sweetie. Now, help me with the curds."

Three months later, as promised, Helmut Drucker joined them, having passed the Oberstdorf farm over to his cousin, and he worked for Daniel Schwegler as a woodsman.

Midsummer, news drifted through of landings in Normandy by American, British and Allied forces, and eventually, of the fall of the Vichy Government and the loss of France with the Allies' liberation of Paris in late August. In Switzerland, however, the talk was more of the collapse in Italy, with Italian and German deserters and refugees crossing the border into neutral Switzerland.

When the long summer of 1944 had passed, the four Jewish children at the Schwegler farm were enrolled at the Protestant School in Bishchofszell.

Chapter Six
The End and New Beginnings
1945–1946

Kurt Moeller and the 10th Army had been chased up in Italy by British and American forces after the loss of Rome, but they established a line to make a final stand to protect the remaining parts of the northern Republic of Salo, where from Milano, a chastened Mussolini still held loyalty to the Axis with Hitler.

Kurt was surprised when he received a letter in the officer's Reichspost from his mother saying that his father had been conscripted and sent to defend the Polish border on the Eastern Front. *Good grief, the man is fifty years old,* he thought as he stared at the letter. *He'll never come out of that hell alive. Damn Hitler! What has the Fuhrer done to us?* Kurt thought back on the days when he had so admired the man, and how in his innocence he had served in the Hitler Youth so enthusiastically. Germany had been transformed then. But ever since he had seen those Jews incinerated in that synagogue in Poland, he had questioned things more and more. His brother had died in the African desert. His sister had spoken of Hitler's fury…that was when his friend Captain Heinz Groth had innocently claimed Mount Elbrus for the Third Reich. *We thought we were doing the right thing, something for the glory of Greater Germany. We climbed one of the highest peaks in all of Europe and renamed it for Hitler.* He mulled it over in his troubled mind. *But the Fuhrer apparently suggested that we should be court-martialled at the Reichskriegsgerich, probably taken out and summarily shot.* Fortunately, it had never happened, as assuredly he would have been implicated…and poor Groth…he was killed at Stalingrad. *After the hell of 'the Ukraine', thank God, we had those few days of joy in the Caucasus before that horror,* he reasoned.

Kurt sat on a bench outside his Division Headquarters in Milano, the crumpled letter in his hand. *Why did they fail?* He thought as he reflected on the

July plot that had almost succeeded in killing Hitler at the Wolfsschanze Nazi HQ in Poland. The plot, headed by Colonel Count Claus von Stauffenberg in July was the talk of his fellow officers.

Over the following weeks, Himmler's Gestapo, driven by a furious Hitler, had rounded up nearly everyone who had the remotest connection with this plot, including many army officers. The discovery of letters and diaries in the homes and offices of those arrested revealed other plots of 1938, 1939 and 1943, and this led to further rounds of arrests. Under Himmler's new Sippenhaft laws, many relatives of the principal plotters were also arrested in the immediate aftermath of the failed plot—more than seven thousand people altogether—and half of them had been executed.

The word among Kurt's fellow officers was that very few of the plotters tried to escape or deny their guilt when arrested. Those who survived interrogation were given perfunctory trials before the People's Court—a kangaroo court that always seemed to decide in favour of the prosecution. In propaganda films, the court's president, fanatical Nazi, Roland Freisler, was seen shouting furiously and insulting the accused at the trials. It was reported that the plotters were stripped of their uniforms and given old, shabby clothing to humiliate them for the cameras. The officers involved in the plot were tried before the Court of Military Honour, a drumhead court-martial that merely considered the evidence furnished to it by the Gestapo, before expelling the accused from the army in disgrace and handing them over to the People's Court. The first trials had been held in early August. Hitler had ordered that those found guilty should be 'hanged like cattle'. Many of those arrested had taken their own lives prior to either their trial or their execution.

A late November report on the background of the plot even stated that the Pope was somehow a conspirator, specifically naming Pope Pius XII as being a party in the attempt.

"What a shame, Major Kurt Moeller," repeated to himself. "If only it had succeeded."

* * *

In Berchtesgaden, Hilda Moeller was let go from her position at the Berghof. After the July assassination plot, Hitler ordered that the Berghof should be closed down for the foreseeable future. Only a skeleton staff was maintained.

It was a comfort for Delphine Moeller to have Hilda back home now that Manfred was away in Poland defending the Greater German Reich from expected Soviet advances. Together, they reopened the Gästehaus for refugees from the horrendous bombing raids that now rained down on Germany's northern cities.

Ever since the Battle for the Ruhr in 1943, the people of Northern Germany had been under attack. In a succession of massive raids through 1944, both the American Eighth Air Force and Great Britain's Bomber Command firebombed a multitude of cities, killing some six hundred thousand civilians and injuring many thousands more. Many refugees from these attacks, where almost everything they had known had been destroyed, made their way to Germany's safer south.

In late 1944, Frederick Trotter and his daughter Marlene arrived in Berchtesgaden. They had been caught in the second major attack on what little was left of Hamburg after the original disastrous firebombing of 1943. Frederick Trotter had lost both his young wife Eugenie and his mother Ursula in that disastrous raid, and he had brought up young Marlene in his father's house in the one part of the city that was still more or less unscathed. Frederick's father, industrialist Alfred Trotter, ran a factory on the outskirts of Hamburg, and Frederick, working for his father, had avoided conscription because of the importance of their work.

It was early December when the Trotters arrived in Berchtesgaden. At the refugee administration office, they were billeted to the Moeller Gästehaus.

Sitting in the parlour with Delphine and Hilda Moeller, Frederick Trotter regaled their story. "On the night of the sixth of September, one of the many random raids on Hamburg resulted in my father's factory being completely destroyed…Ironic really, when you think about it, as we were working on the Fuhrer's new 'Vengeance' rockets…flying bombs that were being launched from the Low Countries in a stand against Britain. They don't have to be carried in planes, and they are terrifying London…they just drop out of the sky unannounced. We made electronic components for those bombs." Frederick looked down at the floorboards. "Sadly, my father was working late that night. He was killed in the raid. What made it even worse was that when I carried Marlene home from the shelter the next morning, before I even knew my father was dead, we found that our house was just a pile of rubble still burning in its ruin."

Delphine reached out to Frederick. "We are so sorry," she said, "that must have been dreadful for you."

"It was," he said slowly. "Of course, we then went to the factory finding it almost totally destroyed, and we were informed that Marlene's grandfather was dead." He paused…"I decided right there and then that I had to take Marlene and get us out of Hamburg."

"So, where did you go?" Delphine asked, her brow furrowed with compassionate concern.

"We walked through the woods out into the countryside and at dusk, took refuge at a friendly farmhouse." He looked up at her. "That's how we travelled the last two months…from farmhouse to farmhouse, borrowing a change of underwear here and there until we reached Munich. I didn't trust cities any more, however, and before registering there, I got us on a train to Freilassing. I then saw this little train scheduled to run to Berchtesgaden…the end of the line. We took it and I felt a great relief to finally be in the mountains."

"Well, you're safe in the mountains now," Delphine said. "My husband though, he's somewhere facing the Russians on that Eastern Front."

"Oh! That's terrible…the worst," Frederick gasped.

Hilda then showed them to their room. The geraniums and petunias had finished in the window boxes, but the view out of their little window to the Watzmann in a fresh cap of snow gave them hope.

On their long journey from Hamburg to Berchtesgaden, Frederick had got used to doing farmyard chores to help out those who had helped them out on their way. It was only natural, therefore, that he continued these tasks in Berchtesgaden. He worked on the farm next door to the Gästehaus, mucking out the cowshed and chopping wood for Hannes Stack. At least it kept him warm in the cold Bavarian winter.

When Frederick was out on the neighbour's farm, Hilda spent much of her day taking care of his little girl. Marlene was five years old and would soon be celebrating a birthday, and she was becoming very fond of her new friend. The child had barely known her mother, Eugenie, being only four when her mother and Grandmother Ursula Trotter were killed. Hilda Moeller was fast becoming her mother figure.

Listening to the German news in the parlour in mid-February, they heard of yet another massive Allied bombing, this time in Saxony, and much further east. American and British bombers had pounded the beautiful old city of Dresden.

Frederick shuddered at the news, but in his heart he realised, knowing the part he had played in preparing those dreadful flying bombs, that this was an increasing and pointless round of tit-for-tat. He remained silent and moody until comforted by Hilda, who put her arm around him and lightly kissed him on his cheek.

There had never been an attack on Berchtesgaden, but on 20 February 1945, the valley suddenly roared to the sound of fighter bombers. The aircraft attacked a train but encountered heavy anti-aircraft fire from the Bahnhof and disappeared as quickly as they came. There was no time for the people of Berchtesgaden to take shelter, but many watched, their mouths agape, as the explosion and ball of fire rose in a wooded area along the river close to the railway station. It was enough to make people nervous, and over the next few weeks on a regular basis, the mayor ordered a series of rehearsals for the use of the air-raid shelters.

In early April as spring began to thaw the mountain snows, the Moellers and Trotters celebrated Marlene Trotter's sixth birthday with the luxury of cake and biscuits, such as Hilda remembered when first she had been invited to one of Adolf Hitler's tea parties for Berchtesgaden children at the Berghof in the 1930s. *If only they could all go back to those days and this war had never happened,* she thought. *There was such hope, and now there is only despair.* It seemed hard now to believe that for five years she had been in service up at the Obersalzberg estate. *I wonder what happened to Fraulein Eva Braun. She had said that she would go back to Munich.*

A late snowfall fell over Berchtesgaden in the early hours of 25 April. After breakfast, Hilda and Marlene went out with a sledge to slide down the bank below the Gästehaus. Marlene laughed as the sledge turned over, tumbling her into the wet snow, when suddenly the misty air filled with the buzz of bombers. The mayor's air-raid sirens wailed. A wave of American and British bombers was flying over the Berchtesgaden area. It was about 9:30 a.m. The bombers orbited around the valley. Hilda grabbed Marlene, abandoning the sledge, and called out to Delphine as they all headed down into the beer cellar to take cover.

Returning from the direction of Salzburg about twenty minutes later, the bombers started to drop their cargo on the Obersalzberg. Wave upon wave came over. Massive explosions resounded from the mountain. A second series of waves bombed between 10:42 a.m. and 11:00 a.m. Two British Lancaster bombers were shot down by Waffen-SS anti-aircraft guns. An aircraft from the Royal Australian Air Force was hit shortly after dropping its bombs, all of its crew surviving after the pilot made a forced landing near the town of Traunstein. They were made prisoners-of-war, along with the British crew of an aircraft from No. 619 Squadron RAF. Of that bomber's crew, four were killed and three were taken prisoner.

After the all-clear sounded about noon, the buzz on the streets of Berchtesgaden indicated that it must have been a massive attack on the Obersalzberg as there was no damage to their old town. Their suspicions were soon confirmed as they could see the coils of black smoke rising from the mountain when the snowy skies opened up. The mountain peaks were clear again against a blue sky. The Kehlsteinhaus could still be seen, undamaged on its mountain perch. The citizens of Berchtesgaden felt relieved that they had come away from the unexpected raid unscathed.

Locations near the Obersalzberg had also been attacked, including Freilassing, Hallein, Bad Reichenhall, Salzburg and Traunstein. Considerable damage was inflicted on several train stations, gasworks and hospitals in these towns. More than three hundred civilians were killed.

* * *

Hitler's vice chancellor, Herman Göring, emerged from his private bunker on the Obersalzberg to see the smouldering ruin of much that had been his home. Dazed, he shuffled into what was left of his mountain retreat. The smell of charred wood and blackened plaster greeted his nostrils. He started to aimlessly pick at his strewn possessions. There was now a deathly silence over the Obersalzberg. Slowly, he made his way down to the Berghof. *It looks like it has survived*, he perceived. SS guards were running in and out of the building as if they were looting the place.

Göring learned that most of the approximately three thousand people at the Obersalzberg estate had sheltered in the bunkers below the Berghof. Over thirty were known to have been killed, including several children. It was quickly revealed, however, that the bunker network wasn't seriously damaged, and Herman could see that much of the Berghof was still standing, but severe damage had been done to most other areas, including the Waffen-SS barracks.

The vice chancellor realised he had to stop the looting. *It was the Fuhrer's orders that if the Obersalzberg was attacked, he must see that everything left should be destroyed before the enemy had time to advance into the area.* "Stop!" he yelled. "The building must be destroyed! That's an order…that's the Fuhrer's order! Nothing must be left for the enemy."

He ordered petrol cans from the bunkers to be brought up and used to start the conflagration. In no time, the great chalet was ablaze. A tear swept a line across the grime of Herman Göring's cheek as he looked up at the funeral pyre of the Third Reich. He had done his duty, but a fearful lump filled his throat. Then, he turned to the stunned SS guards.

"It's every man for himself," he shouted. "Go!"

* * *

Major Kurt Moeller watched in fearful horror as the German 10th Army began to crumble in the Republic of Salo. The Italian Piedmont population had no desire to fight on, often acting against the forces of Mussolini and the Germans. More and more German soldiers risked a chance to reach the Swiss border and escape the inevitable end. Piedmont mountain guides showed them the way. Several went missing from Kurt's division. The major turned a blind eye, more fearful of the summary executions that such desertion meant. *They'll just shoot them like they murder the Jews,* he thought.

What news came through to the troops was only bad. The stand in Belgium had collapsed. French and American soldiers were now in the fatherland, and worst of all, the Soviets were fast making gains on the Eastern Front. It seemed that all was lost. *Why are we holding on to Savoy?* Kurt questioned. *Wouldn't it be better to just let the men go home to see their families before the inevitable dreadful end?*

On 28 April, astounding news surfaced. Benito Mussolini had been assassinated.

On the evening of Mussolini's capture, Sandro Pertini, a Socialist partisan leader in northern Italy, announced on Radio Milano: '*The head of this association of delinquents, Mussolini, while yellow with rancour and fear and trying to cross the Swiss frontier, has been arrested. He must be handed over to a tribunal of the people so it can judge him quickly. We want this, even though we think an execution platoon is too much of an honour for this man. He would deserve to be killed like a mangy dog.*'

Kurt was astounded at what he heard. *Surely this will be the end,* he thought. *Now, they must send us home.*

The bodies of Mussolini and his mistress, Clara Petacci, and the other executed fascists were apparently loaded onto a van and transported south to Milano. On arriving in the city in the early hours of 29 April, the bodies were dumped on the ground in the Piazzale Loreto, a suburban square near the main railway station.

By 9:00 a.m., a considerable crowd had gathered. The corpses were pelted with vegetables, spat at, urinated on, shot at and kicked. Allied forces began arriving in the city during the course of the morning, and an American eyewitness described the crowd as 'sinister, depraved and out of control'. After a while, the bodies were hung by their feet from the metal girder framework of a half-built Standard Oil petrol garage.

At about 2:00 p.m., the recently arrived American military authorities ordered that the bodies be taken down and delivered to the city morgue for autopsies to be carried out. A U.S. army cameraman went to the morgue and took photographs of the bodies for publication, including one with Mussolini and Petacci positioned in a macabre pose as though they were arm-in-arm. On 30 April, an autopsy was carried out on Mussolini. Four bullets near the heart were given as the cause of death.

* * *

Earlier on the day that Adolf Hitler learned of Mussolini's execution, Hitler had recorded in his *Last Will and Testament* that he intended to choose death rather than be captured by the enemy or fall into the hands of 'the masses' to become 'a spectacle arranged by Jews'. Eva Braun had joined him at the bunker and they were quickly married. The following day, Hitler committed suicide in Berlin, shortly before the city fell to the Red Army.

At first, the word was put out that the Fuhrer had died nobly fighting 'the Bolsheviks', but a few days later, the truth came out that he and Eva Braun had committed suicide together after testing cyanide pills out on Hitler's favourite German Shepherd dog, Blondi. Blondi died, but Hitler was now sure he could commit suicide and join Blondi in the hereafter. Blondi had recently had a litter of five puppies. After Hitler and Eva Braun poisoned themselves, the Fuhrer's personal dog trainer shot all five puppies in the garden next to the bunker.

Hilda Moeller gasped and buried her head on Frederick Trotter's shoulder. "Blondi…not Blondi. She was a wonderful dog, Frederick…I loved her. She was always so gentle…not fierce at all. Oh no!" she sobbed. "Blondi and her pups… that's dreadful! How could Hitler do that to Blondi?"

In accordance with Hitler's prior instructions, his own body was immediately burnt with petrol, leaving virtually no remains. With Vice Chancellor Herman Göring presumed to still be in the ruins of the Obersalzberg above Berchtesgaden, Grand Admiral Karl Dönitz was announced as the new Nazi Leader as Berlin was overrun by the Russians. In days, Dönitz sued for peace. The Third Reich crumbled.

* * *

Major Kurt Moeller crossed the border into Switzerland, climbing up the ravines north of Lake Como and making his way towards Lugano. He kept to the woodland paths wishing to avoid being seen in his German uniform. The beauty of Lugano, with its multi-coloured Italianate façades beside a clear glacial lake all untouched by the pockmarks of war, seemed like a dream. The smell of fresh-baked bread drew Kurt to a side-street café, where he sat and begged for food. The owner spoke German and treated him kindly.

"You need to ditch that uniform," the baker suggested. "Let me give you trousers and a shirt. A lot of you boys have come through here, but you need to be careful. Not all these Italian Swiss are sympathetic. I'll help you get on up into the north-east. Where are you trying to go?"

"Bavaria," Kurt replied.

The baker's eyes lit up. "I'm a Bavarian! I got out in 1939…saw what was coming. My family was from Garmisch."

He ordered them a couple of beers, but he never revealed his name nor did Kurt ask.

The next day, this generous man took Kurt to the railway station and saw him onto a train bound from Lugano to Lucerne. It seemed a long way as the train chugged its way through the two main ranges of the Swiss Alps, but the snow-capped mountains brought a rush of excitement to Kurt. He was particularly excited to eventually see Mount Eiger on the left. The peaks reminded him of the Watzmann and home. "I wonder how much Berchtesgaden has changed?" he asked himself. Still tired, he dozed off and dreamed of carefree days before he had joined the Hitler Youth when the Berchtesgadenland Mountains were his world. He laughed as the train jolted him back into consciousness. The image of the cows, crowned in those headdresses, their bells clanging as they stampeded their way home from their Alpine meadows, filled his mind. Could the world ever be like that again?

From Lucerne, he knew that he must head towards Liechtenstein or Lake Constance—the areas where Switzerland was closest to Bavaria. Kurt was lucky to get a lift in a lorry carrying produce from Lucerne to Zurich. He was running out of funds and had to rely on the kindness of others in the market stalls, who from time to time gave him berries and fruits and occasionally a Swiss crêpe. From Zurich, he walked about forty kilometres through undulating farmland to St Gallen. At the market there, he met Daniel Schwegler, a cheesemaker, who took pity on him and drove him back to his farm on the outskirts of the very pretty village of Bischofzell.

In the kitchen at the cheesemaker's farmhouse, a lady was making Swiss pancakes. The smell of cooking permeated the house.

"Francine…this is Kurt," the cheesemaker said. "He's on his way back to Bavaria, but he's starving. I thought we could help him out for a couple of days."

Francine handed him a plate with a fresh chicken and asparagus pancake oozing with Swiss cheese. "I'm making these for the children when they come home from school. You're welcome to join us."

"Thank you, so much," Kurt said as he took a bite out of the crêpe. "So, how many children do you both have?"

"Oh…they're not my children," Schwegler said. "Francine and the children are refugees from Bavaria."

Kurt's eyes now lit up, "Where in Bavaria?"

"Oberstdorf," Francine answered. "We are Jewish, not practising…actually Lutherans, but it wasn't safe for us anymore. Anybody of Jewish heritage wasn't safe. We knew in time that someone would find out who we really were and report on us. We escaped and settled here with Daniel. My husband will be home soon. He's a woodsman, but I help Daniel here with the dairy…the children do, too, on the weekends and school holidays."

Kurt froze. He thought of Merla Finkelstein in Berchtesgaden, and how his own brother had assisted in her arrest and mysterious disappearance. Then, the horror of that burning synagogue in Poland in which he had played a role loomed before him yet again. He looked at the floor and held his head in his hand.

"Are you all right?" Francine asked.

"Yes…I'll be okay. Just give me a moment…I came over a bit faint." He took another bite out of the crêpe. The melted cheese dribbled from the corners of his hungry mouth. It tasted so delicious. "Did you know Heinz Groth or Gerd Aurich?" he asked as he wiped the cheese away with the back of his hand.

"In Oberstdorf?" Francine shook her head, "I don't think so."

"I just wondered…I knew them on the Eastern Front. They were Oberstdorfers. I served with them. They were both killed."

Francine looked a little nervous, but she heard the children chattering away outside. They were back from school, and they would be ready for their crêpes.

The children only wanted to know from Kurt what it was like being a soldier in Italy.

* * *

In the last days of the Third Reich, the people of Oberstdorf were fearful. It was known that the French were not far away. Occasional shell fire rumbled around the mountains. The struggle between die-hard Nazis and those simply wanting to surrender and carry on with their lives was leading to summary executions. On the day that Hitler committed suicide, the French with armoured tanks entered Immemstadt, just a few miles down the road from Oberstdorf. Karl Richter, one of Oberstdorf's most successful businessmen, who was the self-proclaimed leader of the anti-Nazi resistance movement, raised a white flag of surrender on the church spire. Mayor Fink immediately ordered it to be taken down but made no attempt to have Richter arrested. Members of the resistance openly wore blue and white armbands waiting to welcome the French as liberators, but in reality, for the most part, they just wanted to protect their homes, their village and their Bavarian way of life.

After a successful coup, where arrests of prominent Nazis, including the mayor, were made by the resistance in a midnight raid, the Nazi leaders were all locked down in the cellar of the town hall. A prominent French aristocrat and former ambassador to Berlin, who had been detained as a prisoner-of-war under house arrest at the Ifen Hotel in Hirschegg, a hamlet only nine miles from Oberstdorf, was sprung. He was asked to write a letter on behalf of the people of Oberstdorf, pleading that their little town might be spared for their surrender.

The letter was delivered to Karl Richter who was determined to get it to the French as soon as they closed in on Oberstdorf. He bit his nails as he waited in a snowstorm on the road leading north out of the town. He knew that American troops were also making their way through the Allgau region.

In the silence of that afternoon, Karl Richter finally heard the rumble of tanks. They appeared out of the snowstorm, and they were French. With a white flag, Karl approached the first tank with the ambassador's letter. The tanks then rumbled on towards Oberstdorf, but not a shot or shell was fired.

* * *

Later that evening in the town hall, now nineteen-year-old year Janne Heizz stood with her parents anxiously wondering what might become the fate of their town. The French commander accepted Thomas Neidhart as the new mayor, who had been Oberstdorf's last non-Nazi mayor before Nazification in 1933. He also put Richter in charge of law and order allowing his Heimatschutz resistance members to keep their arms. The next day, French Moroccan troops in black-tasselled, red fez hats marched into town.

Janne looked at her father. "So does this mean that now we're all French?"

Her father frowned. "Perhaps," was all he said.

The Americans moved on to Upper Bavaria.

* * *

About midday on 4 May, Americans of the U.S. Seventh Army, meeting little resistance, reached Berchtesgaden. Their jeeps rattled over the cobbled stones in the old town, and some of the soldiers handed out chocolate bars to curious children in Palace Square, but they didn't stay, making their way to the Obersalzberg.

Delphine looked across the valley at the mountains. The Kehlsteinhaus could clearly be seen at the top of the ridge.

"It's funny that they never bombed that place," she said to Hilda. They both stared up at the familiar mountain.

"Were you ever up there?" Delphine asked. "I've often wondered what it was like."

"I was only ever there once," Hilda replied. "Fraulein Eva Braun asked me to help out up there for a wedding party last summer…one of those important Nazis married her sister. I waited on them, but I can't really remember his name…Fenegel, or something like that. They were actually married in Salzburg, and of course, they came back to the Berghof. There were wedding parties for a couple of days, but the only one I was serving at was the party that Fraulein Braun gave for her sister. Hitler didn't come to that…actually, he very rarely ever went up to the 'Eagle's Nest' as we used to call it."

"It must be a fantastic view from up there."

"It is."

"Is it true that you have to take a golden lift from inside the mountain to get there?"

"Oh yes, that's true, but apart from the view over the Alps, I didn't think it was all that special. The Berghof was much nicer."

They stared at the mountain a little longer, wondering why the Americans had all gone up there.

On 8 May, it was official; the German Third Reich surrendered to the Allies—the United States, Great Britain, France and the Soviet Union—but as yet there was no official government, just foreign soldiers. A day later, the word was out in Berchtesgaden that Herman Göring, Hitler's commander-in-chief of the Luftwaffe, president of the Reichstag, head of the Gestapo, prime minister of Prussia and designated successor as vice chancellor was taken prisoner by the U.S. Seventh Army when he was found hiding in the loft of a barn close to the ruins of his Obersalzberg home.

"The war's over…Your father might be coming home," Delphine said to Hilda. "We can only hope and pray that he is still alive."

* * *

As Allied troops moved across Europe in a series of offensives on Germany in April 1945, they began to encounter and liberate concentration camp prisoners, many of whom had survived death marches into the interior of Germany from camps in the east, and who told of the horrors of places like Auschwitz.

U.S. forces liberated the Buchenwald concentration camp near Weimar on 11 April. Earlier that day, before the arrival of the Americans, apparently an underground prisoner resistance organisation seized control of the camp and prevented atrocities from being committed by retreating camp guards. On their arrival, the Americans found some twenty thousand prisoners, mostly Jewish, in various stages of starvation. The U.S. forces then went on into Bavaria, and in April and May liberated further camps at Dachau, Dora-Mittelbau and Flossenbürg, where Professor Herman Finkelstein had been sent to work at the Messerschmitt factory and mysteriously disappeared in 1943. The last camp the U.S. Army found was Mauthausen, about the same time that they reached Berchtesgaden—the time of the surrender.

British forces liberated camps in Northern Germany that included Neuengamme and Bergen-Belsen. At Bergen-Belsen near Celle, they found some sixty thousand prisoners, also mostly Jewish, in critical condition because of a typhus epidemic. In their weakness, many of them apparently died within days of their liberation.

It was a month or two later before the Russians revealed some of the horrors that they had found earlier in their march across the eastern parts of Greater Germany. Apparently, they had discovered Majdanek near Lublin in Poland as early as the summer of 1944, but the camp had been abandoned. They reported on evidence of the mass murder committed in these camps by the Nazis. Six months later, the Soviets claimed that they had liberated Auschwitz, which turned out to be the largest Nazi concentration camp. As at Majdanek, there was abundant evidence of mass murder. The retreating Germans had destroyed some of the warehouses at Auschwitz but had no time to destroy the gas chambers and crematoria. The Soviets found the confiscated possessions of the Nazi victims, that later when they invited journalists in after the surrender, included thousands of men's suits, women's garments and more than fourteen thousand pounds of shorn human hair. After the Soviets overran Berlin, they liberated Stuttof, Sachsenhausen and Ravensbrück.

Slowly, these horrific revelations were uncovered. Among many of the ordinary German people, however, where there was still a lot of systemic anti-Semitic feeling, the reports were treated sceptically as the propaganda of their new masters.

In Oberstdorf, where there had been more tolerance of Jews than in most areas, the plight of Jews first came home to the villagers when Emil Schnell, a prominent citizen, committed suicide on receiving the summons that he was to be sent to the Jewish ghetto at Theresienstadt. One by one, even Oberstdorf's Jews had been sent away.

Janne Heizz was curious as she discussed the matter with her boyfriend, Arne, as they walked along the banks of the Breitach River.

"Where did they take them?" she asked.

With a leer, Arne grimaced at her, "To a place where if they died, their teeth were broken out to get the gold from the fillings, their hair was shaved off, and their scalps were made into lampshades. Then, they boiled their bones to make soap."

She giggled. "Oh, don't be so silly, Arne. You're just trying to scare me."

"No…it's true," Arne insisted. "They say that's why Herr Schnell committed suicide."

Janne's eyes looked crossed. "I don't think I'll ever use soap again."

* * *

Helmut Drucker drove Kurt to the Border Mountains. "How come you know so much about Oberstdorf?" he finally asked.

"I trained with the 1st Mountaineers at Sonthofen…before we were sent to the Eastern Front," Kurt revealed. "I travelled with several Oberstdorfers at that time. We climbed Mount Elbrus when we were in southern Russia together, one of the highest mountains in Europe." He stared ahead of him at the narrow road leading into the mountains. "That was before we were sent up to Stalingrad."

Helmut Drucker stopped the car where a grassy footpath came down through the forest to meet the road. "It's quite a long way, but eventually this will take you to Mittenwald where you can descend to Garmisch-Partenkirchen," he said. "You will then be in Upper Bavaria, but you will probably have avoided American checkpoints." They shook hands. "Good luck!"

It was, indeed, a long walk in the woods and Alpine meadows of the passes through the Austrian Alps to reach Mittenwald. Luckily, Kurt found a cow byre in which to stay the night. The second night, after he had passed Mittenwald and the border and was making his way down from the Bavarian Alps to Garmisch, at sunset he rested up in another byre set in the meadows of a large Schloss near Krun. Nobody disturbed him, and the cows were outside enjoying the rich late-May grass of the Alpine meadows. It was comforting to Kurt to hear the bells clanging around their necks again as they moved about. At times, Kurt could also hear their breath, but the nights were now too warm for the cows to come into the shed. Comforted by the sounds, Kurt smiled and laughed to himself, *Things seem pretty normal here. It's good to be finally going home.*

He hitched a ride on a timber train taking pine logs down to the plain. It just kept going all the way to Munich, but it seemed to be the only train on the line that day. From Munich, he hoped he could get a train to Freilassing. There was chaos at the Munich Bahnhof, but after several people had informed him that there was a train going to Vienna, he approached the suggested platform. For confirmation, he walked up to the engine. "Vienna?" he asked the driver. The man nodded. *This should stop at Freilassing,* he reasoned before seeking confirmation, "Will you stop at Freilassing?"

"Freilassing?" the driver repeated.

"Yes."

"All right, I'll stop for you at Freilassing."

Nobody appeared to have tickets and there seemed to be no timetable. Trains seemed to move just on the freewill of their drivers. Kurt clambered up into a compartment in the first crowded carriage. Steam up; the engine pulled the train out of the station.

The train moved very slowly, but it didn't stop, at least not until it reached Freilassing about three hours later. In a cloud of steam, Kurt descended to the platform. The train driver looked back from his cab and seeing Kurt on the platform gave him a wave. A few people climbed on board, and then with a series of loud puffs in a mixture of steam and coal smoke, the train moved on.

Kurt slept the night on a railway bench. *Not much chance of a train from Freilassing to Berchtesgaden, but I know the road,* he thought to himself. In the morning, feeling very stiff, Kurt started to make his way towards Bad Reichenhall and the road to home. Several hours later, Kurt walked up through Berchtesgaden until he reached the Moeller Gästehaus. When Delphine and Hilda saw him, he looked totally exhausted with dark circles around both of his eyes.

After Kurt had surprised his family with his sudden appearance in late May 1945, the reality hit him that neither his mother Delphine, nor his sister Hilda, had any idea where his father was. All they knew was that Manfred Moeller had been serving on the Eastern Front somewhere in southeast Poland. Apparently, there had been no letters since Christmas, when Manfred had written that they were celebrating in a Polish village as they retreated from the advancing Soviets. The very thought of a Polish village made Kurt shudder.

"A Jewish village?" he asked.

"No, like the letter said, they were celebrating Christmas. Apparently, they roasted a pig," his mother answered. "Now, if they were Jewish they would never have roasted a pig."

Kurt felt a wave of self-pity. He started to uncontrollably cry. His mother couldn't console him, but Hilda came over and sat beside him. "Did you see the camps?" she whispered. "Did they have camps for Jews in Italy?"

"No…I never saw a camp…but I saw worse. I carried out orders. I locked Jewish villagers up in their own wooden synagogue when I was in Poland. Then, we soaked the building in petrol and we set it ablaze." He put his head in his hands.

Hilda put her arm around her brother's shoulders. "It wasn't your fault. They were orders."

He looked up at her. "Yes…but I was the sergeant in charge." Then, he shouted, "Leave me alone, Hilda…Leave me alone!"

Startled, Hilda released him.

Kurt heard his mother call his sister. "Leave him, Hilda. Prepare his room. we need to get him upstairs. We need to get him up there before Frederick comes home and Marlene is out of school."

The next thing Kurt remembered was waking up the following morning in a bed with sheets and blankets—a luxury that he had almost forgotten. He could smell the pine wood of the walls and he could see the geraniums blooming outside in the window box, and the mighty Watzmann looking down on Berchtesgaden.

* * *

As the summer wore on, more and more reports surfaced of the horrors that the Allies had found at the concentration camps—whole lines of ovens in the crematoria, whole trenches of mass graves, those piles of boots and shoes, the emaciated skeletal bodies of the liberated. The first photographs bore witness to this killing machine.

At first, however, led by the Americans, the Allies embarked on the immediate problem of hunting down the Nazi leaders and a program of the denazification of local governments. In Northern Bavaria in the summer of 1945, they set up a military court at the old mediaeval city of Nuremberg for this purpose. In Berchtesgaden, it was known that the Americans had captured Hermann Göring at his home on the Obersalzberg. It was not known where they kept him prisoner, but it was assumed, if he was still alive, that he was held in the old Wehrmacht barracks on the edge of the town that had become the American headquarters. In October, it was revealed that he had been taken to Nuremberg. Hermann Göring was the highest-ranking Nazi officer on trial at the International Military Tribunal. It was Göring who ordered Security Police Chief Reinhard Heydrich to organise and coordinate a 'total solution' to the 'Jewish question'. The Nuremberg Tribunal charged Herman Göring for crimes against peace, war crimes, crimes against humanity and conspiracy to commit such crimes. He was convicted by the joint military tribunal and sentenced to death.

Frederick Trotter became nervous as more and more Nazis were imprisoned. *What if they ever link me to my father's name…to our part in assisting Hitler in building the electronic circuits for those 'Vengeance' rockets?* He thought of his own city, Hamburg, totally destroyed with thousands of civilians killed. *This is so unfair*, he thought, sweating in the safety of his bed. *They committed the same war crimes we did. They killed millions of civilians…these hypocrites have obliterated two huge cities in Japan with single bombs. What right do they have to judge others?*

Frederick kept these thoughts to himself. He was falling in love with Hilda Moeller. His daughter was happy in Berchtesgaden and she loved Hilda. They loved the mountains. He loved his new life. *No…nobody must ever know.* All he now said when asked by others was that 'he had owned a factory that made wireless parts'. Now, he was a farm-hand. *That's all anyone needs to know.*

Whether it was on the rebound from these thoughts—a means for his greater security—he asked Hilda to marry him. He didn't have a ring, but as they walked in the fresh snow looking out to the Untersberg above the Moeller Gästehaus, he kissed her and went down on one knee as he held her hand.

A beautiful smile came across Hilda's face. "Of course…Yes!" she said. "We must tell Marlene right away." She started to laugh. "Get up…your trousers will get soaking wet."

"But I haven't even asked you yet," he said.

She helped pull him up. "You don't have to. I've given you my answer."

In Oberstdorf, denazification was also causing distress. The Moroccan French troops were withdrawn from the town in late 1945, and the Americans took over Swabia. They set up the Prechamber in Sonthofen—a new kind of tribunal but run by Germans—that was supposed to separate the Nazis from the non-Nazis. It was grossly inefficient, however, as its judges could see that in practice most Germans were now utterly disillusioned with National Socialism, deeply weary of conflict and far from plotting against the Allies. They were thinking only of where they could find their next meal. After registration, those summoned to the Spruchkammer were required to produce their own witnesses and supporting documents and were then judged into five categories—major offenders, offenders, lesser offenders, followers and exonerated persons. For the most part, no more than fines were given out.

Janne Heizz's boyfriend, Arne, was called to the Spruchkammer in Sonthofen.

"Why…you're not a Nazi?" Janne pleaded after they had fed her cows from their precious crop of last summer's hay. But Arne looked shifty as if he really was hiding something. "I'm not. I've never been a member of the party," he insisted.

"Then, why are they calling you?"

Arne was shaking. "I don't know! What have we now?" he shouted. "No country, no government, no money, precious little food! Damn the Americans! Damn them! We were once a great country. What are we now?"

Janne had never seen him this angry. She felt a little scared. "When do you have to go?" she asked.

"I don't know…as soon as possible, I suppose." He walked out of the cowshed. "Things will never be how they were," he muttered, looking up at the setting sun streaking out a fan of beams as it lowered its orb behind the Alps. He started down the path, and Janne thought she heard him curse 'those sneaking, snivelling Jews'!

Arne disappeared from her life. He went to Sonthofen but he didn't come back. Through the gossip channels, Janne later heard that he had been sent to a prison camp as an 'offender', all something to do with him informing the Waffen-SS during the last two years of the war on the whereabouts of Oberstdorf's Jews. As a result, many were deported to Theresienstadt in Bohemia.

In 1946, news filtered through to Bavarians about the Nuremberg trials as sentences began to be handed out to the captured Nazi leaders. Twelve were condemned to death by hanging, including Martin Borman, Albert Speer and Herman Göring, all of whom Hilda Moeller had known by sight at the Berghof. Borman was condemned *in absentia,* as he was missing, and Göring reportedly committed suicide through poisoning the day before he would have been hanged. Albert Speer was at first condemned to death, but after two days his sentence was changed to twenty years' imprisonment.

"He always seemed rather nice," Hilda confided to Frederick Trotter. "I mean, I didn't personally know him, but at the Berghof, he didn't shout and get angry like some of the others. Whenever I served him he actually said 'Thank you'. None of the others did."

Frederick, still holding his own dark secret, put his fingers to his lips. "Shss! Don't talk about those days, Hilda. You don't want to get the call to a Spruchkammer."

"I'm no Nazi!" she assured him.

"Good…Now, how's your mother getting on with that dress for Marlene? She's so looking forward to being your flower girl."

The wedding of Frederick Trotter to Hilda Moeller took place in the Maria Gern Roman Catholic church perched on a little hill on the road leading out of town in the folds of the Kneifelspitze. The Trotters were Lutherans, but in Bavaria, Frederick had adopted Catholic ways. The little church with its exquisite baroque interior was the perfect setting for this small family wedding. The congregation was made up mostly of Marlene's school friends all longing to see her as a bridesmaid or flower girl. Delphine had made both the bride's and the young girl's dresses. They were simple with the austerity of the times, but the nuns at the Convent of the Sacred Heart had provided the white lawn cloth that Delphine had sewn. The silky cotton made an excellent background for the late autumn flowers that Hilda and Marlene had picked from the fringes of the woods above the Gästehaus—pink sedums and blue augustifoliums mixed with orange rose hips from the climbers at the house. The nuns also contributed to the lace veil.

Frederick and Kurt were in their best Lederhosen and Delphine in a Dirndl.

A little after 3:00 p.m., on a mild October day with the sun streaming through the windows enhancing the gilded splendour of the church, Father Sebastian proclaimed Frederick and Hilda to be man and wife. Marlene threw out late rose petals with autumn gentians and colchicums as they passed down the little aisle between the pews, carpeting the stone floor in pink, blue and white. Outside, Hannes Stack had his two heavy workhorses tethered to his wagon, ready to take the bride and groom home as the golden light of late afternoon lit up the Watzmann. The others followed, piled into Manfred Moeller's pre-war DKW.

Silently, alone in her room as the wedding revellers filled the parlour, Delphine asked herself, "Where is my husband…Where is Manfred?" They had still not heard a word.

Chapter Seven
Nightmares and Dreams 1947–1949

In 1946, the United States and Great Britain merged their occupation zones, and in 1947, some of the shortages and hardships of the German people were alleviated when the United States Government began a massive programme which pumped dollars and goods into Europe to aid in recovery. The Soviet Union prevented the countries along the Soviet border in Eastern Europe, many of which had experienced the rise of communist leadership in the wake of the war, from taking part in this arrangement. Instead, the Soviet Union offered its own post-war program for economic aid within a communist system. This divide between the Soviets and their allies did not bode well for Germany's future.

Stalin imposed a blockade from 24 June 1948, cutting off all land and river transport between the joint American and British zones and the Soviet zone. As Berlin was landlocked in the middle of the Soviet zone, but was still officially the capital of all Germany and itself divided into four zones that included a French zone, this action crippled the capital. The Americans and British then created an airlift to bring food and goods from their western zones into their Berlin zones. Even coal was airlifted this way. Costly, but effective, the airlift lasted until 12 May 1949. Within two weeks, the American, British and French areas of occupation jointly became the Federal Republic of Germany establishing the capital in Bonn. Some four months later, the Soviets proclaimed their area of occupation as the German Democratic Republic firmly allied to the Soviet bloc of nations within a communist system. The division between East and West was now formed.

* * *

As all this was unfolding in the military and diplomatic circles of the Allies, a measure of order returned to ordinary German life. Assuming that Manfred Moeller had been killed on the Eastern Front, Delphine made the Moeller Gästehaus over to her daughter and new son-in-law, and they opened up for guests again.

Delphine's new step-granddaughter Marlene Trotter wanted a pony for Christmas—rather beyond Delphine's means, but somehow the miracle occurred. Delphine arranged it with Father Sebastian and they hatched a plan. When the three kings knocked at the Moeller door at Epiphany to bless the Gästehaus, they had a small pony with them. When Marlene saw the pony, her eyes lit up.

One of the kings then led the pony up to the girl. "This pony has come a very long way and is awfully tired. I don't think she will get to Bethlehem, so perhaps you can take care of her?"

"Oh my…of course!" Marlene said joyfully. "I'll call her Maria after the mother of Jesus." She looked up at Delphine. "That was just what I wanted. It's a miracle!"

Maria then became the centre of Marlene's life. Hannes Stack helped to teach her to ride the pony, and her school friends sometimes came around to help with grooming and mucking out. 1949 looked promising for the child.

Kurt, however, withdrew more and more into himself, accepting the Trotters but not fully embracing them. He made himself useful at times, helping out here and there, but his only real outlet was escape—escape to the mountains. What little money he earned came from acting as a guide, especially after the American and British-occupied zones became one administration. Northern Germany was still heavily scarred from the war, and Germans from the north started to move more freely to Bavaria as an escape from their drab lives. They re-discovered the beauty of the Bavarian Alps. A few were experienced skiers and climbers, and for them, Kurt ventured to the Jenner or the Watzmann, but for most of them it was more leading them along the paths and trails that he knew so well to give them views of the mighty peaks. The 'non-fraternising' rules of 1945 had long been relaxed, and by 1949, there were quite a number of American tourists among Kurt's clients. Most of them knew little about the Obersalzberg, but once they realised that this had been Hitler's home, curiosity beckoned. All they wanted to do was to go there. The area was still off-limits, so Kurt knew he couldn't take them.

He kept asking himself, *Why are they so fascinated with Hitler? They fought against him. He ruined our country and he was a mass murderer.*

The thought of all those extermination camps haunted him because of his own secret guilt. Often he couldn't sleep or he awoke from violent dreams where he saw Jews shot into mass graves, and always those scenes from Poland came back to haunt him. The flames…the smell of burning flesh…the final screams from within as the roof caved in…it was he who had ordered the first match to be struck. It was he who had burnt them to death. There must have been near to a hundred of them crammed into that synagogue—men, women and children— pretty much the whole village. And yet it was all nearly ten years ago. *When will this ever go away?*

As he tossed and turned in his attic room at the Gästehaus, he made a decision. *I must leave Berchtesgaden. The stench of Hitler is too strong here. I'll go back to Oberstdorf. I have yet to climb in the Allgau. Yes…I must get away. I'm going to Oberstdorf. I wonder if Gerd Aurich's family is still there.*

* * *

Janne Heizz often joined friends at a beer garden just outside Oberstdorf on the road to Birgsau that looked out across the river at the twin peaks of the Rubihorn and Nebelhorn. On a warm evening in early June of 1949, there was a noisy group of young mountaineers a couple of tables away. It wasn't long before one of them came over and asked if she and her girlfriend might join them. Janne looked at her friend.

"Why not?" Gretel said, and they picked up their tall glasses of Lowenbrau and joined the mountaineers.

Janne was seated next to a climber she really hadn't seen before.

He introduced himself. "My name's Kurt…Kurt Moeller. I'm visiting…from Berchtesgaden."

"Welcome to the Allgau," she answered. "I'm Janne and my friend here is Gretel."

Gretel, however, with her 'bedroom eyes' was already busy raising a glass with one of the more rowdy ones.

"So, how long have you been here?" Janne asked Kurt.

"About ten days…doing a bit of climbing…tackled the Rubihorn a couple of days ago, but we really want to have a crack at the Grosser Kottenkopf. Do you climb?"

"A little…mostly in the foothills," she said. "We take our cows up to the alms every summer."

"So, you farm?" Kurt asked.

"Yes…mostly Hinterwälders. My family has had Hinterwälders forever. I think grandfather Heizz started the herd when he came back from the war."

"The first war, you mean."

"Of course…He fought for the Kaiser. He was proud of it…won some fancy medal. Were you in this last war?"

Kurt was slow to reply. "Weren't we all," was all he said.

He picked up his stoneware stein and quaffed on it. He called over the barmaid. "Two more, please," he ordered.

"Schöne frau," he said to Janne, "just like you."

Janne blushed. "It's the Dirndl. You men are all the same." Then, she looked right into Kurt's eyes. "It must have been terrible for you," she said, "the war."

Kurt looked away. "Yes…it was. I really don't want to talk about it."

They sat in silence for a while as the golden light of evening hit the peaks of the Rubihorn and the Nebelhorn. Gretel and the others were raucous and laughing, but for both of them, the mountains had such meaning. "It's very beautiful here," Kurt finally said. "I might stay awhile."

The barmaid returned with their beers.

"Where are you staying?" Janne asked.

"With the Aurichs…I trained with the great mountaineer at Sonthofen when I first came here during the war. I was with Gerd when he was killed in 'the Ukraine'. Another valuable life lost almost as soon as we reached the front-line. His son Chris, though, he'll make a good mountaineer. He came with us when we tackled the Rubihorn the other day."

* * *

On 15 June, Manfred Moeller aged and weak, dozed in the compartment as his train wound its way through the Bavarian Alps. At Bischofsweisen, his senses sharpened. It had been five years of hardship and despair, but now he really was coming home. It had been impossible to communicate with Delphine from the

Soviet interior. Captured in Belarussia at Borisov during fierce fighting during the German retreat in July 1944, he had been sent to a labour camp in the Don.

He watched the white water of the river beside the railway. Nothing had changed. Nothing was destroyed. At the Berchtesgaden Bahnhof, that had originally been built for the Fuhrer's train, everything looked the same except that the long red banner with the black and white swastika of the Third Reich no longer hung over the station's façade.

Manfred boarded a bus that took him up to the town. After seeing the total devastation of Russian cities and Belarusian villages, it seemed strange to see the quaint cobbled streets, the façade of the ducal palace, the twin spires of the mediaeval Stiftskirche and the bell towers of the Franziskanerkirche and of St Andreas all still intact. *The Allies haven't bombed Berchtesgaden. The Moeller Gästehaus is probably still standing,* he realised. He walked up the hill towards the Untersberg and home.

It was a warm sunny day with puffy white clouds slowly moving across an azure blue sky. Goats were grazing in fields among outcrops of rock, and hikers passed him on the road. *Is life really this normal?* he asked himself. *This is so different. It is alive...full of hope.* He reflected on the misery he had endured in the coal mines. The hard labour that had been forced upon him and his fellow prisoners-of-war when clearing the rubble and rebuilding those Soviet cities...*Such primitive methods so lacking in modern technology.* He thought of their rations...*about a litre of liquid soup and three hundred grams of stale bread a day.* The goats reminded him of the very first camp that he had been taken, too...*a front-line camp where we were kept locked in a goat pen, overseen by a junior female Red Army lieutenant.* He smiled to himself. *On those days when we were ordered to chop wood for the Russian field kitchen, sometimes she gave us hot tea for dinner and other treats.*

Looking up from his musings there it was—Moeller Gästehaus—and there were geraniums in the window boxes spilling off the balconies. *Home.*

Some guests were sitting outside under the umbrellas. A barmaid was serving them in a fresh Dirndl, her hair plaited just like in the old days. He smiled at them before going inside where he saw his daughter Hilda. He called out to her.

Hilda looked around. Her draw dropped and her eyes became as big as proverbial saucers. "Mutter!" she shouted.

Delphine appeared from the parlour. She stared at Manfred, then, she ran to him. "This is really you! You're alive! Tell me...this is really you!"

Manfred held her tight. It had been five long years. Tears ran in rivulets over the rough skin of his face.

Delphine, her eyes flashing with excitement, simply whispered, "We thought you were dead."

Hilda had a whimsical look of double joy on her face. "Vater…Mutter…you will be grandparents," she announced. "I'm pregnant."

Manfred broke away from Delphine. "And who is the father?" he asked.

"My husband, of course…Frederick."

Delphine beamed. "Hilda's married, Manfred. She's Frau Trotter now, and very soon her step-daughter will be home from school…our granddaughter. You'll love Marlene. What a wonderful summer we shall all have together."

Manfred looked a little stunned as if he really couldn't take it all in. "Where's Kurt?" he asked.

"Climbing mountains in Swabia," Delphine said. "He'll be back here next month."

A smile spread across Manfred's face…a smile that reminded Delphine of the old days. "So, he's alive?" he said. "Oh, that's so good, Delphine…the best news…the best." He choked on his own happiness.

* * *

Kurt and his friends, including Christian Aurich, Gerd Aurich's now teenaged son, set out from Oberstdorf early on 15 June to climb the Krottenkopf. It would take them two days even though the summit was within sight of the town. The ascent through the wild Trettach River Valley was beautiful early in the day. Wildflowers in the dew of the early morning glistened along the path, and the higher they climbed the better the view was looking back down to Oberstdorf. Following babbling brooks running down to the Trettarch they approached the main ridge now hiding the summit. They reached the ridge about mid-morning. Still snow-capped at 2,656 metres, the Grosser Krottenkopf and the lesser Madelgabel looked majestic glistening in the summer sun framed by those wildflowers. Kurt and Christian stood for a while just admiring the peaks.

"It doesn't get any closer does it," young Aurich commented as they looked up at the mountain.

"She's magnificent, isn't she?" Kurt said as he ruffled the teenager's hair, "the highest peak in the Allgau."

80

"You know what my father used to say?" the youth said. "He used to tell me that a number of evil spirits had been transformed into toads and then been banned to these mountains. That's why they call the mountain, Krotte."

Kurt laughed. "Krotte...toad...very good Christian," he said.

They followed the signed path for about an hour before they reached Kemptner—a mountain hut at around 1,800 metres. They would camp there and tackle the main climb the next day. At the Kemptner Hut, Kurt learned that the peak was named Grosser Krottenkopf by Hermann von Barth. Until then, the whole part of the Hornbach chain known as the Krottenspitzen in the west to Marchspitze in the east had been collectively called Krottenspitzen by the people of Oberstdorf—'the toad mountains'. In 1869, Von Barth had climbed the highest and named it the Grosser Krottenkopf.

An elderly couple that kept the hut, cooked them crêpes filled with diced ham, fresh baby spinach, sliced mushrooms and shredded Swiss cheese. Kurt couldn't help thinking of those crêpes that the Druckers had made for them at their farm in Switzerland, all oozing with that same cheese. After a long day hiking, they tasted especially good washed down with a beer.

The next morning dawned grey and gloomy as a low cloud made its way over the ridge, but by about 10:00 a.m., it lifted. Kurt and his party set off in Von Barth's footsteps, following the map and climbing the northern approach towards the rocky peak. They reached the snowline about 2:00 p.m.—rather dirty snow caught in the crevices and at times a little slippery in the summer thaw. It was all worth it, however, when they finally reached the summit, which they could only access by climbing around to approach from the south—they were standing on the roof of the Allgau Alps. In the mid-afternoon sun now close to midsummer's day, they could see over the mountains all the way to Lake Constance in Switzerland.

It was harder coming down in the parts where they had to traverse the thawing ice, but daylight was with them until 10:00 p.m. and, with barely a slip, they all made it back to the Kemptner Hut before dark.

* * *

Frederick Trotter was a little flustered on finding Manfred Moeller was alive and had returned home. He had morphed rather comfortably into becoming the innkeeper at the Moeller Gästehaus, and now, Hilda was pregnant and they were going to have a new addition to their family. He feared that Manfred would want to take over as 'mein host' as he had for all those years before he had been called up. After all, the property was still in his name, even if Delphine had reopened the hostelry for the Trotters. Over the entrance it still read in German Gothic script 'Herr Manfred Moeller', along with those markings that showed the three kings had visited and brought that Epiphany gift of the little pony—Maria. *When Kurt gets back, the two of them might expel us,* Frederick reasoned. *What would we do then with a baby on the way?*

Manfred's return, however, led to an increase in business. Old friends dropped by from all over Berchtesgadenland to hear Manfred's stories of his Russian ordeal.

"Working conditions in the camps were, of course, dire," Manfred explained as he held court in the parlour. "At first, we had to load two train cars with wood during one work shift, but then the norm was increased to three cars. We were forced to work sixteen hours a day…on Sundays and holidays, also. We didn't return to the camp until nine or ten o'clock in the evening, but often at midnight. We received watery soup and fell asleep so that the next day at five in the morning, we would go to work again. And that was before we were sent to the mines in the Don River Basin…uranium, coal and iron ore…it was back-breaking."

Manfred lit his pipe and took in a draft of the sweet tobacco.

"Working at the construction sites we were actually paid after 1946…all of seven Soviet rubles a month!" He laughed as he held his warm pipe in his hand. "A jug of milk cost two rubles and a pair of shoes 150 rubles!"

One of the older men asked, "How did you survive?"

"Soul and body were sold for a plate of soup or a piece of bread," Manfred answered. "It was the hunger that spoiled us…it turned us into animals. We stole from each other…we couldn't help it. It was even worse in the mines…we weren't paid at all…we were slaves of the Bolsheviks. It was worst in remote areas where we worked on the construction of roads and railways. It was every man for himself."

He raised his stein and drank the last of his beer before passing it back to the bar girl, who went off to replenish it.

"So many never made it," he continued, "thousands died, and mostly of starvation. Yes…the work was back-breaking, but most of my fellow prisoners-of-war…they died of starvation. The Soviets…they just felt they had a right to our slave labour…'reparation' they called it."

Manfred sat with his circle of friends nightly regaling these experiences.

Our experiences in Hamburg were as bad, Frederick thought. *My wife, my mother and my father were killed…our home was reduced to charred rubble…our livelihood was destroyed. We had nothing, too, and we had nowhere to go back to until we ended up here in Berchtesgadenland. I hope that now we can stay here.*

Later, alone with Hilda, Frederick held her in his arms. "Has Delphine said anything yet?"

"No…I think we will be all right. Actually, it's Kurt I worry about more. He will soon be back. Remember, Manfred and Delphine will be real grandparents; to them, you are family now. But Kurt…he might be more of a problem."

* * *

A letter from Kurt arrived at the Gästehaus.

"He's climbed the Krottenkopf…says it was easier than he expected," Delphine said excitedly as she shared the news with Hilda. "Oh…and he's met a girl. Well, I suppose that was to be expected. Maybe that will have lightened him up a bit…made him a little happier."

"Let's hope so," Hilda agreed. "What's her name?"

"Typical…he doesn't say…but he'll be back here in about a week."

"Does he know Vater's back home?"

"Well, I could write back and tell him, but no…he doesn't know. He's never telephoned. You know how he is. I can't guarantee a letter from me would now get to him in time. I think we should keep it a surprise. What do you think?"

"Oh…let's surprise him."

Manfred, of course, knew that his son would soon be home, but Delphine and Hilda watched with excited anticipation as they waited for the train to arrive at the Berchtesgaden Bahnhof. They heard the engine's whistle as it looped around those last curves before coming into the station. Kurt dismounted with his climbing gear.

Manfred shouted his name.

Kurt turned around and shook his head in disbelief. Kurt hadn't seen his father since he himself had left for Italy in 1943. They stared at each other as if their vision was a mirage. Finally, Manfred walked towards him and embraced his son. Delphine and Hilda let them have their moment.

The four of them then piled into the old Moeller touring car, mountain gear stowed in the back, and Delphine drove them through town to the Moeller Gästehaus.

"So…you met a girl?" Delphine finally asked when she had a moment to speak to Kurt alone.

"Yes…I think you would like her, Mutter. Janne…her family have a farm just outside Oberstdorf." That was about all he revealed. Around his family, he was still a man of few words.

* * *

In some ways, it was easier for Kurt to talk to his father as they exchanged their different experiences of the Eastern Front, but the memories then brought back the guilt. The dreams returned as nightmares when he tossed and turned in the room at the top of the Gästehaus that was his personal space.

He retreated to his mountains once again, at first alone, and then with clients. He described only the beauty of Berchtesgadenland when he wrote back to Janne, barely mentioning his family. They were mostly the Trotters now anyway. Soon, there would be another Trotter, his nephew or niece, but Kurt really wasn't as excited about it as his mother and father were. In the pure air atop the Jenner, he dreamed of returning to Oberstdorf, where for a few weeks he had been free of those nightmares. He looked down from the summit to the deep crevasse in the mountains that contained the deep blue water of the Königssee. Through the haze, he could see the red domes of St Batholomew. Yes…the mountains were his world.

As summer turned into autumn, that magic time of warm days and cold nights when the first snows appear on the summits and the leaves start to turn, their yellows and browns contrasting with the dark green pines on the lower slopes, Janne invited Kurt to come back and stay with her family in Oberstdorf. He answered that he would.

Kurt arrived back in Oberstdorf just in time to join Janne and her father in bringing the cows back down from the alms below the Rubihorn. He helped Frau Heizz wash the cows and fasten the crowns and festive belts before leading them through the town on their way back to the Heizz farm. The mayor was at the town hall platform as they passed, and a brass band played in the market square on the steps of the great Church of St John the Baptist. In the evening, Janne and Kurt returned to the Hirsch Tavern and met up with Christian Aurich and his mother. They were dressed in their traditional Bavarian Dirndls and Lederhosen and enjoying a few beers in the aftermath of the annual parade.

Christian wiped the froth from his youthful moustache. "So, are you two going to get married?" he blatantly asked Janne and Kurt.

Janne's eyes sparkled. "Is there something I don't know?"

Kurt took hold of her hand. "Well, what do you think?"

Christian kicked Kurt under the table.

"What do *you* think?" Janne answered.

Kurt looked around and caught Frau Aurich's eye. She was smiling with approval. "All right, Janne…will you marry me?" he said.

"Of course…why do you think I invited you to come back here?"

"Well, I suppose we are going to get married then," Kurt said, and he kissed her to the applause of others in the tavern parlour.

Kurt spent the next two months helping Janne and her father on the farm, feeding the cows and goats, mucking out in the barn, and generally making himself useful as Janne planned their wedding. They would be married at the Roman Catholic Church right before Christmas.

The square around the church was busy with the Christmas market in December, and on 5 December Janne and Kurt were well imbibed with Glühwien when they witnessed the arrival of the Oberstdorf Krampus—terrifying half-man half-goat characters with menacing horns. They were chasing the young girls around brandishing flails of whipping birch twigs. Kurt remembered how they had always come around in December at Berchtesgaden before the war. One of his first vivid memories was of his sister Hilda as a young girl clinging to their mother, terrified by the Krampus.

The legend in Alpine towns was that these Krampus assisted Saint Nicholas in rewarding well-behaved children with gifts such as oranges, dried fruit, walnuts or chocolate on 5 December. Badly behaved children, however, got chased and whipped by the Krampus with the idea that they still might have time to reform their ways before St Nicholas makes his Christmas Eve visit. But the Krampus always seemed to concentrate more on the girls than the boys. A menacing Krampus approached Janne. She feigned fear and clutched onto Kurt. Kurt was certain he saw in the ghastly visage of the Krampus the eyes of seventeen-year-old Christian Aurich, who was menacing Janne, his fiancé, with birch twigs. Grimacing, the Krampus finally left them and went about his duty scaring younger girls and a few timid boys.

"That was Christian, wasn't it?" Kurt said as they returned to their Glühwien.

"I think you're right," Janne agreed. "I always used to hate the Krampus."

"My sister, too."

The night before the wedding on 22 December, Kurt stayed with the Aurichs. Manfred and Delphine Moeller came to Oberstdorf for the occasion, staying out at the Park Hotel. Hilda didn't come as she was now heavily pregnant. Kurt, the Aurichs and his parents had dinner at the hostelry together. It was the first time either of Kurt's parents had ever been in Swabia and they were most impressed with the beauty of the place.

"Those mountains hang over Oberstdorf just like the Watzmann hangs over Berchtesgaden," Delphine observed.

"The Rubihorn and the Nebelhorn," Kurt proudly informed them as if he was now an Oberstdorfer.

"The first time I climbed the Rubihorn was with Kurt last summer," Christian said. "Then we went on to climb the Krottenkopf…the highest mountain in the Allgau." He beamed with pride with those same sparkling eyes that Kurt had seen in the Krampus' mask. *I suppose in a way he now thinks of me as his father, after losing his father in 'the Ukraine',* he thought to himself.

At noon the next day, Janne and Kurt were married in the great church in the square. Janne wore a modified version of the wedding dress that her mother had worn when she had been married some thirty years before, right after the first Great War. She had kept it for her daughter all these years, the white lace having turned cream. Bavarian white hellebores or 'Christmas roses' made up her bouquet, and Gretel was her bridesmaid. A wagon drawn by two black, land horses carried them away from the church to the Park Hotel where they held the wedding breakfast.

Chapter Eight
The 1950s

The fate of the Jewish survivors of the Nazi concentration camps was slow to be resolved. The freed survivors of the death camps, including large numbers escaping from the Soviets, ended up in displaced persons camps run by the United Nations in the British and American sectors of Western Germany. The nearest such camp to Berchtesgaden was at Bad Reichenhall, on the far side of the Untersburg. The Bad Reichenall camp had achieved a large measure of internal autonomy and a variety of Jewish agencies were actively providing the refugees with food and clothing and vocational training, preparing the survivors of Nazi oppression for a new life.

Shortly before Kurt Moeller and Janne Heizz were married in Oberstdorf, Frederick Trotter hired Rachel, a German-Jewish refugee from the Bad Reichenhall camp, as a bar girl. She had arrived at Bad Reichenhall in 1945 after being liberated by the Americans at the Mauthausen concentration camp near Linz. She barely remembered her father before they had been transported, and her mother died of starvation shortly before the Americans arrived at Mauthausen. Now, a pretty if rather fragile girl, she was a maid of all sorts at the Moeller Gästehaus.

"But isn't she Jewish?" Marlene at the age of ten, said to her father's surprise. "Aren't Jews bad people?"

"And where do you get that idea?" her father said.

"Nobody wants them…that's what my friends say."

"Don't you ever say that," Frederick said firmly. "We were refugees once, so we should help other refugees."

* * *

Direct immigration into either Great Britain or the United States was very difficult to accomplish during these immediate post-war years, and there was a strong movement among Jews for the creation of a Jewish homeland in the British mandate of Palestine. The British, however, severely restricted Jewish immigration into Palestine largely because of Arab objections. Many Jewish refugees escaping Europe had, therefore, been placed in displaced persons camps in British Cyprus rather than having direct access to Palestine. This internment of Jewish refugees turned world opinion against British policy.

The Americans put pressure on the British to let at least 100,000 European Jews into Palestine. As the crisis escalated, the British government decided to submit the problem of Palestine to the United Nations. In a special session, the UN General Assembly voted in November 1947 to partition Palestine into two new states, one Jewish and the other Arab, a recommendation that the Jews accepted but that the Arabs rejected. After the withdrawal of British troops, a civil war broke out between the Jews and Palestinian Arabs.

In early 1948, Zionist leaders moved to establish a modern Jewish State. On 14 May, David Ben-Gurion, the chairman of the Jewish agency in Palestine, boldly declared: "The Nazi Holocaust, which engulfed millions of Jews in Europe, proved anew the urgency of the re-establishment of the Jewish State, which would solve the problem of Jewish homelessness by opening the gates to all Jews and lifting the Jewish people to equality in the family of nations." A new nation of Israel was then formed out of the Old British Mandate of Palestine.

Jews then flocked into Israel, including many who escaped from the Soviet Union. They fought hard in the resulting War of Independence that led to the Jewish victory over the Palestinian Arabs in 1949.

* * *

In early May 1950, Kurt Moeller brought his young wife to Berchtesgaden to finally meet his sister and her new baby boy—Klaus Trotter. Marlene was very protective of her baby half-brother and always a little fearful of Kurt, but she took a shine to Janne. Pulling on her arm, she insisted on taking Janne personally out to the stable to meet her pony—Maria.

Kurt was quite surprised that the Trotters had hired a Jewish maid at the Gästehaus, but was drawn to the girl as his conscience gnawed at him yet again.

I wonder what horrors she and her family endured, he thought. And when he got the opportunity he tried to find out.

"My father…I think he was gassed," the maid said. "I never saw him again…that was when we first arrived at Auschwitz. My mother and I…we were on the death march from Auschwitz to Mauthausen. We survived that but almost starved to death after we got there. There wasn't that much for us to do…but there were fewer and fewer guards. The men at Mauthausen often worked at a quarry. Many were lined up at the quarry cliff and shot. Sometimes…so they said…other Jewish men were forced at gunpoint to push them over the edge, awaiting in turn the same fate." The maid choked. "It was mass murder."

Rachel paused and looked away as she wiped a tear from her eye with the back of her hand.

"The hunger was the worst thing for us," she resumed. "There was simply nothing to eat. Sometimes, my mother gave what she scrounged to me, but she…she just wasted away. They made me work in the laundry, but my mother was too weak to work. Inevitably, like so many of the others she just died of starvation…and only two days before the Americans arrived." Tears now welled in Rachel's eyes. "If she had just lived two more days, maybe she would have been alive today."

Rachel pulled a handkerchief from her Dirndl, dabbed her eyes and looked up at Kurt with a pitiful smile.

"The Americans were very nice to us…they fed us properly," she said. "At Bad Reichenhall, we were given everything we needed, but we weren't free. Now, I'm free. Herr Trotter rescued me, for I really had nowhere to go."

Kurt was also crying with remorse. He held out his hand to her. "I hope my sister treats you well," was all he could think to say. "I'm so sorry you had to suffer."

Later, Kurt Moeller reflected on their conversation. *I wonder what she will think if she ever finds out that my sister worked as a maid for Hitler at the Berghof.*

Janne seemed to be getting along very well with Marlene and sometimes she went riding with her and Hannes Stack's boy. *She'll make a good mother to our children,* Kurt thought. *I wonder how soon I might become a father.*

His mother liked her, too, but in his heart, Kurt knew that Berchtesgaden was no longer home. Oberstdorf had become his home.

Shortly after they returned to Oberstdorf, Janne revealed that she was now pregnant. Close to Christmas 1950, Lottie Moeller was born.

* * *

Late in 1951, the new West Germany officially brought an end to denazification. The programme had been enormously unpopular, and since 1949 was carried out in an increasingly lenient and lukewarm way. In the French sector, it was barely observed at all. The denazification process was also often completely disregarded by both the Soviets and the Western powers when it came to German rocket scientists and other technical experts, who were taken out of Germany to work on projects in the victors' own countries or simply seized in order to prevent the other side from taking them.

War was raging again in the Far East. Soldiers from the North Korean People's Army poured across the 35th Parallel, the boundary between the Chinese-backed Democratic People's Republic of Korea to the north and the pro-Western Republic of Korea to the south.

Manfred Moeller was holding court in the parlour at the Moeller Gästehaus in Berchtesgaden. Leaning back in his chair, puffing on his pipe, he pontificated as his guests listened to this news. "They're all commies…the Russians and the Chinese. What's the difference? Cat's poop or dog's poop if you ask me."

Fearful that in time, the Soviets might launch a similar attack on the new West Germany, the Americans encouraged the West German leader, Konrad Adenauer, to re-arm. Adenauer declared that ending denazification was necessary for West Germany's re-armament. The old munitions factories had for the most part been owned by Nazi industrialists.

This Korean War came to an inconclusive end on 27 July 1953. After three years of a bloody and frustrating war, the United Nations, the United States, the People's Republic of China, North Korea, and South Korea all agreed to an armistice, bringing the fighting of the Korean War to an end. Adenauer's plans were well underway, however, and in 1955 the Bundeswehr was formed as the new West German army defence force.

* * *

A few years later, in 1958, just before Kurt and Janne Moeller were to celebrate Lottie's eighth birthday, Kurt George Kiesinger was appointed Minister-President of the state of Baden-Württemberg, the large area of West Germany immediately west of Swabia and Bavaria, just a few miles to the northwest of Oberstdorf.

"Wasn't he in Hitler's Propaganda Ministry?" Kurt said to Janne as they listened to the news. "Didn't he work under Ribbentrop…that Nazi condemned to death at Nuremberg? The Americans even interned him for his connection to Ribbentrop. He spent eighteen months in the Ludwigsburg camp for goodness sake!"

"If you say so," Janne answered, "but that's all in the past Kurt. Don't get angry over the past. It's Lottie's birthday tomorrow. Just think about that."

Janne had got used to his moods and knew how to calm him down when he got angry. She reached for his hand and they turned off the wireless.

* * *

At Bischofzell in Switzerland, the Druckers were also listening to the news. Baden-Württemberg was just the other side of Lake Constance.

"We don't want Nazis on our doorstep again," Helmut said to Francine. "Wasn't Kiesinger anti-Semitic?"

"I believe that was what the French said," his wife agreed. "Kiesinger had been chiefly responsible for the contents of German international broadcasts which included anti-Semitic and war propaganda."

"And now he's in charge of half of Germany. Doesn't anybody ever learn?"

"Perhaps those Jews who made it to Israel are better off," Francine said out of the blue. "You've got to admit the Jews were pretty plucky in that war against Egypt a couple of years ago."

"So, is that what you want to do now…move to Israel?" Helmut asked.

"Well, we're not really Swiss are we?"

"We may not be, but Abigail and Johannes…they seem pretty Swiss now. Look at them going out with a brother and sister. There'll be double wedding bells there before we know it."

Francine smiled. "You're pretty shrewd Helmut…you might be right."

He was right. In the spring of 1959, in the Lutheran church at Bischofzell, Abigail and Johannes Drucker were married to the Gerber brother and sister Aldrich and Andrea. The Gerber family had a large dairy farm on the shores of Lake Constance. Aldrich and Andrea first met Abigail and Johannes at the St Gallen Cheese Fair, when Abigail was crowned the 'Dairy Queen' in 1957. Cheese in many Swiss varieties featured at the wedding feast laid on by the old cheese maker, Daniel Schwegler, at the Gallo Hotel in St Gallen not far from the fairgrounds. Because Abigail had been a reigning 'Dairy Queen', many St Gallen people came to the reception, including the mayor and his entourage.

After it was all over, but before the two couples went their separate ways, Abigail said to her brother, "Now...I'm definitely no longer a Finkelstein... because I've had to change my name to Gerber."

"I think that I'll remain a Finkelstein Drucker," Johannes answered her.

Abigail and Aldrich left in his father's Mercedes that he loaned to them for their honeymoon. They chose to spend a few days at Oberstdorf, whereas Johannes and Andrea took the train from St Gallen to Lake Lugano, staying in Switzerland.

* * *

On their Oberstdorf honeymoon, Aldrich and Abigail Gerber stayed at the Park Hotel. Chatting with the concierge, Aldrich expressed an interest in the Bavarian hinterwälder cattle. "Dairy and beef all in one," he said, "I think I'd find that interesting."

The concierge admitted that there weren't too many Hinterwälders in the Trettach Valley, but that the Moellers had a herd. "Their cows are often the most admired when they come down from the mountains in October...won a few rosettes, too. I can put you in touch with them."

So, it was that Aldrich and Abigail met Kurt and Janne Moeller and their daughter, Lottie. Lottie was now attending the convent school attached to the Basilica of St John the Baptist. She had just been collected by her grandfather when the Gerbers arrived at the old Heizz farmstead.

Kurt and Janne took the honeymooners out to the barn to see some of the herd. There were several young calves with the cows, even though the nights were still cold.

"Shortly after Easter, we'll let them out in the meadows here, and then in late May, they'll go up on the alms, so you chose a good time to come to see them," Janne explained.

"Dairy and beef," Aldrich repeated, "milk, cheese and veal?"

"Yes, especially the veal…all those Wiener Schnitzels," Janne said with pride, "you've probably had some of ours at the Park." She still looked younger than she was—the clear skin of youth with the rosy cheeks borne out of the mountain air. Her hands, however, gave her away. They had the toughness of the farming life.

"We have a large herd of brown Swiss at Lake Constance, mostly for cheese," Aldrich said. "That was how we met. Abigail is a cheesemaker…she was the Dairy Queen at the St Gallen Show two years ago."

Janne made a light curtsey. "You should try some of our cheese curds then…that is if Lottie hasn't already scoffed them."

They all went back inside. Indeed, Grandfather and Granddaughter were both already eating the curds that Janne always left for them when they came back from the convent in the afternoon.

"So, what did you do today?" Janne asked her daughter.

Lottie picked up a piece of paper. "Look…I learned to write 'Lottie Moeller'," she said, and then the nuns taught us to sing 'Alleluias' for Easter.

Janne looked at the paper with its spaced-out letters. "Very good," she said.

"Would you like to climb the Nebelhorn?" Kurt asked Aldrich. "You can go up on the ski lift most of the way, and there's not much snow there at the moment…patches here and there, but on a fine day like today, there are nice views along the ridge to the Grosser Krottenkopf and across to the Kleinwalsertal range."

"We were thinking of riding up there."

"Well, let's go together."

The next morning, they met at the bottom station of the ski lift, and in minutes the four of them were silently and slowly gliding over the alms taking them up to the escarpments of ranges above. At the ridge nearly three-quarters of the way up, they moved over to the final lift taking them up over the ragged rocks above the tree line. Drifts of snow still lay in their shadows and crevices. The views were spectacular, especially looking back down on the ridge leading to the larger Krottenkopf. At the top station, it was only a short climb along a well-worn path to reach the Nebelhorn summit.

"I mean, it's not the Matterhorn, but it's pretty spectacular up here," Kurt said with pride. "It's a great ski run down in the season, but there's not too much snow now. The sights of the blue gentians though…aren't they beautiful?"

"Little Switzerland," Aldrich agreed.

Abigail bent down to look closer at the blue flowers. "Any Edelweiss," she asked.

"Too early," Kurt replied. "You'll find it up here in July and August, but even then it is usually in rather out-of-the-way spots. It likes the limestone crevices."

"It's funny, but we really don't know much about the mountains even though we're Swiss," she said. "Where we live, its rolling hills down to Lake Constance…very pretty country, but not mountainous. We can see the mountains in the distance, but they are quite a long way off."

After a pause, Abigail looked up from the gentians. "I remember these mountains in my childhood…after my brother and I came to live with my Aunt Francine. That's partly why I wanted to come back here and show them to Aldrich."

Kurt looked surprised. "You lived here?"

"For a year…during the war, before we moved to Switzerland."

"To escape from the war?"

"Well, in part. I'm Jewish you know, at least my family was Jewish. We're Lutherans now, but it wasn't safe in Germany for Jews back then."

Kurt's face turned ashen. "No…" he said. "No, it wasn't."

There was an awkward silence as they came back down from the summit to the upper station café.

"Why did you tell them that?" Aldrich asked when Kurt and Janne went to order refreshments. "You're not Jewish now."

"No…but Johannes and I really are. Our name was Finkelstein. We came to Bischofzell as Jewish refugees from Oberstdorf. We took my uncle's name Drucker…we're really Finkelsteins. I mean it's all legal…our adopted parents are the Druckers, but our real parents…we don't know what happened to them. They lived in Berchtesgaden where we were born, but we've never been able to trace them. They were probably murdered by the Nazis."

Kurt and Janne returned with beers and the subject was dropped.

* * *

At first, the two newly-wed couples all lived in the large Gerber farmhouse near Altnau looking out over Lake Constance. Soon, however, Johannes and Andrea found an apartment in an old house in Romanshorn, close to where the ferries crossed the lake to Baden-Württemberg.

Chapter Nine
The 1960s and 1970s

The North Atlantic Treaty Organisation was created in 1949 by the United States, Canada and several Western European nations to provide collective security against the Soviet Union. The uneasy truce in the Korean War in 1953 was soon followed by further fears of communist aggrandisement around the world. The Western Allies in Europe, on fully withdrawing from their political governance of West Germany in 1955, strengthened their military commitments in fear of Soviet advancement into the fledgling state.

Far closer to home, however, a revolution in Cuba in 1952 created serious concerns for President Eisenhower in the USA. By the end of the decade, the Soviet-backed Fidel Castro finally overthrew the decadent Batista government in Havana. Fearful of a Soviet ally on the very doorstep of the United States, Eisenhower planned an invasion. His successor, President Kennedy launched it.

In April 1961, American bombers attacked Cuban airfields. On the night of 17 April, American soldiers landed on the beach at Playa Girón in the Bay of Pigs where they overwhelmed a local revolutionary militia. Castro swiftly reacted, taking personal control of the Cuban militia. The American invasion force lost its strategic initiative and Kennedy decided to withhold further air support as the international community became aware of the operation. Eisenhower's plan had required the involvement of both air and naval forces. Without further air support, the invasion was being conducted with fewer forces than the CIA had deemed necessary. Thus, the invading force was defeated within three days by the Cuban Revolutionary Armed Forces and surrendered on 20 April. Most of the surrendered American troops were publicly interrogated and put into Cuban prisons.

The invasion was a U.S. foreign policy failure. The Cuban government's victory solidified Castro's role as a national hero and widened the political division between the two formerly allied countries, pushing Cuba closer to the Soviets.

In response to the failed 'Bay of Pigs' invasion and the presence of American ballistic missiles in Italy and Turkey, Soviet leader, Nikita Khrushchev, decided to agree to Cuba's request to place nuclear missiles on the island to deter future U.S. harassment. For thirteen days in October 1962, the world waited. An American spy plane confirmed that the Soviet Union was indeed beginning to install missiles in Cuba that could launch attacks on U.S. cities. The confrontation that followed brought the two superpowers to the brink of nuclear war before an agreement was reached to withdraw the missiles.

In return, Kennedy cleverly traded away those obsolete U.S. nuclear missiles based in Turkey in order to get Soviet nuclear arms out of Cuba and avoid a serious military confrontation with Moscow. Nonetheless, the Iron Curtain between Soviet interests and American interests was now truly evident around the world. NATO missile bases were set up in Italy facing Eastern Europe, and an over four-metre-high concrete wall now separated East and West Berlin and also surrounded West Berlin—a literal concrete curtain. A cold war between the Soviet Union and 'The West' had begun.

* * *

In 1964, Abigail and Johannes' Uncle Helmut and Aunt Francine Finkelstein Drucker left the farm at Bischoffzell and moved to Israel. On arrival, the Jewish government appointed them to the dairy and goat farms at Kibbutz Givat HaShlosha, where they were to produce Israeli laban yoghurts and cheeses. Originally founded in 1925 in the days of the British Mandate, Givat HaShlosha was moved in 1953 to land that was once a Palestinian village. There were about 450 members of the collective, many of them young holocaust survivors from the German displaced persons camps. More were arriving every day. Farming at the kibbutz was highly intensive, with citrus and other crops as well as the dairy. There was also a shoe factory and a plant for building materials. Run very commercially by the kibbutz overseers, Givat HaShlosha was seen as a pioneer property in the fast-developing economy of the young state of Israel. Daily life was lived communally, the kibbutz proudly boasting one of the largest dining halls in the country.

Helmut Drucker had some difficulty adapting to nominal Judaism, but he had always been aware of his wife's Jewish background. When they had first been married in Oberstdorf, before the war back in 1935, there was no shortage of Jewish visitors to the resort. Their marriage was one of many mixed marriages in the town. Francine had happily become a nominal Lutheran, and it wasn't until Hetty Laman and Elizabeth Dabelstein had started bringing Jewish refugee children into the Hoches Licht Children's Home after Kristallnacht, and even more so after Holland was absorbed into the Third Reich, that Francine revived her Jewish interests. There were many Jewish refugees in the town. So long as they were registered as Ayrans, Oberstdorf's Mayor Fink had sheltered them from the worst of Nazi atrocities. When things had got tougher in most of the German Reich, was when the Druckers had taken in Francine's Finkelstein nephew and niece from Berchtesgaden, and a year later, escaped with the two children and their two Dutch-Jewish friends to Switzerland.

Switzerland had been good to them, but then Francine had got this crazy idea that they should now move to the state of Israel. Francine hadn't become a practising Jew, but she had become a political Jew with a fervent passion for this new homeland that had opened up along the Eastern Mediterranean's Levant. Helmut played along with it and accepted the veneer of religious Judaism that was part of the kibbutz life, but it was really the total dedication of these Jews to creating something of their new country that fascinated him. The dairy farm— mostly Holstein-Freisian cows—was incredibly efficient, and the productivity was rewarding. The goats too, fascinated Helmut. He had always rather looked down on the goat cheeses in Switzerland, preferring his round robust cheeses. Here, at Givat HaShlosha, they used goat's milk to make amazing laban yoghurt.

Helmut and Francine adapted to their new lifestyle.

* * *

Tensions ran high between Israel and her Arab neighbours, and many of the young Israelis serving in kibbutzim throughout Israel were also trained to serve in the Israeli army. Ever since the reprise of General Nasser after the Suez crisis of 1956, disputes between Israel and Egypt had arisen over the rights of Israeli shipping to pass through the Suez Canal and the Red Sea. In June 1966, Egypt and Israel's Arab neighbours united in a common cause to reclaim Israel. Thanks to the brilliance of the Israeli minister for defence, Moshe Dayan, in just six days

Israel defeated three Arab armies, gained territory four times its original size and became the pre-emanate military power in the region. Moshe Dayan became the hero of the hour, uniting Jewry and its Western Allies with the lasting image of a black patch over the left eye that he had lost in his youth fighting for Israeli independence.

The war galvanised Helmut and Francine's pride in their newly adopted country. A photograph of Moshe Dayan sat on Francine's dressing table in their bedroom at Kibbutz Giva HaShlosha.

* * *

In 1966, after his eight years as president-minister of Baden-Württemberg, Kurt George Kiesinger was elected to replace Ludwig Erhard as the German chancellor. He formed a grand coalition government in Bonn with Willy Brandt's Social Democratic Party. The student movement in particular, but also other sections of the population, saw him as a politician who stood for the inadequacy of Germans to come to terms with their past.

Marlene Trotter was now a rather Bohemian lady who dabbled in art and found Berchtesgaden a little too old-fashioned for her tastes. In 1966, she had moved to Munich. Two years later, her younger half-brother Klaus came to join her when he became a medical student at Ludwig Maximilian University. There, Klaus became friendly with Jürgen Scholtz, who was a keen supporter of the West German Student Movement. The movement was characterised by the protesting students' rejection of traditionalism and of German political authority which still included many former Nazi officials.

Unrest had started in 1967 when student Benno Ohnesorg was shot by a policeman during a protest against the visit of Mohammad Reza Pahlavi, the Shah of Persia, whom the students considered a right-wing 'Nazi' dictator. The students blamed Chancellor Kiesinger for inviting the Shah, citing Kiesinger's Nazi sympathies. There followed an assassination of the student activist leader Rudi Dutschke, which sparked numerous protests across West Germany. The movement then morphed into protests against the Vietnam War being waged by the Americans in the Far East. Klaus, Jürgen Scholtz and Marlene all took part in the student protests in Munich.

It was with delight that in April 1968, they heard how French Nazi-hunter, Beate Klarsfeld, slapped the chancellor in the face during the 1968 Christian Democrat convention, calling him a 'Nazi'.

Marlene stood up in front of their little TV set in their flat, shouting with joy, "Can you believe it, Jürgen! That feisty Frenchie clocked him one!"

On the TV screen were scenes of ushers dragging Beate out of the convention. Beate was yelling at Kiesinger in French and then shouted in German, 'Kiesinger! Nazi! Step down!' Kiesinger stood there, holding his left cheek with a startled expression.

Jürgen jumped up beside his lover and shouted, "Bravo!"

"That might finish him," Marlene said as she embraced Jürgen.

It did. After the election of 1969, Kiesinger was succeeded by his former vice-chancellor, Willy Brandt.

During the winter recess, Klaus Trotter visited with his cousin Lottie at the Moeller's home in Oberstdorf. Klaus liked to ski, but he also had a soft spot for his cousin, who was now eighteen and had blossomed into a beauty. The first thing he noticed was her mini-skirt.

"It's all right, I'm wearing tights," she said, not taking her eyes off her handsome cousin.

There followed a discussion as to whether it was the French or the British who had invented 'the mini'.

His Aunt Janne stemmed the discussion. "Quant or Courrèges…they should both be ashamed of themselves!" Janne was still a traditionalist, usually dressed in a Bavarian Dirndl.

Kurt came in and changed the topic. "We should go up the Nebelhorn tomorrow. The snow's really good at the moment. You'll find Lottie very competitive now. She's quite the ski bunny."

The next day they took to the slopes.

"A good thing we got rid of the chancellor," Klaus said as he shared the ski lift with his uncle. "The man was a Nazi, he really was."

"Brandt will be better," was all Kurt said.

They turned their attention to the slopes, quite active on this clear winter's day. When they reached the runs, Klaus was impressed at how easily his cousin handled her skis even to the point that they were able to competitively show each other off.

Before supper, Lottie shared her Françoise Hardy records with Klaus, and they both danced to *Tous les Garçons et les Filles*. Lottie was crazy about the French singer and her German look-alike, Katja Ebstein—both with long mousey hair, fringes, pouty lips and bedroom eyes.

Later, when her parents were out in the cow barn, the two cousins stole a kiss and this winter break looked promising.

"Do you ever come down to Munich?" Klaus asked.

"Hardly ever…but it depends if I'm asked?" She answered by batting those flirtatious eyes.

"Well…if I asked you? I mean you could stay with my sister Marlene."

"Is she still crazy about horses?"

"Not as much as she used to be. She paints now…large, rather strange canvasses, but people seem to like them. Will they let you get away?" Klaus pressed.

"They probably would. My parents like you…but it's the farm. Ever since my grandfather passed away, it's been very hard to get away from the farm, at least until the summer. Things quiet down a bit when the cows go up to the alms. Maybe then you might come back here and help with the haymaking."

Klaus kissed her again. "Well, let me know if you are ever to come to Munich. Maybe Oktoberfest…that would be fun?" They heard Lottie's mother and father come in from the barn and they broke their embrace.

* * *

After Helmut and Francine Finkelstein Drucker immigrated to Israel, Johannes and Andrea Gerber had returned to Daniel Schwegler, the cheesemaker, at his farm in Bischofzell, Switzerland. They had a son, Hans, who in 1970 was already ten. He was the first in his generation to have been brought up with television. In Bischofzell, they picked up both the German and Swiss stations. In February, German television had announced that Katja Ebstein would be singing the West German selection for the Eurovision Song Contest. She was tipped as a possible winner. Switzerland hadn't put up much of a challenge and the popular German singer had a lot of German-Swiss backing her. Johannes was excited about Katya's prospects and Andrea teased him about his admiration of her sultry looks.

101

On 21 March, the family was all in the parlour with Daniel Schwegler to watch this annual spectacle—a 'kitsch' event that for ten years, going from black and white to colour television, had nonetheless been a competitive, but unifying force, throughout Western Europe. It had been slightly marred the previous year, when for the first time there was an equal tie between four countries and a rather hurried decision was made splitting the honours. Traditionally, the nation that won the song contest became the host country for the following year, but with a tie, that was impossible. Of the four 1969 winners, with Spain having hosted and the United Kingdom hosting in 1968, only France and the Netherlands were in consideration. A draw of ballots between these two countries resulted in the Netherlands being chosen as the host country. In reaction to this decision, Finland, Norway, Sweden, Portugal and Austria all pulled out of the 1970 contest.

Johannes stood up. "Without the rebels…well, that should make it even better for Katja," he said.

"I'm betting on Great Britain. They always have good songs," his wife chided.

Hans was quiet, but all of a sudden the child shouted out, "What about Switzerland?"

"That would be nice," his mother Andrea agreed, "but I don't think we have a really catchy song."

The Eurovision theme music came on, and after a short introductory film, the Dutch compère began to introduce the contest. '*In order to avoid an incident like last year, a tie-breaking rule has been created. If two or more songs gain the same number of votes and are tied for first place, each song will have to be performed again. After which, each national jury, other than the juries of the countries concerned, will by a show of hands decide which they thought was the best. If the countries tie again, then they will share first place.*'

"Seems fair," Johannes said.

The twelve contestants then started their performances.

An attractive blonde-haired girl named Mary Hopkin, representing Great Britain, performed about halfway through the contest with her song, *Knock, Knock, Who's There?* It certainly looked like a winner, garnering 26 points.

"It'll be hard for Katja to beat that," Andrea admitted.

Katja was the eleventh to sing out of twelve. For Germany, she sang *Wunder gibt es immer weider.* She sang it beautifully, and the Gerbers and Daniel sat glued to their televisions. 12 points, however, were all that the juries returned.

Disappointed, Johannes shook his head. "So, Great Britain wins again," he said resignedly. To close the contest, a schoolgirl from Ireland walked out on stage with the name of Dana Brown, of whom nobody had ever heard. She started to sing the most beautiful and simplistic song titled, *All Kinds of Everything.*

Young Hans started to squeal with delight. "I hope she wins," he said. "She's just a schoolgirl…I really like her."

His mother and father, surprised, looked at each other and smiled.

The simple lilting melody and sugary words finally came to an inevitable end. To everyone's surprise, the juries totalled up 32 points. The schoolgirl, Dana Brown, for Ireland, had won first place, and the sultry Katya Ebstein for Germany was relegated to third place. Dana Brown had certainly won a fan in young Hans.

In Oberstdorf, Lottie Moeller was also surprised and excited by the Irish schoolgirl, but her parents Kurt and Janne expressed their disappointment that Katya hadn't done better.

"She should have got more than 12 points," Janne said. "Why didn't Switzerland give us more than one point, and Italy and France…they gave us no points."

In Berchtesgaden, Kurt's parents Manfred and Delphine were also disappointed, but Frederick Trotter and Kurt's sister Hilda both thought Great Britain should have won.

"The Irish girl had a good song, but she's too young," Hilda expressed. "The British song was actually more catchy than ours. I think they should have won."

In Munich, Klaus Trotter and his half-sister Marlene had watched with some of her artist friends. The 'Bohemians' were all rooting for Katya, but the whole contest wasn't taken too seriously by them. It was just a good excuse for a party. Klaus, however, expressed an opinion on how far technology had advanced in bringing nations together, and he predicted that maybe, one day, Western Europe could all be one federation of independent nations with its common market.

At Kibbutz Givat HaShlosha, nobody paid any attention to the Eurovision Song Contest. In 1970, Israel was not part of the Eurovision programme. Helmut and Francine Finkelstein Drucker, like their fellow kibbutzniks, were far more concerned about the tensions between Israel and Egypt.

The Soviets were stationing troops in Egypt. Israeli jets were repeatedly bombing Soviet and Egyptian positions, and on 8 April, a group of military bases about 30 kilometres from the Suez Canal was bombed. Israeli fighter jets attacked a school in the Egyptian town of Bahr el-Baqar after it was mistaken for a military installation. The building was hit by five bombs and two air-to-ground missiles, killing 46 schoolchildren and injuring over 50. As a result, the Egyptians reconstructed their Soviet missile batteries closer to the canal creating a stronger defence. Soviet MiG fighters provided the necessary air cover. Soviet pilots also began approaching Israeli aircraft. Tensions ran high and fear of another full-blown Arab-Israeli War, with serious Soviet backing of Egypt, became the talk of the kibbutz.

* * *

Klaus Trotter's predictions on Europe came a step closer in the early 1970s. The 1960s had seen the first attempts at enlargement of the original 1957 Common Market. In 1961, Denmark, Ireland, Great Britain and a few months later, Norway, applied to join. However, President Charles de Gaulle of France had seen British membership as a possible means of too much U.S. influence and he vetoed membership. Applications from all four countries were suspended. Greece actually became the first country to join the original European Common Market in 1961 as an associate member, however, its membership was suspended later after a coup d'état established a military dictatorship there. In February 1962, Spain attempted to join, but because Spain was not a democracy but a Fascist dictatorship, all the members rejected the request in 1964. Denmark, Ireland, Great Britain and Norway re-submitted their applications on 11 May 1967, and with Georges Pompidou succeeding Charles de Gaulle as French president the veto was finally lifted. Negotiations began in 1970 under the pro-European government of Prime Minister Edward Heath in Great Britain, who had to deal with disagreements relating to the Common Agricultural Policy and Great Britain's relationship with the Commonwealth of Nations. Nevertheless, two years later the accession treaties were signed so that Denmark, Ireland and Great Britain joined the European Community. Norway, however, held a referendum and finally rejected membership.

Under Chancellor Willy Brandt, West Germany made great commercial gains, becoming equal to France and Great Britain as the strongest industrial powers in the new European Community. In a period of prosperity, the chancellor set out to appeal to both the left and right sides of the political scene. He also set about thawing relations with the Eastern Bloc of Soviet Europe and tried to placate the old guard as well as encourage the students who had grown up in a post-war world. He used the new prosperity to make numerous welfare reforms. He was regarded highly on the international stage, being awarded the Nobel Peace Prize in 1971 for his efforts to strengthen cooperation in Western Europe through the European Community and to achieve reconciliation between West Germany and the countries of Eastern Europe.

An event which moved the world occurred in Warsaw, Poland. During a 1970 visit to a monument to the Jewish uprising in the Warsaw Ghetto crushed by the Nazis in 1939, after laying a wreath, Chancellor Willy Brandt, spontaneously, knelt and meditated. He remained silently in that position for a short time, surrounded by a large group of dignitaries and press photographers. The occasion of Brandt's visit to Poland at the time was for the signing of a treaty between West Germany and Poland, guaranteeing German acceptance of new borders of Poland. The treaty was one of the Brandt-initiated policy steps in his 'Ostpolitik' to ease tensions between West and East during the Cold War.

Kurt Moeller put down his copy of the *Süddeutsche Zeitung* in his lap and held his head.

"What's wrong?" Janne asked.

He handed his wife the newspaper. "Read this!"

"What?" she asked.

"Chancellor Brandt in Poland," he said. He felt tears welling in his eyes and he got up and stared out of the window. It was snowing hard.

Janne read a few lines of the paper. "What about it? So, the chancellor is visiting Warsaw."

"I was there!" Kurt yelled. "Jews died because of me…we herded them into their synagogue in a Polish village and burnt them alive!" He went to his knees and placed his head in his wife's lap sobbing uncontrollably. In his mind, he could smell the kerosene…he could smell the odour of burning flesh. "I saw them being rounded up in Warsaw, too. I played my part in it all."

That night Kurt remained restless, and when he finally slept, he dreamed…

He could see the black skeletal remains of the Polish synagogue as the snowflakes fell and yet he knew that it had happened before the first snows had fallen. The blackened posts and the scene of this mass murder gradually disappeared under a blanket of white, and still the snowflakes fell. Then there was silence…just a menacing silence until…

Kurt awoke with a start and sat up in the dark of their Heizz farmhouse bedroom. Janne was disturbed by his sudden movement. Kurt felt palpitations as he placed his hand on his heart.

"What is it?" Janne asked, rubbing the sleep from her eyes.

Will she never understand? Kurt thought. "It was only a dream, Janne…a dream. Snow…it covered the scene of my crime." He started to cry again as the guilt attacked every organ of his body. "It will never go away, Janne…never. Sometimes, I just feel I need to end it once and for all."

Janne reached for him, but all he could say was, "Don't touch me!"

It snowed in Oberstdorf all night and most of the morning—big white flakes silently floating down, layer upon layer, just like in Kurt's dream.

When it finally stopped, Kurt took the wide shovel that hung by their front door and started to clear the snow from their cobbled yard. *Snow shovelling…it's just part of the Bavarian winter way of life,* he mused. The grey skies lifted, and blue skies returned, but it was too cold to thaw. When he had finished clearing the yard, Kurt looked up at the roof. The snow lay nearly eighteen inches over the eaves. In bright contrast to the sparkling white, the neighbour's ginger cat sat beside the chimney stack looking down at him with wide open eyes. *After lunch, I must start to clear the roof,* Kurt thought, and he went back inside.

Lottie was busy decorating the Christmas tree with silver and gold stars. Janne called them into the kitchen where steaming bowls of knödel, sitting in a rich meaty sauce peppered with lentils, greeted them. Silently, Kurt ate from his bowl as Lottie and Janne gossiped about the Christmas market.

After lunch, he went back outside while the sun still shone. He leaned their old wooden ladder against the house and taking the shovel and scraper, he climbed up onto the roof. The cat had long since gone, and he started to shovel and push the snow off the roof. It fell in great lumps that splattered on the ground below. It was part of the rhythm of Bavarian life. Then, he felt a slight pain in his chest and stopped, raising his hand across his heart. He slipped and slid down the incline, but there was nothing he could grab a hold of. He screamed…then followed a brief moment of silence, and then excruciating pain as he blacked out…

* * *

Lottie ran out of the house having heard him scream.

"Vater!" she shouted, but there was no response. Janne was right behind her. "Mutter! Call Herr Doktor Bloomer!" Lottie yelled. "Vater is unconscious, he might even be dead."

The ginger cat appeared again and sat looking at Kurt's body and licked snow from her paws.

Janne took Kurt's wrist. She thought she could feel just the lightest pulse, but he didn't appear to be breathing. A pool of blood was oozing beneath his head. Janne and Lottie put towels under to soak up the blood that in the cold was already beginning to congeal.

Herr Doktor Bloomer wasn't long in answering the call, but on examining Kurt he looked up at Janne and Lottie. "I'm afraid it's too late," he said gravely, "he's gone. I would think he died immediately after he hit the ground…partly the impact and partly shock. I'm terribly sorry, Frau Moeller, there is nothing that I can do now."

* * *

The coroner's inquest concluded that Kurt Moeller had died of a heart attack. Kurt was buried a few days later in the Oberstdorf Catholic Cemetery after a brief service at the Basilica of St John the Baptist. Delphine and Hilda Moeller came over from Berchtesgaden and to their surprise young Klaus took the train in from Munich, but Marlene wasn't with him. Christian Aurich gave a moving tribute, referring to Kurt as a great climber and his mentor. Most of Oberstdorf's farming community attended as well as many among Oberstdorf's mountaineers, but rumours began to circulate…*How could such an experienced climber have just fallen from the roof?* The possibility that Kurt Moeller might have committed suicide crossed some people's minds, and Janne when she heard such things, began to think it could possibly be true. His words the night that he had awoken from his nightmare reverberated in her head, 'It will never go away, Janne…never. Sometimes, I just feel I need to end it once and for all.' She didn't say much to Lottie, however, as she felt her personal guilt in not understanding Kurt's pain.

* * *

Klaus Trotter was primarily at his uncle's funeral to see his beautiful cousin, Lottie. Only two months earlier, they had shared a happy week together at the Munich Oktoberfest, but there were not many opportunities for them now, gathered among the mourners. Nor had Klaus ever seen Lottie dressed in black. She somehow looked completely different in these changed circumstances, and they only shared a few brief moments together over two beers and Zuckerkuchen cake at the 'Leichenschmaus'—the wake held in the old farmhouse.

After most of the guests had left, however, Klaus and Lottie went out to the barn.

"Thank you for coming," Lottie said almost by rote.

The cows needed to be fed and Kurt was no longer there to do the chores. The first two hinterwald calves of the new season had been born just two days after Kurt Moeller's death.

"They are both boys, so I call them Caspar and Melchior," Lottie said as she opened up the bin of cattle pellets to supplement the byre's hay. She tried to brush away a tear from her cheek. "Mutter may want to give them other names more in keeping with the herd names," she said as she scooped up the pellets, "but they may be all we get this Christmas."

Klaus smiled, "Well, you'd better call the next one Balthazar, then."

She turned towards him. "That depends…the next one might be a girl."

Lottie filled her bucket and started to dispense it to the stalls. "You can start pitching the hay into the racks," she said. "There's a pitchfork on the end wall there."

They worked together in the barn to the smell of urine, straw, hay and dung.

"All right, you can give me a kiss now," she said when they had finished. "Life goes on. Where are you staying?"

"With Grandmother Moeller and Hilda at the Park Hotel," he answered, "but I have to get back to Munich tomorrow. I just felt I should be here for you."

"I was surprised to see you, but thanks," she replied. "I'm probably going to be pretty stuck here until the summer."

Klaus brushed the hay from his now somewhat crumpled suit.

As they walked out into the darkness and back to the farmhouse, he asked himself, *Where has her sparkle gone?* The snow was crisp under their feet.

* * *

Willy Brandt's appeasement policies between East and West came to something of a head in the summer of 1972. In keeping with the chancellor's efforts, Munich was awarded the privilege of hosting the Olympic Games. The Nazi Berlin Olympics of 1936 were still within living memory with their anti-Semitic stance, and the Bavarian authorities and the West German government wanted to alleviate any fears of links with the Nazi games by making the site truly welcome to all. Security was at a minimum, almost with the intent of showing German openness when hosting the world. The open policy backfired, however, when eight members of the Palestinian militant organisation, 'Black September', infiltrated the Olympic Village, killing two members of the Israeli Olympic team and taking nine others hostage. The 'Black September' commander became their negotiator.

Shortly after the hostages were taken, 'Black September' demanded the release of over two hundred Palestinian prisoners who were being held in Israeli jails, plus the West German imprisoned founders of the Red Army Faction— Andreas Baader and Ulricke Meinhof.

Jürgen Scholtz and Marlene Trotter, now living together, waited for news.

"Israel is too much under the thumb of the Americans. I've really had enough of their shenanigans," Jürgen expressed. "I sympathise with the poor Palestinians."

"And maybe we will get Andreas and Ulricke back," Marlene added.

Jürgen Scholtz and Marlene Trotter had both become followers of the Red Army Faction, known among the students as the Baader-Meinhof Gang. The gang members described themselves as communist, anti-imperialist urban guerrillas engaged in resistance against what they deemed to be a fascist German state. The West German government firmly branded the Baader-Meinhof Gang to be a terrorist organisation.

Prime Minister Golda Meir of Israel appealed to other countries to 'save our citizens and condemn the unspeakable criminal acts committed in Munich'. She also stated, 'If we should give in, then no Israeli anywhere in the world shall feel that his life is safe…it's blackmail of the worst kind.'

Golda Meir and the Israeli Defence Committee secretly authorised the Mossad Jewish Intelligence Agency to track down and kill those allegedly responsible for the Munich massacre. The accusation that this was motivated by a desire for vengeance was disputed by the Mossad, who described the mission as 'putting an end to the type of terror that was perpetrated in Europe'.

The nine Israeli hostages and eight 'Black September' terrorists who captured them were flown via helicopter to the Fürstenfeldbruck Air Base, about 30 kilometres from Munich and the Olympic Village, where the terrorists demanded that they and their hostages be flown to a friendly Arab nation. A Boeing 727 was waiting. Five German police snipers proceeded to engage the Palestinians in an attempt to free the hostages. In the ensuing gun battle on the tarmac, all nine Israeli hostages and one German police officer were killed. The hostages died while they were still tied up in the helicopters.

After this botched rescue attempt by Bavarian border guards and Munich police, the West German government was criticised for the poor execution and overall handling of the incident. It was thought by many that West German neo-Nazis probably gave the Palestinians some logistical assistance in the Munich massacre. The bodies of the five Palestinian attackers killed during the Fürstenfeldbruck gun battle were delivered to Libya, where they received heroes' funerals and were buried with full military honours.

Controversially, after a 34-hour suspension, the Munich Olympic Games continued after this attack and breach of security. On 6 September, a memorial service attended by 80,000 spectators and 3,000 athletes was held in the Olympic Stadium. Olympic President Avery Brundage made little reference to the murdered athletes, which outraged many listeners during a speech where he praised the strength of the Olympic movement.

Klaus Trotter and Jürgen Scholtz sat in a Munich café mulling over the recent events.

"This could escalate," Klaus suggested. "Are we really ready for that?"

"I am…I don't know about you, but we must remove the world of capitalist aggression. We don't want it in our own government, too cosy by far with the Americans. The Americans are no better than the Nazis…Look how they support dictators and despots for their own ends, including Israel. The world pays far too much attention to them. I hope they do get kicked out of Vietnam."

On 8 September, Israeli planes bombed ten Palestine Liberation bases in Syria and Lebanon in response to the Munich massacre, killing a reported 200 militants and 11 civilians.

Just over a month later, an act of Palestinian terrorism occurred aimed at the liberation from a West German prison of the three surviving perpetrators of the massacre. German Lufthansa Flight 615 was hijacked by sympathisers of the Black September Organisation during the Beirut to Ankara part of a multi-stopover flight from Damascus to Frankfurt. The West German authorities complied with the demand of having the prisoners released and they were handed over at Zagreb Airport in Yugoslavia before the hijacked aircraft was flown to Tripoli, where all the hostages were released. The liberated Munich attackers were then granted asylum by Libyan leader Muammar Gaddafi.

"It wouldn't surprise me if the government wasn't complicit in this," Jürgen Scholtz said to Marlene as they listened to the news. "They are just like the Americans…they feather their nests for their own interests."

Klaus said nothing. For him, Jürgen and his half-sister were becoming too extreme.

Klaus Trotter was now a serious post-graduate medical student and set his sights on his future profession. With Lottie Moeller now out of the picture, he had met Elsa Homberg, a research student in the psychology department. He became less interested in activism and he and Elsa moved from Marlene's flat into a small Munich apartment closer to the university.

For its actions, the West German government was certainly criticised by Israel and other parties. Allegations were made that the hijacking had been staged or at least tolerated, with theories of a secret agreement between the German government and 'Black September'—the release of the surviving terrorists in exchange for assurances of no further attacks on West Germany.

The Israeli government had publicly launched 'Operation Wrath of God', which authorised the Mossad to track down and kill anyone who had played a role in the Munich attacks.

* * *

In January 1973, The Israeli Premier, Golda Meir, accompanied by the Israeli Ambassador in Rome, spent nearly 80 minutes with Pope Paul VI in a private audience with the hope of brokering some sort of a peace settlement. In fact, little was achieved by this historic visit. The tit-for-tat assassinations continued. A month later, Israeli Air Force jets shot down a Libyan Arab Airlines Flight over Sinai killing all the passengers and crew.

Helmut Drucker became even more fearful that all-out war between the Arabs and Israel was inevitable. He was nervous, as Francine had invited her granddaughter Sabrina Finkelstein Drucker to visit in the summer.

Sabrina Finkelstein Drucker often walked back home from school in Bischofzell rather than ride the school bus. She was sitting down on a bench overlooking the banks of the River Sitter where it meets the Thur. The sun caught her dark-haired plaits held together by matching white bows. *I hope I can go,* she thought. *We hardly ever see Gran and Gramps here, and I've never been there.* She had just had her twelfth birthday and was really looking forward to visiting her grandparents in Israel, but she had never been on a plane and she wondered what it would be like to fly on her own. Her mother had reassured her, saying that one of the El Al 'Aunts' would take good care of her. 'They might even let you see the captain and visit the cockpit where he flies the plane,' she had said. The sound of the rushing waters where the two rivers met soothed her, and she felt reassured. She picked up her satchel and continued on her way home past the orchards to the farm.

* * *

Sabrina's anxious parents Johannes and Andrea Gerber watched the news daily in Switzerland, following closely developments in the Middle East. May was relatively quiet in the Israeli-Palestinian conflict, and there were no reported assassinations from around the world. Her parents decided to let Sabrina go. They drove her to the Zurich Airport at Kloten, where true to her mother's word they were met at check-in by an El Al 'Aunt' who gave Sabrina a badge to wear and a Toblerone bar of chocolate. They watched as Sabrina went through El Al security.

"They say it's the safest airline in the world now," Johannes reassured Andrea. "They have guards on all their planes and all the baggage is security checked…ever since 1968 when this same flight from Zurich to Tel Aviv was attacked. It won't happen again."

Andrea tried to smile. "Well, it would be extraordinary if it did…no I'm sure everything will be all right." She watched as the El Al security men checked Sabrina's travelling bag. Andrea's eyes were moist. "That lady seems very nice…the 'Aunt'," she choked.

Johannes reached in his pocket for a fresh clean handkerchief and handed it to his wife so she could dab her eyes.

The security man returned Sabrina's bag. The El Al 'Aunt' and Sabrina turned back to them and waved. Johannes and Andrea waved back and Andrea blew her daughter a kiss. Sabrina really looked quite grown-up. She only wore her hair in plaits when she went to school. Now, it was pulled back in a ponytail that contrasted with her yellow dress and a new white blazer that Andrea had bought for her. They watched until she disappeared into the Departure Lounge. Johannes and Andrea waited in the Viewing Lounge having coffee until they saw the El Al plane taxi out to the runway and take off—a sleek white cigar tube rising up into the azure summer sky.

"She'll be fine," Johannes said after they got into their car, and he put his hand reassuringly on his wife's knee. "By the time we get home, Andrea, she'll almost be in Tel Aviv."

About two hours after they got home, the phone rang. It was Gran Francine. 'Just wanted you to know that Sabrina arrived safely at Ben Gurion. The flight landed on time,' the voice said.

"Ben Gurion," Johannes repeated nervously, "I thought she was flying into Lod?"

'Oh…Yes…they changed the name. Of course, most people just say Tel Aviv. Sabrina was one of the first off. They always bring the unaccompanied minors off first with the aunts. Now, hold on and we'll get Sabrina to speak to you and tell you all about it.'

Sabrina came on.

"So, did you enjoy it?" Andrea asked.

'It was beautiful. We could see all the Swiss mountains and then all the puffy clouds. The sea was so blue as we flew into Tel Aviv. And now, guess what Mutter, we're staying at this lovely hotel near the beach. I'll be going swimming in the morning…I can't wait. The sea…it's amazing.'

"I'm sure you'll have a wonderful time, dear. On the plane, did they let you see the captain?"

'No…it wasn't allowed, but I had a good time. They were all very kind to me, and we had a proper meal and everything.'

"Here's Vater…Have a lovely time with Gran and Gramps, sweetheart. So glad you had a nice flight."

'Bye, Mutter…Bye'.

"So glad you enjoyed flying," her father said. "Send all our love to Gran and Gramps Drucker."

'Finkelstein Drucker' Sabrina's voice said loudly from the phone.

"All right, sweetie…Finkelstein Drucker. How long will you be at the seaside?"

'Three days I think, and then we go to the farm.'

"Have a wonderful time. This is an expensive call so much love from Vater and Mutter…Bye!"

'Bye!'

Andrea sat down in a comfy armchair. "Well, that's a relief," she said, kicking off her shoes.

* * *

Sabrina was excited when she awoke in the morning, although surprised that it was already 8:00 a.m. Gramps explained that it was the 'jet lag'…something to do with it being a different time zone here in Israel than in Switzerland. They all had breakfast outside in the open-air restaurant on the oceanfront. It was the first time Sabrina had heard the sound of the surf, and she could smell the sea and the sand. Tractors were raking the long beach running all along the Tel Aviv waterfront. The orange juice, too, tasted different…just like real oranges. "They grow some of the best oranges in the world just north of here…Jaffa oranges," Gran Finkelstein explained.

Later, they went swimming. Sabrina was surprised at how warm the water was after having only known the Swiss lakes, and when they walked along the beach the sand actually felt quite hot under her feet. These were all new and wonderful sensations for her. She also noticed how many of the girls here were wearing the new fashionable bikinis, whereas she still had the old-fashioned swimsuits that most of the Swiss were still wearing. *Perhaps Gran will buy me a bikini,* she thought.

Gramps bought them ice creams, but Sabrina found hers to be a little sour compared with Swiss ice cream.

"It's the yoghurt," Gramps explained. "We make a lot of things with yoghurt here, especially goat's yoghurt. You'll see that when we go back to the kibbutz. We make a lot of yoghurt, don't we, Gran?"

Her gran nodded. Sabrina wasn't sure that she really liked the yoghurt and she added a little sugar to her ice cream. It was refreshing, though, and she thought that maybe she would get used to it.

"It's very good for you…very healthy," Gramps assured her.

They pour this yoghurt over a lot of their salads and tomatoes, Sabrina noticed. *It seems to be the basis of almost everything...this 'laban'.*

Sabrina got used to it, especially after they went inland to Givan HaSholah. She actually came to rather like it. Gran also bought her a yellow bikini that she thought looked 'so good' as she started to get a tan. *'A Gottex' Gran had said, 'one of our great Israeli fashion houses'.*

At the kibbutz, Sabrina was sometimes put to work picking early apples in the extensive orchards as well as helping her grandparents with the dairy. There was a nice swimming pool and they rarely worked in the afternoons, so she often lay out in her yellow bikini and tanned herself. The most exciting event was on Sabbath Eve when the whole kibbutz came together in the huge dining room and it was cleared after supper for dancing.

Everyone seemed to take part, dancing in circles to exciting exotic-sounding rhythms and the teenagers on the kibbutz soon had Sabrina dancing in their circles. Sometimes, when the music stopped, the older boys cracked eggs over the girls' heads. It was all part of the fun, but it was a bit messy and Sabrina was afraid that it might spoil her dress. Her gran thought that it had something to do with an old Sabbath tradition in which Haredi Jews throw stones at other Jews as a protest against what they view as violations of religious laws concerning the Sabbath—like the wearing of immodest clothing by women and similar issues. "Eggs are less damaging than stones," Gran said wisely.

"What are Haredi Jews?" Sabrina asked.

"Very conservative, orthodox Jews, who literally live by every word of the Torah," Gran Finkelstein explained. "In order to prevent outside influence and contamination of values and practices, Haredim strive to limit their contact with the outside world, avoiding, as much as possible, both non-Haredi Jews and Gentiles. Interaction with outsiders is generally confined to things like going to the post office. To be truthful, dear, that's why I think we see so many eggs cracked here on Sabbath Eve. We are farmers...Israelis yes, but not terribly strict Jews. We're not very orthodox. We have rather lax rules. I think the boys crack the eggs rather in mockery of the stone-throwing laws of the Haredi." She hugged her granddaughter. "You know what it really means, sweetie...they're flirting with you. They think you're pretty."

Sabrina started asking more questions about Judaism and her family.

"Who were my real grandparents?" She asked one day when she had her grandmother alone. "I mean you're my gran, but Mutter said that you aren't actually Vater's mother."

"She's right," Francine said. "I'm his aunt." She thought for a moment. "Well, you really should know…My brother was your grandfather Herman…a well-known German professor of engineering in Munich. The Nazis kicked him out of his post at his Munich university. He and your grandmother fled from Munich and settled at Berchtesgaden in the mountains where they felt safer, but it wasn't so. After Kristallnacht, and during the war, Nazis started to arrest Jews and send them off to work camps. Thinking it might happen to them, they sent your father and your Aunt Abigail to stay with me in a safer part of Germany…Oberstdorf, near the Swiss border. Eventually, it wasn't safe for us either, and we fled Oberstdorf one night making it into Switzerland. We were billeted as refugees with Daniel Schwegler, the cheesemaker in Bischofzell. We then made a very good business for him and eventually, a few years later, your father met the Gerbers. That's how you became a Gerber Finkelstein and your Aunt Abigail a Finkelstein Gerber."

"So, what happened to my real grandparents?" Sabrina pressed.

"We don't really know. We assume that they were victims of the Nazi holocaust. Some research did show that your grandfather, Herman, died in a bombing raid on a Messerschmitt factory near Flossenbürg, but there was no mention of your grandmother, Merla. She was probably sent to Ravensbrück, near Berlin, but we don't know. Six million innocent Jews were murdered by Hitler and the Nazis in those camps. Nowadays, we know that most of them were gassed and incinerated. That could be what happened to your grandmother."

Sabrina frowned and looked very solemn as she tried to hold back tears. "Gassed and burnt! Why? What for?" And then, the tears came.

Gran Finkelstein held her close, comforting her. "That was one of the main reasons why we decided to come here. Thousands of survivors have come to Israel from the German displaced persons camps set up after the war…This is a great country, Sabrina. We will survive!"

After these revelations that did not totally surprise her, Sabrina started to ask her gran more and more about what it meant to be a Jew. "Can I be a Jew and still be a Lutheran?"

"I don't see any reason why not. We're not really Jews…we were Lutherans, too…but we are Israelis!"

The window of Israeli-Palestinian peace didn't last long after Sabrina returned to Switzerland. Just two days later, Yosef Alon born Josef Plaček, also known as Joe Alon, an Israeli Air Force officer and military attaché to the United States, was mysteriously shot and killed in the driveway of his home in Chevy Chase, Maryland.

The fact that this was an assassination right in the heart of America was greeted with pleasure by the left-wing communist students of the Baader-Meinhof group in Munich. On 1 July, several members met at Marlene Trotter's apartment, including her lover, Jürgen Scholtz.

The American news was announced on German television:

'On the night of 30 June 1973, 44-year-old Yosef Alon and his wife Dvora went to a dinner party for a departing Israeli embassy staffer. At roughly 12:30 a.m. on 1 July, the couple entered their Ford Galaxie and drove home to Chevy Chase, Maryland, arriving about a half-hour later. Dvora exited the vehicle and walked twenty to thirty feet to their porch, while Alon gathered up his sports coat on the backseat.

'At this moment, Alon was shot in his chest five times with copper-jacketed military bullets shot from a foreign-made revolver, either an F.I.E. Titan Tiger or a German Arminius. One shot that pierced his heart would soon prove to be fatal, while the other shots caused only minor wounds. Dvora rushed inside and called the police, seeing only a light-coloured car drive away, and then she returned to the front yard. She attempted with her eighteen-year-old daughter Dahlia to stem her husband's bleeding with towels. Alon was taken to a hospital, where he died at 1:27 a.m.'

Joe Alon's family accepted President Richard Nixon's offer to repatriate Alon's body to Israel. An aircraft left the United States from Andrews Air Force Base in Maryland, arriving at Ben Gurion, Tel Aviv, with his family on board.

Later, the Cairo-based Voice of Palestine broadcast that 'After the assassination of martyr Mohammed Boudia at the hands of the Zionist intelligence elements in Paris, Colonel Yosef Alon…was executed…His is the first execution operation carried out against a Zionist official in the United States.'

"Black September!" Jürgen Scholtz shouted excitedly. "This is a blow against Israel and the United States."

Marlene poured them all a glass of wine.

* * *

In October 1973, at the time of the Jewish festival of Yom Kippur, a surprise attack of Arab and Palestinian forces broke into Israel.

Francine Finkelstein Drucker looked at the photograph of Moshe Dyan still displayed on her dressing table. "I hope if we now go to war again we will have somebody like you to lead us," she said. "The whole world seems to be against us now."

Helmut came in. "Did you hear the news?" he said. "We are under attack in the north again. Egyptian and Syrian-led troops are gaining ground on the northwest frontier." He held his wife. "Maybe we made the wrong decision. Perhaps it would have been better if we had stayed in Switzerland?"

"Have faith," Francine answered. "The Americans will back us. We will win like we always do."

It was true—the Americans were supplying the Israeli Air Force with fighter jets. And Francine was right—after a few days, the Israelis started to repel the Arab attack.

Life at Kibbutz Givat HaSlosha continued in its agrarian way, although the younger members were heavily drilled in military preparedness. The October attack was successfully overcome, the Arabs were pushed back into their own terrain, but around the world, assassins on both sides were scoring points.

* * *

In May 1974, Willy Brandt resigned as chancellor when one of his closest aides, was exposed as an agent of the Stasi—the East German secret service. Perhaps, 'Ostpolitik' had gone just a little bit too far. Helmut Schmidt who had a part-Jewish background then became Chancellor of West Germany.

In Israel, a Palestinian terrorist attack occurred on 15 May, involving a two-day hostage-taking of over a hundred Israelis, which ended in the murders of 25 hostages and six other civilians. It began when three armed members of the Democratic Front for the Liberation of Palestine entered Israel from Lebanon.

Helmut and Francine Finkelstein Drucker listened at Kibbutz Givan HaSlosha as the Israeli news was broadcast:

'Soon afterwards, they attacked a van, killing two Israeli Arab women while injuring a third and entered an apartment building in the town of Ma'alot, where they killed a couple and their four-year-old son.'

"Close to the Lebanon border in West Galilee," Helmut said.

'From there,' the Israeli newsreader continued, *'they headed for the Netiv Meir Elementary School, where they took more than a hundred and fifty people hostage, including a hundred and five children. Most of the hostages were teenagers from a high school in Safad who on a Gadna Camp field trip, were spending the night in Ma'alot. The hostage-takers issued demands for the release of twenty-three Palestinian militants from Israeli prisons, or else they would kill the students.'*

With so many children involved, Israelis hung on their radios and TVs awaiting further news.

'On the second day of the standoff, the Israeli counter-terrorism unit Sayeret Matkal stormed the building. During the takeover, the hostage-takers killed children with grenades and automatic weapons. Ultimately, twenty-five hostages, including twenty-two children, were killed, and sixty-eight more were injured. It appeared the three hostage-takers were Palestinians dressed in Israeli Defence Forces uniforms.'

"Thank goodness, Sabrina isn't with us now," Francine said. "Many of our teenagers from here are taken to the Gadna camp. There might even have been some of ours on that trip."

* * *

In 1974, the United States had been embroiled in a massive scandal surrounding President Nixon over the theft of tapes after a break-in at the Watergate Office Building in Washington. The scandal stemmed from the Nixon administration's continual attempts to cover up its involvement in the 1972 June break-in there of the Democratic National Committee headquarters. The House Judiciary Committee approved three articles of impeachment against Nixon for obstruction of justice, abuse of power and contempt of Congress. With his complicity in the cover-up made public, and his political support completely eroded, Nixon resigned from office on 9 August 1974. Gerald Ford immediately assumed the presidency.

As president, Gerald Ford signed the Helsinki Accords, which marked a move towards détente in the Cold War. With the collapse of South Vietnam nine months into his presidency, United States involvement in the Vietnam War ingloriously ended, and there was a mood to turn away from militarism to peace.

In Israel, however, peace still seemed a long way off.

At 11:00 p.m. on the night of 4 March 1975, eight Palestinians in two teams landed by boat on the Tel Aviv beach. As they landed on the shore, police officers spotted them in a patrol vehicle that was passing by. The officers in the car opened fire on them, and one of the boats, stocked with weapons, was hit and exploded. The militants escaped from the beach onto a street corner. They crossed onto Herbert Samuel Street, where they shot randomly and threw grenades. Then they tried, but failed, to break into a cinema. Continuing down the street, they took over the Savoy Hotel. During the takeover of the hotel, three people were killed. Three others managed to escape in the confusion, but most of the guests and staff were taken hostage.

Private Moshe Deutschmann, a soldier from the Israeli army's Golani Brigade on home leave, grabbed his weapon and ran to the hotel. Meanwhile, some militants attempted to leave. Deutschmann saw them at the entrance and engaged them. In the exchange of fire, Deutschmann was hit. He managed to crawl away, but later died of his injuries.

Israeli security forces then arrived. The Palestinians barricaded themselves inside the hotel with their hostages, detonating an explosive charge which caused part of the building to collapse. They threatened that if Israel didn't release 20 Palestinian prisoners within four hours, the hostages would be executed. Tracer bullets streaked through the night air. The four-storey Savoy Hotel, illuminated by floodlights, was surrounded by troops, local police and border officers in full battle regalia. Military vehicles, armoured cars and personnel carriers clogged the surrounding streets. Red Magen David ambulance crews administered first-aid to wounded civilians on the pavements and in the street gutters. The blinding light of magnesium flares revealed naval patrol boats cruising just off the beach.

The Israeli security forces conducted negotiations with the militants. Speaking Arabic, one hostage became a mediator between the security forces and militants. During the negotiations, she provided the security forces with detailed information on the militants.

Early the next morning, the Israeli Sayeret Matkal stormed the hotel, killing seven of the perpetrators and capturing the eighth. Two Sayeret Matkal were also killed. Five hostages were freed, while five died. A few hours after the rescue operation, the boat that had transported the militants was captured at sea. Its crew was arrested.

"That was the hotel we stayed in when Sabrina was with us," Francine said as they listened to the morning news.

"Yes…it was…that was a nice hotel. When is this ever going to end?" Helmut answered.

Due to such audacious responses, however, the international reputation of Israel rose.

* * *

Later in the summer, Israel's reputation was further enhanced, thanks in large part to an amazing display of boldness. On 4 July, an Air France Flight, originating in Tel Aviv, took off from Athens, Greece, heading for Paris. It was hijacked by four terrorists, two from the 'Popular Front for the Liberation of Palestine' and two from the radical German militant group, 'Revolutionary Cells' which had morphed out of the 'Baader-Meinhof' gang. The hijackers had the plane flown to Entebbe in Uganda and the perceived safety that they thought would be given to them by the Soviet-backed Idi Amin regime. Israel then performed a rescue mission to free all the passengers and crew members held hostage at Entebbe Airport. Acting on information from the Mossad, the Israeli Defence Force flew to Entebbe carrying commandos over 2,500 miles. The operation on the ground lasted just 90 minutes. Of the hostages, 102 were rescued and three were killed. Five Israeli commandos were wounded, and one Israeli unit commander was shot dead. All the hijackers along with 45 Ugandan soldiers were killed and eleven Soviet-built planes of Uganda's air force were destroyed. This was the boldest move by one of the smallest of countries to counter nearly two decades of the international hijacking of planes. The determination of Israel to survive was on display to the whole world.

In Switzerland, Sabrina Finkelstein Drucker was ecstatic. "You've got to hand it to those Jews, they are plucky," she said to her mother as they worked in the Bischofzell farm dairy. "It gives me great hope for Israel. Gran and Gramps must be very proud."

It was a little different in Munich. Jürgen Scholtz and Marlene Trotter had enjoyed a particularly hedonistic night together before finding out details about the Entebbe raid.

"Wilfried and Brigitte," Jürgen said as he poured Marlene black coffee. "That's a serious blow to the cause. It's hard to believe that we were all together in Frankfurt just a few weeks ago."

Marlene chuckled. "Wilfried Böse," she said, "the evil one! That's what they'll say about Wilfried."

Jürgen put his arms around her, feeling the warmth and smelling the musk of their recent tryst. "You're bad…bad joke!" And he slapped her backside.

"Böse…evil. I think it's rather funny because that's his name and that's what they'll think."

"He wasn't evil…he was convinced. He was no Nazi, but one of us…an idealist, a believer. And Brigitte Kuhlmann…she was totally convinced of everything we stand for. For many in 'The Cells', she was their leader. Remember what she said in Frankfurt, 'We carry out terrorist acts in West Germany because the ruling establishment has taken Nazis and reactionaries into its service. Our beef with the Israelis is not racial hatred of Jews…it's about the injustice of the Israelis to the Palestinians!' Might isn't always right! And remember it's those damned Americans who are backing them!"

Marlene could feel Jürgen trembling. She reached up and kissed him. "And that's why I love you," she said, "your passion!"

* * *

In the autumn at the United Nations, the Arab League recognised the Palestinian Liberation Organisation as the representative body for the rights of the Palestinian people. Yasser Arafat, the PLO leader then addressed the United Nations General Assembly. Later in the session, the United Nations General Assembly adopted a resolution, which recognised the Palestinian right to self-determination, officiated the United Nations' contact with the Palestine Liberation Organisation, and added the 'Question of Palestine' to the United Nations agenda, allowing the PLO to participate in all Assembly sessions thus paving the way for peace talks.

In the 1976 Republican presidential primary campaign in the United States, Gerald Ford defeated former California governor, Ronald Reagan, for the

Republican nomination, but narrowly lost the presidential election to the Democratic challenger, former Georgia governor, Jimmy Carter—truly a peacemaker. After taking office on 20 January 1977, Carter's first task was to pardon all those who had evaded the Vietnam draft. There was a totally different tone in the White House.

Despite sporadic assassinations around the world on both sides, in September 1978, President Jimmy Carter was able to bring together Israeli Prime Minister Menachem Begin and Egyptian President Anwar Sadat at the rustic presidential retreat in Maryland. There, they signed the Camp David Accord, in which Israel agreed to withdraw from the Sinai Peninsula in exchange for peace and a framework for future negotiation over the West Bank and Gaza Strip.

"There will be peace now," Francine Finkelstein Drucker assured her husband, but Helmut wasn't so sure. "It's a start," was all he said.

Chapter Ten
Sabrina 1979–1990

The peace treaty between Egypt and Israel was signed after intense negotiations in Washington in March 1979. The main features were mutual recognition, cessation of the state of war that had existed since the 1948 war, normalisation of relations and the withdrawal by Israel of its armed forces and civilians from the Sinai Peninsula which Israel had captured during the Six-Day War. Egypt agreed to leave the Sinai demilitarised. The agreement provided for free passage of Israeli ships through the Suez Canal, and recognition of the Strait of Tiran and the Gulf of Aqaba as international waterways, which had been blockaded by Egypt back in 1967. The agreement also called for an end to Israeli military rule over the Israeli-occupied territories and the establishment of full autonomy for the Palestinian inhabitants of the territories.

The normalisation of relations between Israel and Egypt went into effect in January 1980. Ambassadors were exchanged in February. The boycott laws were repealed by Egypt's parliament the same month, and some trade began to develop, albeit less than Israel had hoped for. In March 1980, regular airline flights were inaugurated. Egypt also began supplying Israel with crude oil. It looked like the long Arab-Israeli struggle was coming to an end.

* * *

Sabrina Finkelstein Drucker left the Bischofzell School for the last time in a happy mood as she walked home along the riverbank. She wore her dark hair long these days with a fringe that from time to time she blew back from her eyes. She expressed her freedom, *No more school. Now I am free*! She was looking forward to going back to Israel to visit Gran and Gramps. In a week she would be leaving, and this time, she would be staying a month. Gran Finkelstein had told her that they would go down to the Red Sea. It all sounded rather exotic.

She arrived in Israel in early June, and four days later, they were driving through the Negev on their way to Eilat. For the most part, the countryside seemed rather boring to Sabrina—a flat area pierced with rocks, and it looked like they were driving miles away from anywhere. She rather wished that they were going back to Tel Aviv, but Gran Francine reassured her.

"That beautiful hotel we visited before was destroyed by the Palestinians," her gran explained. "I'm not sure how safe it is there now. But, Eilat is opening up. Many new hotels are being built there now that we have peace with Egypt and hopefully soon with Jordan. They say the water there is really clear and the coral reefs in the Red Sea are spectacular."

The closer they got, the more mountainous the terrain became—quite jagged treeless mountains that had a purple cast in the haze of the hot sun. The road wound through the mountains, slowly descending as it dropped down to the blue waters of the Gulf of Aqaba. Many palms had been planted, and there was a lot of construction, but along the waterfront were some of the many new hotels, sitting in a green oasis against the backdrop of those barren mountains. The sea sparkled, reflecting long white blobs on rich blue waters.

Sabrina's doubts disappeared. "Oh, this is beautiful, Gran. It looks so clean…so neat…so luxurious."

They pulled into the Leonardo Plaza Hotel—one of the first to have been built on the north beach, facing directly down the gulf. The hotel seemed to Sabrina to be the lap of luxury. The great white façade shimmered in the sun looking out on groves of palms surrounding a beautiful pool before leading out to an incredible beach. At the far end, a few old, almost Arab-like dhows were leaning on their sides, bringing character. Sabrina couldn't wait to get her feet into the sea. Later, she tested it. It was really warm.

Sabrina spent much of each day snorkelling, where not far out there were stunning coral reefs teeming with exotic fish. In the evenings, they often dined under the stars, and there was a band that played exciting music. It wasn't long before the boys came around. At eighteen and sultry, Sabrina looked like a good catch, but she didn't speak much Hebrew—just a smattering of words relating to life at Kibbutz Givan HaSholah, along with a little schoolgirl English.

There were German-Jewish families staying at the hotel, however. Most of their young men spoke Hebrew, but some of them remembered their German, having been born in Israel at a time when their émigré parents still mostly spoke German. Their German wasn't very good, but it was enough for them to be able to make themselves understood. Sabrina was easily won over by a rather handsome young man about two years older than her, David Schwartz. When Gran and Gramps retired for the night, it wasn't long before David and Sabrina were kissing under the stars. And after a couple of days, they were making love in a double hammock under the palms.

Sabrina started to giggle as in one of their moments of passion she felt the knots of the hammock push into her buttocks.

"Shss!" David whispered. "That guard's coming around again."

They froze in a compromising position, the hammock swinging, until the night watchman patrolling the beach had passed. The night was romantic, especially in the afterglow as they looked up at the stars through the tracery of palms, but it was not the most comfortable.

The next day, David and Sabrina shared an umbrella on the beach and spent much of the morning snorkelling. Holding each other in the water was somewhat comical in flippers and face masks. *The fish must think we look very strange,* Sabrina observed.

It had all been great fun, but when the time came for David and his parents to leave, Sabrina felt a strange feeling of remorse. *I hope I'm not pregnant* she said to herself as she looked in her bathroom mirror. Fear hung over her for much of the rest of her stay, and she became moody and kept herself to herself.

"Are you all right dear?" her gran finally asked as they lay beside each other under their beach umbrellas. "You don't seem yourself. It might be better not to lie out in the sun so much. It's very strong here."

"No, Gran, it's all right. I'm fine…just a little tired. You're probably right, the sun makes one sleepy. I'll take a walk." She picked up her towel and under a large sun hat that her gran had bought for her, she went off along the shoreline to where the dhows were beached.

She sat in their shadow and those aching feelings of fearful guilt welled up within her again. *I really might be pregnant. Oh my God! I can't be pregnant! Please, God, don't let me be pregnant,* she prayed, and she rarely prayed.

A day or two later after they got back to Givan HaShlosha, her period commenced. "Oh! What a relief! Thank you, God…Thank you, God!" she prayed as she got dressed for Sabbath Eve. Despite the discomfort, her joy was obvious when the dancing commenced, it wasn't long before an egg was cracked over her head.

On her return to Switzerland with an amazing suntan, she overheard her parents on the terrace below her window.

"It looks like she had a good time. She's really grown up over the past month," Johannes said.

"Not our little girl any more, but our grown-up daughter," Andrea agreed.

If only they knew, Sabrina thought. *Thank God, I'm not pregnant*!

Now that she had finished school, in the autumn Sabrina joined her mother and father on a trip to Bavaria to visit King Ludwig II's castles. Johannes had never been back to Bavaria since their escape, so their first stop was naturally to take Sabrina to Oberstdorf.

"So…this is where your Gran and Gramps came from," her father said as the small town came into view nestled below the Allgau Alps.

The trees were just beginning to turn in those beautiful weeks of late September and early October before the real autumn starts. Ahead of them, there was a dusting of snow on the high peaks, but in the valley, it was still gloriously warm.

"Gran told me how beautiful it was and she was right," Sabrina said as they got closer.

Her father nodded. "Of course, your Aunt Abigail and I remember it from the war years and our escape."

"Didn't Aunt Abigail and Uncle Aldrich honeymoon here?" Sabrina asked.

"Yes, they came here and we went to Lake Lugano." Johannes smiled at his now adult daughter. "You might even have been conceived there," he jested.

Momentarily, Sabrina thought of David Schwartz.

They drove through the pretty old town to the Park Hotel where they had reservations for two nights. The next day, her father tried to find the old Drucker farmhouse for them, but his memory was rather vague. Today it could have been one of several now along the road running north from the town. "That's the Hohes Licht Home," he said as he slowed down the car. "It looks like it's a Gästehaus now. I can't believe that was all thirty-five years ago," he recalled as he described the night that they had left with their friends Pieter and Hendrick, crammed into the backseat of Gramps' old car with their rucksacks on their knees.

"What happened to them?" Sabrina asked.

"After the war, they went back to Holland. They didn't really like working in the dairy. That was one of the reasons why we moved back to Bischofschell shortly after you were born, so we could help old Schwegler out."

It wasn't that far to drive on from Oberstdorf to Füssen—close to two of 'mad' King Ludwig's castles. The Swiss travel agent had booked them into the old Hirsch Hotel close by Füssen's Hohe Schloss—not one of Ludwig's, being centuries older. Apparently, once it was the summer residence of the Prince-Bishops of Augsburg. They learned that known for its artwork, the Hohe Schloss in Füssen was also one of the most important secular buildings of German Late-Gothic architecture, and in part, it was easy for the Finkelstein Druckers to see where Ludwig II got the idea for his Gothic romantic fantasies. Apparently, in 1291, the Bavarian Duke Ludwig der Strenge illegally began building a castle. The bishop of Augsburg stopped the construction work, acquired the castle hill and had the unfinished castle extended. In the last decade of the fifteenth century, the castle was completely redesigned to look as it now did. Apparently, during 'the secularisation', and Sabrina had no idea what that really meant, Füssen Castle had fallen back into the Kingdom of Bavaria, but the kings preferred the nearby Hohenschwangau Castle built by King Maximilian II where 'Mad' Ludwig spent much of his childhood. That was where they visited the next day.

They listened as the German guide at Hohenschwangau told of how Ludwig came to live here rather than at the grand palace in Munich where he was born.

"Hohenschwangau, the 'high region of the swan', was the official summer and hunting residence of Maximilian, his wife, Marie of Prussia, and their two sons Ludwig and Otto both later kings of Bavaria," the guide explained. "The young princes spent many years of their adolescence here. Queen Marie, who loved to hike in the mountains, created an Alpine garden with plants gathered from all over the Alps. The King and the Queen lived in the main building, and the boys in the annexe."

As the tourists marvelled at the huge frescoes of swans inside the castle, the guide explained that the mediaeval Lohengrin, the Knight of the Swans, had led to Ludwig later seeing himself as 'The Swan King'. "This became the start of his lifelong friendship with Wagner, starting with the composer's opera *Lohengrin,* and leading later to Tchaikovsky possibly modelling his ballet *Swan Lake* on 'The Swan King' and where the neighbouring lake to Hohenschwangau was known as 'Swan Lake'."

Being close to the guide, Johannes Drucker asked, "I imagine seeing all this mediaeval folklore around him every day here must have had a huge effect on the impressionable young Ludwig?"

"Unquestionably," the guide agreed, "that…and his almost total separation from his parents." The guide then re-addressed the group.

"Ludwig and his even madder younger brother Otto were not close to either of their parents. King Maximilian's advisers had suggested that 'on his daily walks he might like, at times, to be accompanied by his future successor, Ludwig'. The King apparently replied, 'But what am I to say to him? After all, my son takes no interest in what other people tell him.'" The guide paused and looked around at her audience. "My son doesn't either," she said.

There was laughter before she continued.

"Later, when he was king, Ludwig would even refer to his mother as 'my predecessor's consort'. He was far closer to his grandfather, the deposed and notorious King Ludwig I. He was also very close to his cousin, Duchess Elisabeth in Bavaria, and later Empress of Austria."

Sabrina found it all rather overwhelming. *Too many names of past kings, princes and folkloric characters from legends of long ago,* she thought as she looked out of one of the windows at the view over terraces to the curving Swan Lake beneath the magnificent mountains. *Now this view…that I can appreciate.* But Hohenschwangau was only the start. *Tomorrow we'll have to climb up to that neighbouring Neuschwanstein Castle,* Sabrina realised and she sighed. The group was moving on to the next room. *I'd better not get left behind,* she realised, and she trailed after them.

At dinner that night back at the hotel, the sight of a handsome young man at the table across from them was a lot more exciting. Sabrina caught his attention as she flirted with her eyes and blew back her fringe. It worked…he smiled at her, and after dinner, he asked her if she'd like to share a 'Schnapps'.

As she recalled her day at the castle with the young man over their shots, he eventually raised his glass. "That King Ludwig wasn't just mad, he was as queer as a coot…a raving homosexual," he said.

"Really!"

"Stark raving!" The young man knocked back another Schnapps. "Throughout his reign, Ludwig had a succession of close friendships with men. He used his creepy groom at the Royal stables to procure young boys to keep him amused. Never got married you know. He was engaged to some duchess but called it off. I don't think he liked 'pussy' much." He put his hand on Sabrina's thigh. "You're gorgeous…I imagine you like to fuck!"

"Yes…" she said cautiously, "but not tonight. I think I'd better go or I won't be able to climb up to that other castle tomorrow."

Discreetly, she left him, hoping he wouldn't follow her up to her room.

She locked her door after she reached the room. She smiled at herself in her bathroom mirror standing there in her underwear. *Now, if he hadn't had all that Schnapps, well maybe I would have.* She pirouetted in front of the mirror. *I think he might have been pretty good.*

The next morning, however, she hoped that he would not be at the breakfast table. It would be best to forget him. He wasn't there. Perhaps he was sleeping it off.

Sabrina and her parents joined the tour bus to take them up to the base of the hill on which King Ludwig's extraordinary castle was perched. Wisps of autumnal mist were shrouding the turrets when they got there, and they started the considerable climb up the pathway to the entrance.

"Neuschwanstein," the guide said, "the new swan stone castle."

The swans again, Sabrina realised. *The Swan King and his new swan stone castle…perhaps he quarried the stone from the area of the lake?* Apparently, however, Ludwig built the castle on the site of a much older stone castle named Schwanstein, and that was why he called it New Swan Stone.

The guide continued. "In 1832, Ludwig's father King Maximilian II of Bavaria bought its ruins to replace them with the comfortable neo-Gothic palace known as Hohenschwangau Castle that you see below here."

Sabrina smiled. *Where we were yesterday…The things I'm learning,* she thought. *Vater thinks it's important for me to know all this stuff. He really thinks it's important 'Otherwise you'll just be a dairy girl forever', so he said.* She shook her head. *What does he know?*

The guide rambled on. "The ruins above the family palace were known to the crown prince from his excursions. When the young king came to power in 1864, the construction of a new palace in place of the ruined castle became the first in his series of building projects. Ludwig called the new palace New Hohenschwangau Castle; it was only after his death that it was renamed Neuschwanstein. The confusing result is that Hohenschwangau and Schwanstein have effectively swapped names: Hohenschwangau Castle replaced the ruins of

Schwanstein Castle, and Neuschwanstein Castle replaced the ruins of the two Hohenschwangau castles."

There was a smattering of laughter from others in their group. *I suppose that is quite funny,* Sabrina thought.

The guide reassembled them in the entrance hall. "The inspiration for the construction of Neuschwanstein came from two journeys that Ludwig took in 1867—one in May to the reconstructed Wartburg near Eisenach, another in July to the Château de Pierrefonds, which Eugène Viollet-le-Duc was transforming from a ruined castle into a historic palace. The King saw both buildings as representatives of a romantic interpretation of the Middle Ages, as well as the musical mythology of his friend Wagner, whose operas *Tannhäuser* and *Lohengrin* had made such a lasting impression on him."

Sabrina frowned. "That'll be the next thing…they'll take me to the opera," she muttered to herself. She felt the guide's eyes catch hers.

"In February 1868, the death of Ludwig's grandfather, King Ludwig I, freed up the considerable sums that were previously spent on the abdicated King," the lady continued. "This allowed Ludwig II to start the architectural project of building a private refuge in this familiar landscape far from Munich so that he could live out his idea of the Middle Ages. In a letter to Richard Wagner, in May 1868, Ludwig wrote:

'It is my intention to rebuild the old castle ruin of Hohenschwangau near the Pöllat Gorge in the authentic style of the old German knights' castles, and I must confess to you that I am looking forward very much to living there one day, and you know the revered guest that I would like to accommodate there! The location is one of the most beautiful to be found, holy and unapproachable, a worthy temple for the divine friend who has brought salvation and true blessing to the world. It reminds me of *Tannhäuser* and *Lohengrin'*.'"

They say Wagner's operas are really long, Sabrina mused. *When we're in Munich, I would much rather they took me to Oktoberfest!*

"The building design was drafted by the stage designer Christian Jank and realised by the architect Eduard Riedel," the guide droned on. "The king insisted on a detailed plan and on personal approval of each and every draft. Ludwig's control went so far that the palace has been regarded as his own creation, rather than that of the architects involved."

As they were guided through the palace, they saw the shapes of Romanesque, Gothic and Byzantine architecture and art mingled in an eclectic fashion and supplemented with nineteenth-century technical achievements. Characteristic of Neuschwanstein's design were theatre themes: Christian Jank drew on coulisse drafts from his time as a scenic painter.

"The basic style was originally planned to be neo-Gothic," the guide explained, "but the palace was primarily built in Romanesque style in the end. The operatic themes moved gradually from *Tannhäuser* and *Lohengrin* to *Parsifal*."

Sabrina yawned. *Yet another Wagner opera*!

"The foundation stone for the palace was laid on 5 September 1869. In 1872, its cellar was completed, and in 1876, everything up to the first floor, the gatehouse being finished first. At the end of 1882, it was completed and fully furnished, allowing Ludwig to take provisional lodgings there and observe the ongoing construction work. In 1884, the King was able to move into the new building.

"The palace was erected as a conventional brick construction and later encased in various types of rock. The white limestone used for the fronts came from a nearby quarry. Marble from the Untersberg near Salzburg was used for the windows, the arch ribs, the columns and the capitals."

One of the other tourists asked, "How did they carry all these materials up here?"

"The transport of building materials was facilitated by scaffolding and a steam crane that lifted the material to the construction site. Another crane was used at the construction site. In the end, Ludwig II lived in the palace for a total of only a hundred and seventy-two days."

"What a waste!" Sabrina muttered under her breath, but just loud enough for a fellow tourist to turn around and smile.

The next day they drove to Linderhof, a smaller palace set in beautiful gardens that appealed much more to Sabrina.

They learned that King Ludwig II already knew the area around Linderhof from his youth, when he had accompanied his father King Maximilian II of Bavaria on his hunting trips in the Bavarian Alps. Ludwig II inherited the so-called Königshäuschen from his father, and in 1869, began enlarging the building. In 1874, he decided to tear down the Königshäuschen and rebuild it in its present-day location in the park as the Linderhof Palace. The building was designed in the style of the second rococo period inspired by Louis XV at Versailles. The guide then explained how Ludwig was obsessed with the French monarchy and he referred to Herrenchiemsee where Sabrina knew they would also be going—apparently, a replica of the central part of Versailles.

That evening they drove to Schloss Elmau in the mountains above Garmisch. The Swiss travel agency had recommended this as their next hotel where they stayed just one night. It was a magnificent setting, but the hotel itself was quite sparsely furnished. Sabrina was surprised by rather erotic paintings on the walls, but apparently, the whole property belonged to a family with liberal Bohemian trends. Dinner was served in the dining room on long tables each presided over by an older guest who was addressed as 'Madame President'. Young girls with fresh faces, no older than Sabrina, served in pretty Dirndls. Apparently, they came from all over Europe to wait on the guests at Elmau, more or less as a trade-out for a holiday in the mountains. These 'helferinnen', as they were called, when they were not working either as chamber maids or waitresses, had a lot of freedom on the property.

After dinner, there was a dance in the concert hall, and the helferinnen were actually encouraged to join the guests. Most of the dances were progressive waltzes, and it was all supervised by an elegant gentleman who was the Tanzmeister. The younger male guests were happy to dance with the helferinnen, who for the most part were better skilled at these old-fashioned dances than they were. Some of the youths took great joy in stamping their feet like in a St Bernard Waltz as they faced a new partner, but the Tanzmeister was soon onto them. "Nicht stamfen!" he shouted out loudly, "No stamping!" But they didn't pay much attention to him.

Sabrina befriended one of the helferinnen. Her name was Michelle, from Lucerne, and although her first language was Swiss French she could converse in Swiss German.

"How did you learn about this place?" Sabrina asked.

"From a barman in Lausanne…he sort of recruits for the owners here," she said. "Many important international businessmen come to Lake Geneva, and many of them also know this place."

"But it's all above board," Sabrina asked, "nothing shady…if you know what I mean?"

Michelle's eyes sparkled with laughter. "Oh no…nothing like that…that's entirely up to you. I think it is just that the Muellers, who own this place…they like to attract a liberal clientele who appreciate music and the beauty of this landscape, and they try to make things very informal for their guests. It is more

like coming to visit their home when you stay here. It's the same for us…once
our work is done they want us to feel free to treat this as our home. It's very
unusual, but this is a wonderful place."

"It is beautiful here," Sabrina agreed. "I'd think I'd like a job like yours."

"I can get you an application form," Michelle said. "They quite like Swiss
girls as most of us can speak German, unlike the English girls."

Before Sabrina and her parents left for Munich the next morning, Michelle
gave Sabrina an envelope with all the application details. She stuffed it in her
bag and took one last look at the heavenly view from her window. *I think I would
like to work in a place like this,* she thought. *Maybe next summer?*

Munich now sounded fun, as her mother and father had promised to take
Sabrina to Oktoberfest and not an opera. But, of course, there was also another
palace to visit—the one where 'Mad' King Ludwig had actually been born—the
Nymphenburg Palace. Sabrina was surprised when the guide informed them that
'the present head of the House of Wittelsbach, the Duke of Bavaria, still lives in
a small corner of this colossal palace'.

The palace was vast. The guide said it was one of the largest in Europe, and
it sat in a huge park with statues, parterres, lakes and fountains like Versailles.
The Marble Hall was most impressive, and there were endless magnificent rooms
on the upper floor, but what impressed Sabrina most was the Carriage Museum.
It contained this amazing collection of beautifully preserved carriages and
sleighs that had belonged to King Ludwig II.

"The King used to drive that sleigh through the mountains between
Linderhof and Hohenschwangau like Good King Wenceslas," the guide
explained. "At every village and hovel in that magical part of his kingdom, he
would stop the sleigh and give out little bags of money to his people. Naturally,
therefore, he was loved by his people, but he didn't actually spend much time
here in Munich. He didn't much like state business. Perhaps you could say that
he was 'the people's king' and his people were in the mountains."

I'm beginning to like this man, Sabrina thought. *He had passion and
compassion*!

The sleigh was huge and richly decorated, looking like it might have been a
worthy conveyance of either Good King Wenceslas or 'St Nick'.

In the evening, Sabrina finally got to the famous beer halls of Munich's
Oktoberfest. This annual festival was held over a two-week period ending on the
first Sunday of every October. The festival apparently originated to celebrate the

marriage of the crown prince of Bavaria, who later became King Ludwig I, to Princess Therese von Sachsen-Hildburghausen. For Sabrina and most visitors, however, it was simply one of the greatest beer festivals in the world. It made the St Gallen Cheese Festival look small, as the long tables of revellers stretched out endlessly through the vast Munich fairground. The bar girls didn't have the fresh faces of the Elmau helferinnen, being jaded professionals with beer-stained Dirndls who could tout three or four steins in each hand. The noise at the tables was deafening and, truthfully, Sabrina being stuck with her parents really didn't find it as exciting as she had hoped. *I think I would rather be a Helferin at Elmau,* she thought.

"Well, just one more castle to go," Johannes Drucker said as they drove out of Munich the next day through rolling farmland interspersed with patches of thick pine forests. "This one is on an island in a lake…'Mad' King Ludwig's version of Versailles, except he never finished it."

All this talk about Versailles, his daughter thought, *that must really be some place. All I remember in school was that it was where Marie Antoinette said, 'If they haven't got bread let them eat cake.' I think perhaps Ludwig in the end was more sensible than all of them.* Sabrina pondered on what she had learned on this trip. *They say he drowned in a lake with his psychiatrist. They don't know whether he was murdered or committed suicide. It's all a bit of a mystery. Poor Ludwig…he was a good man, a man of peace who thought about the lives of his peasants and provided for them. He was no Nazi, he didn't like war and suffering…he just wanted beauty, art and peace.*

They arrived at Prien am Chiemsee and they could see the island sitting out in the lake with the Bavarian Alps in the background. A ferry took them across. They had arrived at Ludwig's 'Versailles'. They had a little lunch at the old castle restaurant looking out as sailing boats circulated the neighbouring Fraueninsel Island. Deciduous trees were turning yellow and bronze. After lunch, the afternoon sun exaggerated the coloured foliage as they made their way from the old castle through the park to Ludwig's masterpiece. A break in the trees and they came out on the parterre. Two giant fountains played in the midst of the reflecting pools. Statues, still partially gilded, spewed water like a cockatrice. The great façade of the palace loomed in front of them. Behind them, further fountains and a long canal led through the trees towards the lake and Prien.

Inside, they learned that Ludwig never completed this project at Herrenchiemsee. The walls of the north grand stairwell were still the rough brick of construction, the shell that in all these castles and palaces was hidden by the baroque marvels of plaster and marble. On the upper floor, however, doors opened into magnificent rooms dazzling in Roccoco gilt, mirrors and crystal chandeliers, all culminating in the splendid Hall of Mirrors—a gallery that like the one at Versailles ran the whole length of the façade.

"Today, many concerts are held in this gallery," their guide explained, "but in King Ludwig's time, he spent only eight days at Herrenchiemsee."

Next, they entered the King's bed chamber, a nearly exact copy of that of the 'Sun King'—Louis XIV of France.

Towards the end of the tour, they were shown the King's dining room with a 'magic' table, similar to one that they had seen at Linderhof. By ingenious pulleys, the whole dining room table could be lowered down through the floor into the kitchens below, where servants could replenish hot food and the table be pulled back up to the King above. Sabrina shook her head in amazement. *The man was not mad, he was a genius,* she thought, but for the benefit of the tourists, the guide continued to refer to 'Mad' King Ludwig II.

"Poor Ludwig, I actually think I would have liked him," Sabrina said to her mother and father as they walked back through the golden woods to the old castle and the landing stage. That night they stayed at a Gästehaus in Prien, but they were there in time to see the most incredible sunset settle over the lake against the dark silhouette of the Bavarian Alps.

They decided to extend their tour for a couple of days and drove to Salzburg across the border in Austria. Of course, there was another castle—the fortress Hohensalzburg enthroned on the Festungsberg high above the rooftops of the baroque centre of the city. This was not one of Ludwig's, however, but much older—the largest fully-preserved castle in Central Europe. From walls and windows, there were views in every direction. Apparently, it was built for the Prince Archbishops of Salzburg. The original purpose of the fortress from 1077 was to protect the principality and its archbishops from hostile attacks, and in a thousand years, it had never been captured by foreign troops.

Castled out by now, however, Sabrina was more interested in the story of the Von Trapp family and *The Sound of Music.* "They really were from here, then," she said to her father as they sat at a café in the old city. "They had to flee from the Nazis just like us. Just like us, they went over the mountains to Switzerland." And she started humming a few bars of *Climb Every Mountain.*

Her father agreed, "But, they had much further to go than us. We could almost see Switzerland from Oberstdorf, but the Von Trapps had to cross the entire Bavarian Alps."

On their way back, they drove into Berchtesgaden and stayed one night at a Gästehaus above the town. It was run by a Frederick Trotter and his wife Hilda, although it was called 'The Moeller Gästehaus'. The pretty town was dominated by the twin towers of the principal church and yet another palace, still apparently a home of the Wittelsbach family. They were ready for something different now, however, and Hilda Trotter told them about the cows.

"Today, they'll be bringing the cows home for the winter," she said. "It's quite a ceremony. The best place to see it is at Königssee. They have to bring the cows from the remote alms at the far end of the lake by boat, and then they crown them in Königssee before walking them home to their winter pastures and sheds in the Schönau Valley. It's quite a spectacle. If you go, you should get there about 10:00 a.m."

It was a rather grey start to the day as the cloud drifted over the valleys between the twin-peaked mighty Watzmann and the Untersburg. After the really nice 'Indian summer' days of their tour, it felt decidedly cooler. There was already quite a crowd waiting at the slipway in Königssee for the arrival of the cows. Fog hung over the lake and there was dampness in the air. Then, came the muffled sound of cowbells, and like magic the pontoon ferry appeared out of the mists in a burst of hazy sun. After they landed, there was much excitement as the cows were decorated in their finery to make the journey home. Finally, they were off. There was quite a stampede as the young cowhands, all in traditional Bavarian dress, tried to guide their beasts that wrestled with their harnessed crowns as they charged up the street.

The Finkelstein Druckers laughed at the frantic scene. "I think our brown Swiss are better behaved," Johannes said, "more docile."

Sabrina agreed.

When quiet returned to Königssee, Johannes suggested that they had better 'get going'. "It's a long drive back to Switzerland."

* * *

Early the following summer, Sabrina set out on her adventure. She had been accepted as a Helferin at Schloss Elmau. She travelled by train from Konstanz to Munich and was now on her way to Garmisch. The train wound its way through the foothills of the Wetterstein Mountains and the high peak of Zugspitze in the Bavarian Alps. At Garmisch, an Elmau housekeeper, Frau Doppler, greeted Sabrina at the station and they drove up through the woods and high meadows to the Schloss with its tall tower and steep roofs.

"Keeps the roofing from accumulating too much snow," Frau Doppler explained, "but it's the same for you in Switzerland, isn't it?"

"Oh, yes."

"We do get a lot of English girls because of our music programmes. People like Benjamin Britten have played here. The British…they don't really know much about snow, do they? So…you're from St Gallen?"

"Bischofzell," Sabrina answered, "between St Gallen and Lake Constance."

Frau Doppler took Sabrina to one of the staff houses just around the corner from the Schloss. "You'll be staying here with three of the other girls. One is Swiss…the other two are German…one from Bonn and the other from Munich. They'll get you started tonight, but first, we must get you your uniform. You'll need a day Dirndl and an evening Dirndl. If you drop off your things here, I'll take you over to housekeeping."

The evening Dirndls were a little brighter than the daytime ones. Housekeeping gave her a pale blue and pink one for day use, but a bright red, green-and-golden trimmed one for the evenings. "That will look good with your beautiful dark hair," Frau Doppler observed.

Back at the staff house, after taking a shower, Sabrina changed into the evening Dirndl and admired herself in the mirror, adjusting her little white blouse. *I so rarely ever wear my Swiss national costume,* she pondered, *only at the cheese festival, and that's more for the tourists. I don't think I've ever seen Vater in Lederhosen.* But she remembered a photo at home of her mother Andrea, all decked out as a St Gallen Dairy Queen. She felt good as she looked at herself, and she blew at her fringe and saw her eyes sparkle in response. She turned sideways to the mirror and smiled at herself. *I think this is more revealing,* she decided. The summer looked promising.

Sabrina learned about her employers. The Schloss was originally built at the beginning of the First World War for the religious philosopher and writer Johannes Mueller. He wanted to offer his guests the possibility to take a vacation from themselves—become aware of the silence in the mountains as the true essence of their being, along with the essence engendered by dancing and listening to classical music. Sabrina remembered the first time last October when she had experienced Elmau when she danced under the direction of the Tanzmeister and the beady eye of the present Mueller owners, Bernard and Sieglinda.

Founder, Johannes Mueller, was critical of individualism, materialism and capitalism, making him quite a radical. He also opposed the established church as well as meditation and anthroposophy. For him, Jesus was 'the conqueror of religions' and 'the childlike oblivion of the self', the prerequisite for fulfilling the promise of salvation on earth contained in the Sermon on the Mount. The imposing complex served as a cultural and theological meeting point for his followers and their liberal philosophy. Much of this went over Sabrina's head, but what really piqued her interest was the revelation that after the Second World War, the property had become a displaced persons camp for Jewish holocaust survivors.

She learned that in 1947, a Doktor Auerbach took possession of the Schloss, and concerts, literary events and Jewish Holidays brought new life and purpose to the place. Sadly, anti-Semitic charges of misappropriation caused Auerbach to be imprisoned, where he committed suicide in 1951. After his death, the Schloss was returned to the Mueller family, which was when Bernard and his sister took over, with Sieglinda's husband as the hotel manager.

I wonder if any of the Jews from here emigrated from Germany to Israel, Sabrina asked herself.

She had been at Elmau about a month and was sitting outside on an afternoon break looking up at the magnificent Wetterstein range when she met Martin Husselman—one of their guests, who came up to her and asked if he might share the bench. He said he was a farmer from Schönau in Berchtesgadenland. Sabrina recalled to him how she and her parents had watched the Schönau cows return from the alms the previous October at Königssee when they had visited Berchtesgaden. Martin said that his parents had a herd of Bavarian Hinterwälders.

"We have brown Swiss," Sabrina said enthusiastically. "My father is a cheesemaker, and my mother and my sister-in-law were both once 'Dairy Queens' of St Gallen."

Martin smiled. "I bet you'd make a beautiful Dairy Queen."

She smiled. "I thought about it two years ago, but there were lots of girls prettier than me competing that year and I was more excited about a trip I was making to visit my grandparents in Israel." She then looked directly at Martin. "I'm Jewish you know."

Martin blinked as if surprised, but made no comment. Martin was a blonde Ayran from a well-established Berchtesgaden farming family. "We were farming in the Schönau Valley before the first war," he said, "and my grandfather carried us through the second war. He died three years ago, and my mother and father run the farm now. I help out…after all, one day the farm will be mine, but I also work in a Berchtesgaden plant nursery."

"So, you don't mind that I'm Jewish?" She said as she blew at her fringe.

"Why should I…it doesn't matter to me. I'm a Roman Catholic, but I don't pay a lot of attention to it."

"Well, I'm actually nominally a Lutheran," Sabrina revealed. "My grandparents were Jewish, but they disappeared…"

"What do you mean?"

"You know…the Nazis…"

"Oh…I'm sorry." Then, he reached for her hand. "Will you be at the dancing tonight?" he asked.

"Would you like me to be there?"

He blushed but didn't let go of her hand. "What do you think?"

She pulled her hand away from his, but she smiled at him coyly and said, "I'll be there. I love to waltz. I hadn't much until I came here."

Once dinner service was over, Sabrina hastily went back to the staff house to reapply her make-up. She wanted to look at her best. Satisfied, she winked at herself in the mirror and almost skipped out of the house to go back to the Schloss. As she came up the stairs, she could hear the music coming from the concert hall, but she knew she hadn't missed much.

She entered the hall in the midst of a quadrille and so sat it out on one of the side chairs. She saw that Martin Husselman was engaged in the progressive dance and she caught his eye. As soon as the quadrille came to its close, he made his way over to her. He held out his hand in a mocking gallant gesture. "May I have the next dance?" he asked.

Sabrina smiled. "Of course, especially if it's a waltz."

The pianist started to play a slow waltz and many of the older guests took to the floor led by Sieglinda and her husband. The concert hall resounded with the gliding feet of the dancers. Sabrina and Martin joined them. Sabrina realised once she was on the floor that Martin really was a good dancer, actually better than her. They waltzed around the room, and Sabrina felt she could detect a nod from the Tanzmeister. She was glad that she was still wearing her evening Dirndl—the skirt twirled as she whirled! Martin seemed to want to dance almost every dance, until at length, she begged him for a respite and a cool soft drink. In the concert hall, they only served soft drinks, but they were more refreshing when they were dancing.

When the dancing finally ended, Martin stood in front of Sabrina holding her hand, "One one three," he said. Sabrina looked into his eyes and nodded. She knew the Elmau code.

Martin left, and Sabrina made her way back to the staff house.

"Well?" her Swiss roommate Erika asked.

"Yes!" Sabrina replied.

She changed from her evening Dirndl into the pink and blue day one. She also changed her underwear from cotton to shimmering satin and lace.

As she was about to leave, Erika handed her a small packet of condoms. "Just to be safe," Erika said. Sabrina tucked them into her shoulder bag and left their room.

Back in the castle, she knocked on the door numbered 113. Martin let her in.

* * *

After Martin Husselman left Elmau, he wrote to Sabrina many times.

"I don't know what you did to him, but he's got it bad," Erika said.

"We just clicked…you know how it is sometimes," Sabrina said with that flick of her hair as she read the latest letter. "Oh my…he wants me to meet his family in Berchtesgaden," she looked closely at the page, "this summer…before I go back to Switzerland…this could be the real thing, Erika."

"So…will you go?" Erika said, "I mean it won't be until mid-September."

Sabrina thought for a moment. She put the letter down. Her face was smiling more than Erika had ever seen it glow before. "Yes! I will! What have I got to lose?"

Erika laughed. "Well, obviously not your virginity!"

"Oh, that was long ago…but we really did get along very well."

Erika noted for the remainder of their time at Elmau that Sabrina didn't flirt as much with the guests. She took long walks alone in the mountains, but sometimes they both went together as the high summer moved into the pretty days of September.

"So, have you finally arranged to visit his family?" Erika asked.

"Actually, yes…I told him I'd go straight to Berchtesgaden when we sign off in two weeks…just for five days. We'll see how it goes."

They rested, seated on a rock beside a small lake alongside the track between Mittenwald and Elmau, when Erika suddenly asked, "Does he know that you're part Jewish?"

"I told him…he didn't seem to mind. He just sort of shrugged it off, but he's a Roman Catholic and I'm a Lutheran."

Erika laughed. "A Lutheran…but a Lutheran Jew."

Sabrina turned towards her. "Does that really matter…does it matter to you!"

Erika was surprised by her testy reaction. "Of course not…I'm sorry…but what if he asks you to marry him?"

"Well, it doesn't matter to him, so why should it matter to me!" Sabrina yelled.

They sat in silence for what seemed like a long time. Birds hovered over the lake.

Sabrina finally stood up. "I'm so sorry," she said, "I didn't mean to shout at you. We'd better start back now or Frau Doppler will be onto us. We're both on service tonight."

* * *

Sabrina watched the scenery as the Berchtesgaden train wound its way along the River Saalach, making its way from Freilassing. It was so majestic…so beautiful, a gorge running through the mountains—less austere than the Wetterstein range at Elmau. She had telephoned from the station at Freilassing. Martin would meet her off the train at Berchtesgaden. As the sunlight played through the trees along the riverbank it caught the rushing water.

When the train pulled into the Bahnhof at Berchtesgaden, Sabrina saw Martin on the platform. He was dressed to impress in a Tyrolean jacket and khaki trousers and wore a feather in his felt hat. She had worn Dirndls so much at Elmau that she had forgone tradition, travelling in tight-fitting stretch jeans that Gran Francine had bought for her in Israel, along with a flouncy white top. She pulled her suitcase from the train and Martin came to her.

Martin kissed her. "You made it? Welcome to Berchtesgaden!" He then carried her suitcase out to his waiting car.

It was only a short drive up a hill close by the Bahnhof that took them to Schönau, but the farm was across the valley on the lower slopes of the Hochschwartzeck.

"My parents will love you…I told them that you were a dairy girl," he said as they approached the farm. Some of the hinterwälder cattle were grazing in the meadows, but Martin explained that most of them were still on the high alms at the far end of the Königssee. "We will be bringing them down early next month," he explained. "The cows here…they're our milking herd."

Sabrina laughed. "I remember…I saw the cows come down last October. It's funny when you think of it. I might have seen you leading one of the cows, but I didn't know you then."

The farmhouse loomed into sight, backed by the turning trees and conifers climbing up the steeper slopes. It was traditional—a large sprawling chalet, half of which incorporated a cattle barn. "Most of our calves are born right below us when the snow is piled up…but it's probably the same for you in Switzerland."

"Not really," Sabrina answered. "Bischofzell isn't in the mountains…gentle rolling hills along the shores of Lake Constance. Our cows are actually out most of the winter."

Martin's parents were waiting, seated in the sun at a bench table outside the front door. Sabrina felt just a little nervous. *The inspection,* she thought. *I hope they approve.* She actually felt a little overdressed in her designer jeans and top. Martin's parents looked rather simple folk.

"Mutter and Vater, meet Sabrina," Martin said with old-fashioned courtesy.

His mother smiled. "We've heard a lot about you, dear."

"Would you like a Lowenbrau?" his father said. "Let me get you both one."

"Bring the Kuchen, then," his wife said before turning to 'the girlfriend'. "Now, sit down, dear. I understand you're a Swiss dairy girl?"

When Herr Husselman came back with the beers and cake, things became more informal. The view from the farmhouse across the valley was stunning, and Sabrina began to feel more at home.

The five days went by fast, with walks through the forests, and a boat trip to St Bartholemew on the Königssee, where the monastery cooked the freshest of fish, but there was little opportunity for them to celebrate their love as they had so freely in the liberal atmosphere of Schloss Elmau.

Martin's parents were old-school conservatives steeped in Catholicism, and moments even to steal a kiss at the farmstead were nigh impossible. Their most romantic encounter was a teenagers' backseat tryst in Martin's parked car high on the Rossfeld. It wasn't comfortable, but it relieved their frustrations.

One evening, however, they were able to have dinner together at the Moeller Gästehaus terrace on a fine evening with that magnificent view of the Watzmann. They were served by a middle-aged waitress named Rachel.

"She's Jewish," Martin said after she had served them. "She was a refugee from the East. The Moellers brought her here from one of those displaced persons camps."

"I know…I met her here last year. She told me then, but I don't think she recognised me tonight."

Sabrina had mixed feelings when Martin took her to the Bahnhof. It hadn't exactly been the romantic five days she had been expecting, and her friend, Erika would have been disappointed as there was no sign of a proposal. But she thought that Martin's parents had liked her, and she really loved Berchtesgadenland.

* * *

Only two days after Sabrina arrived back home in Bischofzell, there was a telephone call rather late at night. She thought it might be Martin, and her heart flushed a beat. Her parents had gone to bed, so Sabrina picked up the phone.

"Hello!" she said excitedly.

A voice sounding more like Gramps down the phone said, 'Is that you, Sabrina?'

"Yes."

'It's your grandmother…I am so terribly sorry, but your Gran Francine died this evening. I went up to the room and she was lying on the bed, fully clothed, but gone. It looked like she had been sitting on the bed and just slumped back, her feet still dangling over the edge. I think it was her heart, sweetie…I think it was her heart.'

"Oh no!" Sabrina cried.

Her father came out to the top of the stairs. "What is it?"

"Gran Francine…she's dead," Sabrina informed him.

Johannes ran down the stairs and grabbed the phone. "Helmut! It's Johannes…are you sure…Aunt Francine is gone?"

'Yes…quite suddenly early this evening. We hadn't even gone in for supper.' Gramps then let him know all he knew and that the kibbutz medical officer had confirmed that she was dead and that it was probably her heart.

Andrea joined them at the bottom of the stairs.

"It's Gran Finkelstein," Sabrina said, tears welling in her eyes. "She's gone!"

* * *

After he had buried his wife, Helmut Drucker made arrangements to leave Israel and return to Switzerland. They had both retired from the dairy work at Givan HaShlosha in 1980, and he really saw no great reason to remain away from family and all that he had known. It was Francine who had been so bent on coming to Israel. He'd had a good life with her there, but roots now drew him back. He arrived in Zurich shortly before Christmas, and Johannes, Andrea and Sabrina all came to the airport to meet him. It was dark on the journey home to Bischofzell, but Helmut felt he could smell the fresh mountain air after the years in the dry dust of Israel.

* * *

During his chancellorship, Helmut Schmidt won the esteem of many West Germans and became one of the most respected and influential of Western Europe's leaders. In foreign affairs, he sought reconciliation with the Soviet bloc countries of Eastern Europe while at the same time maintaining West Germany's partnership with the United States. He similarly cultivated closer ties with the German Democratic Republic of East Germany while maintaining West Germany's pivotal membership in the European Community and the NATO military alliance. But ironically, considering he had a partially Jewish background, it was the Palestinian conflict with Israel that became his downfall.

While visiting Saudi Arabia in late April 1981, Schmidt made some unguarded remarks about the Israeli-Palestinian conflict that succeeded in aggravating the delicate relations between Israel and West Germany. Asked by a reporter about the moral aspect of German-Israeli relations, he stated that Israel was not in a position to criticise Germany due to its handling of the Palestinians, and 'That won't do. And in particular, it won't do for a German living in a divided nation and laying a moral claim to the right of self-determination for the

145

German people. One must then recognise the moral claim of the Palestinian people to the right of self-determination.'

On 3 May, Israeli Prime Minister Menachem Begin denounced Schmidt as 'unprincipled, avaricious, heartless, and lacking in human feeling,' and stated that he had 'willingly served in the German armies that murdered millions'. Menachem Begin was also upset over remarks that Schmidt had made on West German television the previous week, in which he spoke apologetically about the suffering Germany inflicted on various nations during the war but made no mention of the Jews. Chancellor Schmidt told his advisers that war guilt could not continue to affect Germany's foreign relations.

Caught between the left and the right factions within his coalition government, in February 1982, Schmidt actually won a motion of confidence that pleased, but rather surprised, Jürgen Scholtz and Marlene Trotter and their left-leaning pro-Palestinian friends.

In Bischofzell, Switzerland, Helmut Drucker championed Israel, criticising the West German stance. "The Palestinians will never win in Israel," he said confidently.

Sabrina agreed, but Johannes and Andrea really didn't like getting involved in these political discussions. They had also got used to running the Bischofzell dairy their way and they disliked all the new-fangled Israeli ideas in the dairy industry that 'old man Helmut' now tried to foist upon them.

Concerned after the Soviet invasion of Afghanistan earlier in 1979, and the Soviet superiority regarding missiles in Central Europe, Schmidt also issued proposals resulting in the NATO Double Track Decision, concerning the deployment of medium-range nuclear missiles in Western Europe, should the Soviets not disarm. This decision was unpopular with the German public. A mass demonstration against the deployment mobilised 400,000 people in October 1981, and once again, Jürgen Sholtz and Marlene Trotter were on the streets with the demonstrators in Munich.

* * *

Martin Husselman was quite a letter writer. It was hard for Sabrina to keep up with him as he waxed eloquently about the coming spring and the Alpine flowers—the beautiful blue gentians blooming away among the rocks and the crannies of the Bavarian Alps. He made it all so appealing and Sabrina felt slight tinges of what she could only describe to herself as 'homesickness'—homesickness for a place in which she had only spent a handful of days. Eventually, Martin persuaded her to make a second visit to Schönau.

This time, he was bolder. He took Sabrina to Salzburg where after a romantic carriage ride they stayed overnight at the Altstadt Hotel Weise Taube in the old city. Away from the prying eyes of Martin's parents, they renewed the love that they had fostered at Elmau.

Back at the farmhouse, Martin also shared his love of horticulture with Sabrina. It was mid-May and time to plant out the balconies at the farmstead. As he was still working part-time at the nursery, he was able to make a great selection from the rows and rows of pots that he had himself cultivated. Between them, Sabrina and Martin planted out every balcony at the old farmstead making several trips to the Berchtesgaden nursery. This ingratiated Sabrina to Martin's mother, who was very proud of their annual display. With coming summer, the balconies would become rich in shades of pink, white, purple and green—geraniums and petunias flowing over the balustrades in joyful abundance.

Martin waited until the last day, but as they stood on the main balcony looking across the valley to the Bavarian Alps, he went down on one knee and took a small box out of his pocket.

Oh my...this is it, Sabrina realised as her heart fluttered and her face flushed.

Martin uttered those amazing words, "Will you marry me?" as he proffered a small diamond ring.

Sabrina threw her arms around his neck, emotional tears forming in her sparkling eyes. "Of course...of course...yes!" And they kissed passionately before calling out to Martin's parents to give them the news.

In June, after the cows had gone back to the alms, Martin made the inevitable journey to Switzerland to meet Sabrina's family.

Johannes and Andrea had more liberal views than Martin's family. The guest room at the farm in Bischofzell was made into a honeymoon suite before the honeymoon. Johannes was delighted with his prospective son-in-law, feeling a lot more at ease with him than with 'old man Drucker' as he discussed their traditional farming methods. They also shared time with Aldrich and Abigail at the Gerber farm beside Lake Constance. Martin was impressed with the brown Swiss herd, but Sabrina was more excited about the news that her uncle and aunt revealed about her cousin Hans.

Hans had gone back to Oberstdorf, and he had also recently announced his engagement. He was marrying Lottie Moeller, whose family had farmed near the farm that the Druckers had once owned in Oberstdorf. Lottie's family also had hinterwälder cattle like Martin's family, and at a time when these herds were becoming quite a rarity in Bavaria.

Martin smiled. "Maybe we will be able to exchange bulls?"

They exchanged wedding vows in early September in the Lutheran Church in Bischofzell. It was a simple service and there was no suggestion in the ceremony that Sabrina was of Jewish descent. She was an Israeli sympathiser, but she had always been a Lutheran, at least as long as she had been a Finkelstein Drucker. In reality, she couldn't remember much about her life with her parents, except what Gran Francine had passed on to her.

It was Martin's parents' first visit to Switzerland, but they were a little disappointed not to see the high mountains—great pointed peaks like the Matterhorn. The Lake Constance landscape looked so tame, not what they had imagined. But they did acknowledge that the Druckers made wonderful cheese.

"Of course, when you get back from your honeymoon, we will see if we can also get Father Leopold to bless your marriage," Martin's mother said before they left.

Sabrina and Martin spent their honeymoon at Schloss Elmau. Martin even managed to arrange for them to have Room 113. It was a whirl of waltzes and walks, making love, and catching the last rays of summer around the rather unpretentious swimming pool set in a meadow below the castle. Sabrina wondered if she would see Erika, but her friend was no longer a Helferin. Sabrina didn't recognise any of the Helferinnen.

Back at the farm in Berchtesgaden, they were both put to work making new crowns and belts for the return of the cows. The foliage started to turn and the morning mists hovered over the Königssee—this year, Sabrina Husselman would be assisting her husband and mother-in-law in bringing their cows home from the alms. In a very simple ceremony, Father Leopold also blessed their marriage in front of the high altar in the Roman Catholic Stiftskirche St Peter und Johannes der Täufer.

* * *

On 17 September 1982, Chancellor Schmidt's coalition finally broke apart. Schmidt continued to lead a minority government composed only of Social Democratic members, while the Free Democratic Party negotiated a coalition with the Christian Democrats and the Bavarian Christian Socialists. On 1 October 1982, parliament approved a constructive vote of no confidence and elected the Christian Democrats' chairman, Helmut Kohl, as the new chancellor. Kohl was seen as more conservative than his two more chameleon predecessors.

Following a summer involvement of Israel, allied with Lebanese Christians, in launching 'Operation Peace for Galilee'—an invasion of southern Lebanon against Palestinian Liberation Organisation, Syrian and Muslim Lebanese forces—there continued sporadic assassinations of Jews around the world. The most notable of these was an attempt to assassinate Israel's ambassador to the United Kingdom.

In September, Lebanese Phalangists massacred some 3,000 civilians, mostly Palestinians and Lebanese Shiites, in Sabra and the Shatila refugee camp. While no Israeli soldiers were present in the fighting, Israeli Defence Minister, Ariel Sharon, was found to be 'indirectly responsible by negligence' for the massacre and was asked to resign his position. A month later, on the very day that the Husselmans were busy bringing their cows down from the alms above Königssee, armed Palestinian militants attacked the Great Synagogue of Rome. A two-year-old Italian toddler was killed in the attack along with 37 civilians. The death of the little boy caught the imagination of the world once again.

When the Husselmans heard the West German news on their return to the farmhouse, with all the cows happily home in Schönau relieved of their accoutrements, Martin's mother expressed shock.

"Something should be done!" she shouted.

Sabrina smirked. "It will, you can trust the Israelis…they won't let them get away with it."

Frau Husselman looked intently at her daughter-in-law. "It's not the Jews that's my concern…it's that poor innocent little Italian boy."

Sabrina caught her husband's eye.

Later, back in their bedroom, Martin held Sabrina tight and stroked her long black hair. "It's all right, but we just mustn't ever mention the Jews around my mother. Remember, she doesn't know you have a Jewish background. There's no need to tell her you've been to Israel and that you had an Israeli grandmother.

To them, you're a Lutheran," he chuckled, "and that's bad enough…but thanks for agreeing to Father Leopold's blessing…that made them happy."

Two years later, the hot news was that the Palestine Liberation Front had hijacked an Italian cruise ship, the *Achille Lauro,* redirecting the ship to Syria and holding its passengers and crew hostage. They demanded the release of 50 Palestinians in Israeli prisons. One passenger on board was murdered—Leon Kinghoffer, a Jewish American who was celebrating his 36th wedding anniversary with his wife on the cruise. He was shot in the forehead and chest while sitting in his wheelchair and dumped overboard. This signalled to the world that something did have to be done, but again there was very little international response beyond calls for much greater security on travel, both at airports and onboard cruise ships.

Violence, riots, general strikes, and civil disobedience campaigns by Palestinians spread across the West Bank and the Gaza Strip. Israeli forces responded with tear gas, plastic bullets, and live ammunition against the demonstrators.

In 1988, Shaikh Ahmed Yassin created Hamas from the Gaza wing of the Egyptian Muslim Brotherhood. Until that point, the Muslim Brotherhood in Gaza had enjoyed the support of the Israeli authorities and had refrained from violent attacks. However, Hamas quickly began attacks on Israeli military targets, and subsequently, Israeli civilians. The Israeli army killed over a thousand Palestinians in this 'infanta uprising' while only 164 Israelis were killed. However, it was later reported that almost half of the total Palestinian casualties were caused by internal fighting among Palestinian factions.

Chapter Eleven
The 1990s

The combination of Chancellor Helmut Kohl, United States President Ronald Reagan, and the thawing of their relationships with the Soviets under Mikhail Gorbachev, caused momentous changes in the late 1980s.

On a visit to West Germany, President Reagan and his wife arrived in West Berlin on 12 June 1987. They were taken to the Reichstag where they viewed the Berlin Wall from a balcony. Reagan then gave a speech at the Brandenburg Gate. Shielded by two panes of bulletproof glass with the wall as a backdrop, President Reagan declared to the West Berlin crowd and in front of both the German president and the chancellor.

"There is one sign the Soviets can make that would be unmistakable, that would advance dramatically the cause of freedom and peace." Then, he fictitiously addressed his Soviet counterpart. "Secretary General Gorbachev, if you seek peace…if you seek prosperity for the Soviet Union and Eastern Europe…if you seek liberalisation: come here, to this gate…Mr Gorbachev, open this gate…Mr Gorbachev, tear down this wall."

In 1989, a series of revolutions in nearby 'Eastern Bloc' countries, in Poland and Hungary in particular, caused a chain reaction in East Germany. In particular, the opening of a crossing between Hungary and Austria set in motion a peaceful development during which the 'Iron Curtain' largely broke. The rulers in the East came under pressure, the Berlin Wall crumbled and finally the 'Eastern Bloc' fell apart.

After several weeks of civil unrest in 1989, the East German government announced that all East German citizens could visit West Germany and West Berlin. Crowds of East Germans climbed onto the Berlin Wall, joined by West Germans on the other side in a celebratory atmosphere. Over the next few weeks, souvenir hunters chipped away parts of the wall, and just before Christmas the

Brandenburg Gate was opened for free passage between East Berlin and the West.

Hans Gerber was a lover of classical music, but he was also excited about this rather sudden reunification of the German people. In Oberstdorf, Hans and his wife Lottie were emotionally moved as they watched a televised concert broadcast from a free Berlin. Leonard Bernstein was conducting. The concert featured the Bavarian Radio Symphony Orchestra, to which Hans had often listened on the wireless. They were supplemented by musicians from the New York Philharmonic, the London Symphony, the Orchestre de Paris, the Staatskapelle Dresden and the Orchestra of the Kirov Theatre, finally bringing together all of Germany and its opposing allies of the war years. The concert's highlight was a performance of Beethoven's Ninth Symphony, where the German words for 'Ode to Joy' became 'Ode to Freedom' changing 'Freude' for 'Freiheit'.

"Phew!" was all Hans could say as tears of emotion rolled down his cheeks.

Lottie was less demonstrative. She didn't share her husband's love for the classics, preferring the Bavarian brass bands with which she had been brought up. But she admitted that the event was stirring. She spent much of the concert wrapping up little gifts for their daughter Angelika, who would be expecting a visit from the Christkindl angel on Christmas Eve. Fortunately, they had avoided a visit from the Krampus, and Angelika, just four years old, believed that she had been a good little girl.

The Berlin concert was repeated on Christmas Day when Bernstein conducted it from East Berlin celebrating the total freedom of movement between the East and the West. This 'fall of the Berlin Wall' paved the way for Germany's reunification, which formally took place on 3 October 1990.

Jürgen Scholtz and Marlene Trotter were less enthusiastic about reunification. The 'Revolutionary Cells' movement saw this as the death-throw to their activities. Without a separate East Germany, the now Berlin-based Kohl government would probably pander to the right. The collapse of the Soviet Union in the aftermath of the fall of the Berlin Wall, along with the 'perestroika' policies of Mikhail Gorbachev and Boris Yeltsin, gave the left little hope of a socialist utopia. Jürgen and Marlene's causes were drying up.

* * *

In September 1993, Palestinian leader Yasser Arafat and Israeli Yitzhak Rabin signed the Declaration of Principles on Interim Self-Government in Oslo, brokered by the new American president, Bill Clinton.

This Israeli peace accord pleased Sabrina Husselman in Berchtesgaden, but Martin and his parents were more concerned about the German reunification issue. They had fears that a flood of East Germans into what had been West Germany might disrupt the economy and their way of life.

"They're like refugees," Martin's father proclaimed, "cashing in on all our welfare benefits and contributing nothing. Keep them in East Germany, I say. I mean…the wall's come down, but keep them in the East."

"We can't," Martin said, seated on one of their small Bavarian chairs with backs shaped like a heart. "The genie's out of the bottle now. They're Germans just like us and they'll be everywhere. There are some of them already here in Berchtesgaden."

Later, Sabrina sat up in bed, her long black hair falling around her, while Martin undressed. "Thank you for speaking out in front of your father," she said. "Remember, my family was also once refugees."

They heard a cry from the next-door room. It was their son Wilhelm.

"Check on him, Martin," Sabrina said. "Maybe, it's another nightmare."

Martin left and then returned with the seven-year-old boy who jumped into bed with his mother.

"What was it?" she asked.

"The Krampus," the boy replied, "will they come?"

Sabrina smiled. "Not now," she assured her young son. "The Krampus only come in early December…before Christmas. You just had a bad dream."

"They scare me, Mutter. I hate the Krampus."

Sabrina cuddled him. "Well, you don't have to worry about them for a while. Christmas is still a long way off."

* * *

Doktor Klaus Trotter and his wife Elsa, now also had a young son, Florian. They decided that they would spend Christmas 1995 at Oberstdorf. Like his Uncle Kurt Moeller, Klaus was a good skier. Since his uncle's fatal accident and funeral, he hadn't been back to Oberstdorf.

"I think it's just as good as Garmisch," he said to Elsa, "and it will be fun to take Florian with us. I think he's old enough now to enjoy the mountains in the winter."

"He'd love it," Elsa agreed.

A nervous smile crossed Kurt's face. "Of course, he's never met his cousin Angelika and you've never met Lottie," he said.

"Oh, your first great love," Elsa teased, "now, that might be interesting."

They embraced, and Elsa kissed him passionately. "Was she as good a kisser as I am?" she asked.

Klaus looked sheepish. "That was all some time ago. It was all before I met you. So, do I detect just a little jealousy?"

"Of course not…I'm just teasing you. All of us have a past."

They arranged to drive to Oberstdorf as soon as their son Florian got out of school for the Christmas holiday. The Munich travel agent had recommended a family run-hotel in the Trettach Valley—Gästehaus Christlessee. About three miles south of Oberstdorf, it was reasonably close to two ski lifts up to the Kleinwalsertal range. In December, the valley was a winter wonderland, leading right up to the famed Grosser Krottenkopf that Uncle Kurt had spoken about. In front of the chalet-like Gästehaus, there was a small partially-iced lake—the Christlessee. They were certainly not disappointed when they were shown up to their hotel room. Everything was very cosy and it had the most magnificent mountain view, reflecting the day's last rays of winter sun.

On the drive up the valley, they had passed Lottie and Hans Gerber's farm. One of the first things Hans did at the Gästehaus was to telephone his Gerber cousins and invite them all to lunch at Christlessee the next day. Elsa had now become very curious to meet this cousin of Klaus who had so smitten him a few years ago.

"It's not so much about Lottie," Klaus said. "It's more about their daughter, Angelika. It will be nice for Florian."

Angelika was one year older than Florian—a pretty girl with ringlets of mousey hair, but she was rather shy. Florian was slow to engage with her until after lunch. He coaxed her out into the snow where they made 'snow angels' and they finally started talking to each other.

Elsa squeezed Klaus' hand. "She's still very attractive," she whispered.

"Angelika?"

Elsa laughed. "No…Lottie, of course."

Lottie was still fresh-faced, vivacious and with a pretty good figure. Hans, however, seemed rather dour—he talked mostly about their cows—Hinterwälders, but he had a few brown Swiss, too. "Better for cheese," he said.

It was a happy afternoon as they walked off their lunch in the winter wonderland. By the time they were ready to leave when darkness descended on the valley, an invitation was forthcoming for them to come to the farm for Christmas Day.

On Christmas Eve, the Trotters celebrated 'Heiligabend' at the Gästehaus where the traditional roast pork was served with all the trimmings followed by Stollen and gingerbread. Later, the Christkindl angel visited, leaving a plate of enticing biscuits outside their room. Inside, once they knew that her son Florian was asleep, Elsa carefully placed her bag of Christmas parcels at the end of his bed. "From the Weihnachtsmann," she whispered as she blew her sleeping boy a kiss.

Klaus and Elsa then exchanged their own gifts—two books for him and a new camera for her.

Christmas Day dawned shrouded in winter mists, but Florian was awake early and immediately opened his gifts. "The Weihnachtsmann came!" he shrieked. "Christkindl came!"

"Yes, because you've been a good boy," Elsa said, "Now, today we are going to Angelika's house. That'll be nice, won't it?"

"Yes…but do you think the Weihnachtsmann went to her, too?"

"I expect so…I am sure she'll tell you."

Klaus particularly liked the shiny red toy tractor that was among his gifts and he took it with him when they drove down to the Heizz-Gerber farm.

As soon as Angelika saw Florian, she told him that the Weihnachtsmann had been. She shared with him all the toy farm animals and fences that had been left at the end of her bed.

"I got a tractor," Florian said as he proudly showed it to her. "Now we can play 'farm' together."

The adults sat at the dining table drinking Glühwein and eating wonderful Stollen cake, while the children built their farm on the floor.

The mists lifted. The snow sparkled.

"Let me show you my real pony!" Angelika squealed, and the two of them ran off out into the farmyard, leaving the toy farm in various stages of construction on the floor.

"Well, they seem to be getting along very well today," Lottie said. "I mean, Angelika is pretty shy around most other children, but today she's really opening up."

The next day, they all went up to the ski slopes together. Hans and Klaus made a run or two, while Lottie, Elsa and the children played in the snow outside the café and sledged down the Kinder Run. Trying out her new camera, Elsa took lots of photographs.

I can see why he fell for her, Elsa thought looking at Lottie. *She's just a very natural and rather sweet person…but I don't think she would have ever made a very good Doktor's wife.*

* * *

Not long after Christmas, a double suicide bombing by the Palestinian Islamic Jihad at Beit Lid killed 21 people—one of the biggest attacks which further divided the Israeli public over the peace process. Sporadic suicide attacks continued throughout the coming months. In good faith, an agreement was reached in September, envisioning the establishment of a Palestinian interim self-government in the territories of the West Bank and Gaza, giving the Palestinian Authority some limited powers. It was again brokered by U.S. President Bill Clinton and signed by Yasser Arafat and Israeli Prime Minister Yitzhak Rabin. It wasn't well received by conservative Israelis, and within little over a month, on 4 November 1995, the world was shocked to hear that Yitzhak Rabin had been assassinated in Tel Aviv by a Jewish extremist.

Frau Husselman chuckled. "Well, they can't blame us anymore," she said as they watched the late German news. "Now they're assassinating their own leaders…I really don't care what happens to them anymore."

"How can you say that?" Sabrina shrieked. "That man was a saint…a true man of peace." She got up and left the room.

Frau Husselman looked at her husband. "Oh! What have I said now? You know…at times you would almost think she was one of them."

* * *

Martin Husselman came in from checking the cows in the barn. Upstairs, he found Sabrina sobbing on their bed. "What is it, Sabs?" he asked.

Sabrina turned from the folds of her pillow. "We've got to get out of here, Martin. I can't take it anymore."

Martin handed Sabrina his handkerchief. "Mutter?"

Sabrina dabbed her tears. "Sometimes she's like a Nazi. What would she do if she ever really knew that I was a Jew? Rabin…the Israeli Prime Minister…he was assassinated today…not by the Palestinians, but by one of those Jewish extremists. Your mother…she seemed almost pleased…she hates Jews. I really think she thinks that Hitler was right."

Martin sat beside her. "Maybe we should move out. She's not going to change. She's old-school. I just thought it would be better for Wilhelm to grow up right here on the farm." He shrugged his shoulders. "But…maybe not."

"It would be better for all of us if we were in our own place, Martin!" Sabrina shouted before putting her face down on the pillow again.

Martin shook his head. "I'll start looking," he said, "I really will, but the rental prices around here are shooting up. All these northerners seem to want to come down here now. Half of them only spend a few weeks a year here, but it's pushing prices sky high." He lay beside his wife and comforted her. "We will, Sabs, we'll find somewhere. It would be better for you and for Wilhelm."

Martin did find a traditional chalet for rent in the woods above Berchtesgaden. It was rather dark but it was available at a reasonable price.

"Take it," Sabrina said when they inspected the property. "At least we can be ourselves here."

There was a little garden in the clearing and Martin assured her that he would grow them some vegetables and salads.

Two weeks later they moved in.

"I think my mother was actually quite pleased we moved out," Martin said. "She's going to let us have some of their furniture. We'll make this place beautiful."

"Not too much of theirs, Martin…I want to make this our own."

Her son Wilhelm seemed to take a while to get used to the move. He had liked living with his grandparents at the farm.

"We'll get a doggie," his mother suggested. "You'd like that wouldn't you?"

The boy's eyes lit up, "A big doggie?"

"If that's what you want. Let's see what Vater thinks."

Not long after, Martin learned of a dog rescue centre in Rossenheim that had two young Leonbergers.

"They're huge," Sabrina said, "almost as big as a St Bernard. We saw quite a lot of them in Switzerland."

"They used them to pull carts here in Bavaria," Martin said. "That's why they're scarce here now…so many of them died in both the wars. They used them to pull munitions carts."

"That's awful!"

"Well, it might be a good reason for us taking care of one now. Let's see what they look like."

The three of them drove to Rossenheim.

It only took a moment. As soon as young Wilhelm saw the two dogs, his face lit up with joy. "Big doggies!" he shouted.

They were huge, but they were apparently only two-year-olds. One was a sandy colour and the other darker, more like a lion with streaks of yellows, browns and rusts. It was obvious which one Wilhelm wanted. He went straight to the lion-like dog.

The dog didn't look fierce. He had soft, loving eyes, and his tongue hung out as he started to pant with affection.

Martin knew. "We'll take him," he told the kennel master.

On the way back to Berchtesgaden, there was much discussion as to what they would name him. The dog was so big that he took up the entire backseat of Martin's Volkswagen Golf. Wilhelm had to curl up on a rug behind him in the hatchback. The favoured name turned out to be the obvious—'Leo'.

Back at the chalet, Sabrina took a whole lot of photographs of Wilhelm and Leo. The dog just sat there as if he had always belonged to the family. Seated, he was almost as tall as Wilhelm, and it wasn't long before he was sleeping in Wilhelm's bedroom.

* * *

After the reunification of East and West Germany, back in 1992, Chancellor Helmut Kohl and French President François Mitterand became the architects of the Treaty on the European Union. At Maastricht, they laid out the foundation treaty of the European Union between the twelve member states of the European Communities. It announced 'A new stage in the process of European integration,' chiefly in provisions for shared European citizenship and the eventual introduction of a single currency—the euro. There were also some provisions for common foreign and security policies. This was not popular with everybody and led to some objections within the Gerber family.

"I agree with my father," Hans Gerber said to Lottie as talk of this federal Europe increased, "he doesn't see the Swiss as ever becoming a part of this."

Lottie laughed. "William Tell and centuries of independence, you mean."

Hans looked at his wife. "You are German, I am Swiss, and Angelika…well I suppose she would be free to choose when she's of age, but she was born German."

"But are you really Swiss, Hans? Your mother was born in Berchtesgaden into a German-Jewish family."

Hans sighed. "It's going to be very complicated. Are we all going to end up with European passports?"

"That's what it looks like."

"Look the European Economic Community…that makes sense, free trade between us all, but are we going to become one country like the United States?"

"Maybe…that might be why we're lucky…we still have the Swiss bolt-hole."

Angelika came in from the stable. She was now a teenager. Her ringlets had straightened out into long brown hair, and her passion for the new British 'Spice Girls' competed with her father's love of the classics.

With the fall of the Soviets, German Chancellor Helmut Kohl also became a central figure in the eastern enlargement of the European Union. After the break-up of Yugoslavia, the German government also led the effort to push for international recognition of Croatia, Slovenia, and Bosnia and Herzegovina when those states declared independence at the close of the Bosnian War in 1995. It looked like the European Union would rapidly expand, and almost certainly bring about that common currency.

* * *

On 9 May 1998, Sabrina Husselman sat glued to the television for the Eurovision Song Contest. This year the contest was being broadcast from Birmingham, England. Leo sat below the television, every so often raising his big head and panting.

Wilhelm kept interrupting the show, saying to the dog, "Leo…Leo!"

"Listen!" his mother said as she tried to concentrate. Germany's entry wasn't her favourite. In 1973, Israel had joined Eurovision, and their contestant was now about to perform.

A tall statuesque lady in a long formal dress was ushered on stage to the sound of British ceremonial trumpeters from one of the British Queen Elizabeth's guards' regiments.

Martin had heard the gossip, mostly from his mother Frau Husselman that this Jewess, 'Dana International' as she was called, wasn't actually a woman at all. He chuckled. "Well, I must say, *he* looks pretty good!"

"Don't be silly, Vater, she's a lady," his son said. But when she started to sing the song *Diva,* Wilhelm wasn't so sure. Dana had a very husky masculine voice. The song was good though, and his mother told them both to keep quiet.

Leo looked up at the television screen and continued his panting.

There was real applause at the end of the song.

"What if she was to win?" Sabrina said. "Israel has won almost more times than anybody else...Viva Yitzrael!"

"He or she...*it*...she can't win," Martin said. He was surprised, however, when at the end of the contest, Dana International, singing for Israel, had the most voted points for *Diva* and won. He stood up, staring at the television, mumbling aloud, "A transvestite winning...it shouldn't be allowed."

Leo stood up and nuzzled Sabrina.

"Israel won!" Sabrina said joyfully as she patted the dog's head. "Israel always wins!"

"What's a transvestite?" Wilhelm asked.

"A man who likes to dress like a woman...wants to live like a woman," his father answered. "It's all wrong...it shouldn't be allowed. A man is a man and a woman is a woman." He poured himself a Schnapps.

The German newspapers reported the next day that Arab stations in Jordan had refused to broadcast the Israeli entry, and not just on political grounds, but on perceived moral grounds too.

Chapter Twelve
The New Millennium

Angelika, a fourteen-year-old 'going on seventeen', presented something of a problem for her father Hans Gerber. She was growing up too fast—mad about boys and a magnet for them. Lottie was also concerned but recognised in her daughter some of her own teenage behaviours.

During the millennium year, to console a lovesick teenager, they decided to take Angelika to Munich to experience a performance of ballet at the Munich State Opera House. The Bavarian State Ballet, morphed out of the Opera Ballet had just been founded two years before as an independent company. The highlight of this special 'Millennium' presentation was to be a performance of *The Dying Swan* by guest ballerina, Maya Plisetskaya. After the Soviet Union collapsed, Plisetskaya and her husband from St Petersburg had lived mostly in Germany.

Hans had splurged out for good seats, and the opulence of the opera house undoubtedly impressed Angelika. There was nothing quite like it in Oberstdorf.

After a lengthy millennial tribute performance by the Bavarian State Ballet, the ageing Russian ballerina gave her breathtaking rendering of the death of the swan. She interpreted the swan as elderly and stubbornly resisting the effects of ageing much like herself, but the short dance to Camille Saint-Saëns' music *Le Cygne* from *Le Carnaval des Animaux* was performed to perfection. The audience became hysterical, and Maya Plisetskaya had to dance an encore. To Hans Gerber's delight, Angelika was spellbound.

Her face lit up. "Vater, that dancer…she became a swan…It was magical."

The next day they went to a special 'Millennium' exhibition at the Neue Pinakothek Art Museum in the Kunstareal district. Mounted in the Pinakothek der Moderne gallery were some of the great paintings from the Munich collection showing aspects of the apocalypse and the thousand-year reign of Christ, associated by some with the 'Millennium'. There were also several large abstracts. One in particular seemed to catch Angelika's fancy. On the canvas, amidst bold, purple, red and brown vertical pillars set at crazy angles that looked a bit like abstract trunks of trees, there was in the centre, a thin brilliant luminous line of light. It ran about two-thirds of the way down the canvas where it opened into a little bulb-shaped cavern. There, sat a sprouting brown walnut. Angelika went close to the canvas and stared at the nut tracing the tangible energy that led from the kernel up that ray of brilliance to the frame above.

Hans was surprised that this painting had so captivated his daughter. Personally, he didn't like it much. "Do you see anything in it?" he asked Lottie.

His wife looked in her catalogue. "It's called *The Seed of the Apocalypse.* It's by Marlene Trotter."

It took Lottie a moment, then she gasped. "Hans! Marlene Trotter…I believe that was the name of my father's half-sister…I'm sure it was Trotter. She was some kind of an artist…a bit of a rebel…rather Bohemian if I remember from what my mother said. I seem to remember when I was a bit troublesome, my father used to say 'You don't want to end up like your cousin Marlene Trotter'."

Hans looked at his catalogue. "Well, this rather strange painting was definitely painted by Marlene Trotter." He chuckled. "Fame in the family…we'd better take a closer look."

They joined Angelika below the giant canvas.

"Angelika, you seem to like this," Lottie said. "You know what? I believe this was painted by your cousin…Marlene Trotter…your grandfather's half-sister. She was an artist here in Munich."

"You really think so!" Angelika squealed excitedly "I love it. That single line of light…it's so intense…so powerful."

Hans wasn't so sure. "I prefer those Pre-Raphaelites or even that Titian. At least you can understand them."

"But they don't have the power," Angelika said. "They're the past…this is the power of the future."

Hans looked up at the painting again, and smiling, he shook his head.

* * *

Angelika celebrated her fifteenth birthday two months later in May. It was a rather ordinary day at the farmhouse. Lottie had baked Angelika a cake that they had all sampled on the terrace, but for Angelika, her birthday really didn't begin until her current boyfriend at school, Max Jensen, came around to take her out for a meal at the Oberstdorf Chinese restaurant. Max was almost seventeen and two classes her senior, but his family lived on the same road out of town that led to the Gerber farm and the two of them sometimes walked home together.

The birthday evening started out innocently enough, but Angelika was a terrible flirt. She teased Max unmercifully in the restaurant, playing 'footsie' with him under the table and pressing her toes into the youth's crotch. Then, when the Chinese fortune cookies came around, she read hers out to Max looking at him intensely. "Your love life is about to reach new heights of passion."

Max looked a little embarrassed. "Mine just says, 'Friendship is a precious gift'." He stuffed the little strip of paper into his pocket. The waiter brought Max the bill that he gallantly paid, and the two of them left the restaurant.

"My parents are out late tonight," Max said. "Come to our house. We have wine. Let's celebrate your birthday."

Angelika held him and they kissed before walking back to the Jensen home—one of the newer houses, built on the edge of the town, around which trees and shrubs had not yet matured.

Max took a bottle of wine from his father's rack in the kitchen. He poured out two glasses. Soon, they were on their second glass and kissing passionately. Max had opened her blouse and Angelika felt his hands reach for her breasts. Her stomach churned with excitement. *This could be the real thing,* she thought as her hand reached for his trousers. She could feel that he was aroused, actually rather large. Max put a hand up her skirt. She savoured the tingling moment before releasing him. Max took her hand and led her into the lounge. Instinctively, she lay back on the sofa and pulled down her knickers. Max pulled down his trousers. Angelika's eyes fixed upon the bulge in his underpants. And then, there it was. He straddled her and her lips enfolded around his flesh. She was practised in 'blow-jobs', but she wanted more. First, it was his fingers, but then it was the real thing. It hurt a little, he was so big, but soon she found a rhythm. It was the greatest feeling of ecstasy that she had ever known—frenzied excitement and then warmth, and Max withdrew and kissed her on her forehead.

A blissful silence fell over them. *We've done it…we've really done it!* she realised.

They got dressed in an awkward silence, kissed each other almost by rote, washed the wine glasses and put the bottle in the rubbish bin. Hand in hand, Max walked her home in the dusk as the moon was rising. All he said when they got there was, "You're beautiful," and he kissed her on her forehead. He turned and walked away.

Max passed her at the school lockers the next day. He smiled, but he didn't speak.

Three weeks later, Angelika expected her period, but the bleeding never came or what did come was almost imperceptible. Her mother didn't seem too concerned. "You're still young, sweetheart, that sometimes happens. It will settle down," she said. But it didn't, and Angelika felt funny, a little lightheaded, and she knew possibly why, and she became fearful.

The next month she was certain and terrified.

Max occasionally came around and actually helped her father on the farm. She didn't know whether to say anything to him or not. Then her mother found her crying.

"What is it, dear?" Lottie said. "There's something wrong…tell me…I just want to help you."

"I don't know; Mutter…I might be pregnant."

Her mother's draw dropped. "What!"

"I still don't have my period, Mutter. Sometimes, I feel faint and sick."

Lottie knew her daughter was rather flirtatious—older than her years—but surely not pregnant. "How could you be?" she asked.

"It's possible, Mutter," she said, throwing her arms around her mother and looking up at her through terrified tears.

"How? Who?" Her mother shouted as she pushed her daughter away.

"A boy at school."

"Someone we know?"

Angelika nodded.

"Oh my God! Who?"

"It wasn't his fault, Mutter. We did it…we just did it." She put her arms around her mother again and looked up at her. "I wanted to."

"Are you still seeing this boy?" Lottie said sympathetically.

"No…not really. I mean…I see him sometimes…but we haven't gone out together since…We haven't done it again."

They both heard a tractor drive into the yard. Then, they heard Hans and Max talking outside. "Let's go upstairs," her mother said.

They heard Hans and Max come in for a beer.

Lottie sat on her daughter's bed with Angelika. "We must get an appointment with Dr Kloster…just to make sure that this is all true," she said. "I'll come with you. We don't have to say anything to your father yet. Now, you lie down and get some rest. I'll make the appointment."

Dr Kloster confirmed the pregnancy. He said he could arrange an abortion.

"How long have we got?" Lottie asked.

"Oh, we still have a week or two," the doctor confirmed.

"Now, we have to tell your father," Lottie said as they drove from the clinic. "Then, we can all decide what to do."

Angelika felt scared and hid herself away in her bedroom. She was afraid of what her father might do to Max, and something also told her that she actually wanted to have her baby. She had a fanciful dream that she and Max could get married. Through her open door, she could hear her parents downstairs.

"Who is this boy?" Hans shouted.

"One of her school friends…I don't know myself yet. Look…we've got to be reasonable about this, Hans. She's scared…we've got to keep calm."

"Why didn't you tell me straight away?" Hans said as he went to the kitchen. He seemed calmer when he came back. "All right, what do you propose we do?"

Angelika plucked up the courage and came downstairs to join them.

"What's this I hear…you're pregnant?" Hans said waving a bottle of beer.

"Yes, Vater…I think so," she said moving close to her mother.

"So who is this boy?" her father shouted.

"A friend."

"So, you fuck all your friends!"

"No, Vater! Only him…and only that one time."

"So, what happened…his condom broke?"

Angelika didn't answer.

"Don't tell me he had sex with you without a condom?"

"Yes…it just happened. We did it, Vater. I didn't know we were going to do it. He probably didn't know either."

"So, where did he do this to you…at school…where?"

"At his house…He took me to his house before he brought me home."

"So…he lives nearby?"

"Not far away…and he's someone you rather like." And then she started to cry.

"You'll have to tell us, Angelika," her father said "This could be a police matter. How old is this boy?"

Lottie interrupted Hans. "Look, let's all just sit down and talk about this. Nobody intended this to happen. It's just unfortunate."

"All right…what do you suggest we do?" Hans finally said before swigging his beer.

Angelika looked at her father. "It was…now promise not to say anything…it was Max Jensen."

"Max! He's two years older than you!" Hans shouted.

"Well, so what…" Angelika pleaded. "We've been friends at school for quite a long time."

"The boy who took you out to the Chinese restaurant?" Lottie said. "Was that when this happened?"

"Yes…Mutter…Vater…we love each other. I want to have this baby. Perhaps I can marry Max."

"We'll see about that," Hans muttered. "You're too young to know anything about love, and you're too young to get married. We'll talk with him tomorrow. He's coming back here to stack up the bales." He took another swig of his beer and there was a pregnant silence. Then he opened his arms to his daughter. "I actually do like him…we will find a solution to this mess."

Angelika felt relieved, and Lottie assured her when they were alone again that everything was going to be all right.

Dr Kloster confirmed that there was no obvious reason why Angelika could not handle her pregnancy, and it was agreed that Angelika would leave the Oberstdorf Middelschule. No charges were pressed, and profuse apologies were forthcoming from Max's parents. Max continued on at school to finish his final year, while Angelika went full-term on her pregnancy. On 14 February 2001, her son Carl Valentine was delivered at the Oberstdorf hospital with no complications. The father was recorded as Maximilian Jensen, and it was agreed that on Angelika reaching her eighteenth birthday, they would be allowed to marry. Meanwhile, Lottie ensured that Dr Kloster prescribed appropriate birth control for her daughter. When Max left the Middelschule, Hans employed him on the farm. From time to time, the young man was allowed to stay over with his fiancé and their baby son.

* * *

By the late 1990s, Chancellor Helmut Kohl's popularity had dropped amid rising unemployment. He was defeated by a large margin in the 1998 federal elections by the Minister-President of Lower Saxony—Gerhard Schröder. Kohl had elevated a little-known female politician to federal government—Angela Merkel. In the millennium year, she became the leader of the Christian Democrat Party. After a year or two of difficult levelling up between the former West and East regions of Germany, things had started to progress in a prosperous direction. Germany was becoming the powerhouse of the European Union.

In Berchtesgadenland, Martin and Sabrina Husselman were deeply moved, like much of the world, when on 11 September 2001, they watched on TV horrendous scenes from New York, USA. The Twin Towers, the tallest skyscrapers in the city, were felled by two aircraft that flew into the buildings causing them to collapse. Thousands must have died in the tragedy, and it was revealed that the planes were hijacked by Arab terrorists. A third plane dove into the Pentagon and a fourth that they thought was heading for the White House, crashed in a field in Pennsylvania.

"Palestinians!" was Sabrina's first reaction. "Something must be done about these dreadful Palestinians. This is just because America supports Israel. When is it ever going to stop?"

A wealthy Arab, Osama Bin Laden, claimed responsibility from a group called 'El Qaida'. His henchmen seemed to be Saudi Arabians, but it was apparent that Osama Bin Laden was operating from the extreme Taliban nation of Afghanistan. An irate President George W Bush of the United States was quick to react with his revenge, seeking a 'coalition of the willing' in a 'war on terrorism' to destroy the Taliban and root out Bin Laden. The British Prime Minister Tony Blair was the first to respond and tried his best to get the European Union on board, but only with lukewarm success.

"It's none of our business," Martin Husselman expressed to Sabrina as they saw the helpless Afghans bombed to hell by the Americans. "They've gone after the wrong country, anyway. Shouldn't they be attacking the Saudis? Oh, they won't do that will they…because of American interests…Saudi oil."

Sabrina was less critical of America but agreed that this was not Germany's business, and she rather admired Chancellor Schröder for keeping them out of the fray, despite appeals from Bush for more NATO support. She was even surer, when after seeing the Afghans bombed to smithereens without the Americans even finding Bin Laden; Bush turned his wrath on Iraq and tried to bring the world in with him. In Sabrina's opinion, that 'stupid' British prime minister, Tony Blair, went along with it, but again Schröder paid little attention to NATO pleas.

Deep divisions were opened, however, between Islamic Shia and Sunni factions and it seemed like an Armageddon-like war might rise up between the two. Sabrina feared for Israel.

In the European Union, however, the Helmut Schmidt dream of federation took another leap forward. On 1 January 2002, euro coins were finally introduced in most of the member states. A notable exception was Great Britain which wanted to remain trading in sterling. The day of the changeover went remarkably well elsewhere, however, and ancient currencies disappeared. With freedom of movement, a single market and for most, the one currency, Europe was becoming a federation of friendly states.

* * *

Despite some reservations from his own family, who were not too happy with the way their son had cosied up to the Gerbers, Max was proving to be a good father to his baby son.

Lottie Gerber looked at her husband as they lay in bed late on a Sunday morning. "They're going to be all right," she said as she cuddled up to Hans. "It's funny really, isn't it…Max working for us and all that…"

"Why?" Hans asked.

"It's almost biblical. You know, that story of Jacob working a few years for his father-in-law-to-be before they could get married."

"Oh…that's just an old Jewish story. It's not like that at all. The boy works well and I pay him well. Don't put a guilt trip on me. I'm not a Jew."

"Well, I wasn't. I just thought it was rather funny…but wasn't your mother a Jew?"

"No…she was a Lutheran…a Swiss Lutheran. It was my great-aunt Francine who was a Jew."

"Oh, I'm just teasing you, Hans. We'd better get up now." They could hear young Carl in Angelika's bedroom. "My goodness, he'll be running around soon."

On midsummer's day in 2003, Maximilian Jensen and Angelika Gerber were quietly married in Oberstdorf's Lutheran church. There were just the Gerbers, the Jensens and a few friends. Not long after, however, Max announced a bombshell decision. He would now go to work for his father at their Oberstdorf garage and car dealership. He said that he'd still help out weekends for the Gerbers if necessary. Max and Angelika then rented a small apartment in town. Their real married life now began.

* * *

From Berchtesgaden, Martin and Sabrina Husselman and their teenage son Wilhelm took a summer holiday in the Alps, returning to the place that had first brought them together—Schloss Elmau. They took long walks in the mountains and danced in the concert hall, something that they had not done for a long time.

"Once you know how to waltz you never forget," Martin said as he performed almost as effectively as all those years ago.

Like his father before him, Wilhelm also found a young Helferin to teach him the basics.

Martin and Sabrina watched their son, now seventeen, trying to look as mature with the Fraulein as they fumbled their way around the dance floor.

The stuffy Tanzmeister was no longer lording over all, but Bernhard Mueller was still hosting the guests. He had attracted many to the Schloss for deep and interesting seminars often centred on Jewish affairs. Sabrina observed the brochures of some of the amazing topics that had been discussed in 2003, the most recent having been 'Rebuilding the West in the Greater Middle East' and 'West German Historians and the Holocaust'.

It's a shame we couldn't have been here for these, she thought. *I'll bet they were interesting.*

Revisiting Elmau had been a real tonic for both Martin and Sabrina, and the summer days of late July and early August had been warm and sunny. They went to bed fairly early the night of 6 August in order to pack so that they could leave right after breakfast the next morning for the drive back to Berchtesgaden.

Sabrina awoke in the early hours to the sound of an alarm. She rubbed her eyes. It sounded like a fire alarm. *Surely not,* she thought. Everything seemed normal, but the alarm continued. She opened their bedroom door. The alarm was much louder in the passageway and there was a smoky smell, although she couldn't see smoke.

"What the hell's that?" Martin shouted from the bed.

"Get up, Martin! I think this is real. We need to get out…it's the fire alarm…I'm going over to Wilhelm's room."

Wilhelm had also been awakened by the alarm. He was already half-dressed. "Is it the fire alarm, Mutter…just like at school?"

"Yes, now come with me."

Other people were now out in the wide hallway, slightly bewildered, but the word was out that this was the real thing and the acrid smell was increasing. Now, there were wisps of smoke curling along the ceiling, but the lights were on and there was no real panic.

Martin had pulled on his socks and trousers and the shirt he had worn earlier. Sabrina pulled her dressing gown from the bathroom and hastily put on her sneakers. "Right! Let's go," she said and they followed the others down the hall to the stairs. Some people were beginning to cough as the smoke increased, and reality truly dawned when the sound of the first fire engine clanged its way in from the village of Krun.

The stairs got more crowded as people converged on them from all four sides of the castle. In the lobby, they were joined by others who had escaped the upper floors from the staircase on the far side of the building, bringing them down past the entrance to the concert hall and the Trinkstuberl. The night porter and his staff were busy directing the guests out onto the lawns. Fortunately, even this high up in the Alps, after such a run of weather the night air wasn't that cold. They could now see the fire. Orange glowed from the roof storeys spreading out from the corner opposite from the tower. Thick black and grey smoke now billowed up from the roof.

"It looks like it was all above us," Martin said.

The sound of fire-engine sirens echoed in the valley and the Garmisch fire-fighters arrived with several units. The staff, many now dressed just like the guests in whatever they could put on, ushered everyone back further from the building so that the fire engines could take position. The fire exploded in the roof and burst out in a massive orange ball. It raged fiercely as the fire-fighters extended their ladders and started to shoot their hoses into the blaze.

Wilhelm was looking up, seemingly mesmerised by it all when the young Helferin whom he had befriended in the concert hall found him. She was probably two or three years older than their boy, but she just threw herself into Wilhelm's arms, her dressing robe open to her nightie and no shoes on her feet. She was crying; she was scared.

Sparks now shot up into the air as roof timbers crashed and the fire spread both up and down from the corner not far from the Husselmans' bedrooms.

The people were safe out on the lawn, but the murmurs revealed their instinctive feelings of personal loss as they realised that there was obviously no chance of going back in and retrieving their things. "No sprinkler system," someone noted. Elmau, their holiday resort, was now truly on fire. The trees around glowed with the reflection of the blaze. The stars, one of the beautiful features of the Elmau night sky, disappeared in the brightness.

A first-aid station was set up on the lawn. There were some with respiratory problems, others with knocks and bruises, but by and large no serious injuries. Many from the upper storeys had to be rescued from their windows in the steep roof as the fire-fighters gallantly manoeuvred their ladders up to them. The fire rapidly started to spread its arms around the building as it reached the lower levels, but the worst was still in the roof storeys where almost the entire top two floors were ablaze, mostly staff rooms.

Lives will be lost, Sabrina thought. She saw the young Helferin still in Wilhelm's arms, shivering with shock. "What's your name, sweetie?"

"Lena," the Fraulein said through her tears. She shielded her eyes as she looked up at the burning building. "My room," she sobbed, "it's gone."

Someone came around and took all their names.

The fire-fighters valiantly fought on. It looked like they had saved the tower and possibly the concert hall, but by dawn, most of the building was a shell.

The rumour was that nobody had died and everyone was accounted for. In the daylight, Lena joined her fellow helferinnen with the other staff, and at the Mueller House, Bernhard and Siglinda started to hand out clothing, whatever they had, to those who were without. The guests were then fed at the Mueller House before making their diverse ways home.

On the Husselmans' return home that night, a film of the fire was shown on the German TV news.

'In the early hours a fire broke out at the Bavarian resort, Schloss Elmau,' the commentator reported. *'It is thought it was caused by a faulty electric blanket belonging to the former manager, Ducci Mesirca. The fire destroyed nearly the entire top floor of the main building but without any serious casualties. Ten people, including two fire-fighters were injured.'*

Martin and Sabrina were glad to be home and were able to reassure Martin's parents that they were fine and had all three survived without a scratch. The next day they visited them in Schönau, and Wilhelm was delighted to be reunited with Leo. For Wilhelm, even at seventeen, it had all been a rather harrowing experience. Wilhelm threw his arms around the huge dog. "We could have died, Leo," he said, "we really could have died."

Following the 2005 federal election, which Gerhard Schröder's party lost, and after three weeks of negotiations, Schröder stood down as chancellor in favour of Angela Merkel of the rival Christian Democratic Union.

* * *

Schloss Elmau was rapidly rebuilt under the guidance of the Mueller family, now headed by Bernhard's son, Dietmar. He was determined to keep the Mueller tradition, creating a luxury spa and cultural hideaway with Jewish interests. The new Schloss Elmau was inaugurated in June 2007 with a Schloss Elmau Symposium on 'Islam through Jewish Eyes, Judaism through Muslim Eyes'.

Sabrina Husselman noted the topic with interest in Munich's *Süddeutsche Zeitung*. The Middle East was still very uncertain after the unpopular, and in her eyes irresponsible, American invasion of Iraq. But it wasn't just the Palestinian question with Israel anymore; it seriously looked as if the two factions of Islam manifest in Iraq would become embroiled in their own fight for Middle Eastern supremacy—Shia versus Sunni. By overthrowing the secular even if evil, Saddam Hussein, the Americans had opened a hornet's nest. She handed Martin the newspaper.

Seated in the parlour with Leo at his feet, Martin browsed through the paper. He had different things on his mind as he leafed through the pages. His father was relying more and more on Martin and Wilhelm for help at the Husselman property. Martin had given up working at the nursery and tried to revive the ailing Schönau farm. After a series of weak calves, Martin felt that they needed a new bloodline to enhance their herd. Good hinterwälder bulls were hard to come by, but he saw in the Munich paper an advertisement for the services of a Hinterwälder in Oberstdorf.

"A certain Hans Gerber in Oberstdorf is advertising a hinterwälder bull," he called out to Sabrina, "perhaps we should investigate it. That would bring in a fresh bloodline."

Sabrina came in from the kitchen with cake and tea.

"Gosh, they might be from my family," she said. "My Gerber cousin moved to Oberstdorf and married a girl from there."

Martin still had his head buried in the paper. "This Hans and Lottie Gerber might have the perfect solution to Father's problem."

Leo raised his huge head and sniffed the air.

"Poor old Leo," Martin said putting the paper down. "He's really showing his age now, isn't he? His back legs have all but given up."

"He's nearly twelve," Sabrina said. "For a dog of his size, that's about it."

"So…we should spoil him rotten," Martin said as he proffered the dog much of his cake. A single swipe of the tongue and the cake was gone. Martin ruffled Leo's head.

Herr Husselman, Martin's elderly father, wasn't so sure about his son's suggestion regarding the bull. "Oberstdorf!" he grumbled, "Isn't that in Baden-Württemberg?"

"Not quite," Martin assured him, "but close…Swabia on the western borders of Upper Bavaria…But it might be the very thing we need…a new bloodline. I could take Wilhelm with me and we could have a look. Maybe the Gerbers will be able to help us out. If we don't, we may have to give up the Hinterwälders."

"All right, call them," Herr Husselman said. "Set something up. We're losing too many calves."

When Martin contacted the Gerbers, Hans Gerber confirmed that Sabrina Finkelstein Husselman was the cousin whom he had never met.

Martin and Wilhelm set off for Oberstdorf a few days later.

When they got there, they stayed at the Hotel Alpenhof on the west side of the town where it was easy to park the trailer, and they set out the next morning for the Gerber farm. Hans and Lottie met them, inviting them in for cake and coffee.

"Wow…I can't believe you're the same Husselman," Hans Gerber said, "married to my cousin Sabrina Finkelstein Drucker."

"That's right…and this is our son Wilhelm?"

Wilhelm and Hans shook hands.

"What a shame you didn't bring your mother with you," Hans said. "We've all lost touch."

"It's our dog," Martin chipped in. "He's very old and we can't really leave him anymore. Sabrina's taking care of him."

"What breed?"

"A Leonberger."

"Oh…a really big dog."

"Yes, unfortunately, they don't live very long. His back legs…they've just about given up."

"My daughter and son-in-law are going to join us later for lunch," Hans said. "They have a little boy of their own. How time flies!"

Pleasantries exchanged, they went out into the barn to check out the bull.

"He'd give you a year or two," Hans said. "We had a surplus of bull calves three years ago. He was one of them. We kept him as a bull but the bloodline's a bit too close for us. He might be good for you. There won't have been too much of his blood in Berchtesgadenland…Could be good for cross-breeding, too."

Martin walked around the handsome beast. He looked good. "What are you asking?"

Hans had his dour Swiss look. "Five thousand euros…but for you, keeping him in the family so to speak…" he scratched his head, "let's say four thousand five hundred."

The Husselmans walked around the beast again.

"Want to see him out on the meadow?" Hans asked.

"Yes, let's see him walk," Martin agreed.

Hans paraded the bull.

"I think your grandfather would be pleased with him," Martin said to Wilhelm. "I can see Gramp's miserable face lighting up when he sees this one."

"What's his name?" Martin asked Lottie.

"We call him Nebel…after the Nebelhorn."

Martin smiled. "Sounds like a good name to me. All right we'll take him." He spat into the palm of his hand, rubbed his hands together and then extended his right hand to Hans. They shook on it, and Nebel became the new hope for the Husselman herd of Hinterwälders after Martin wrote the cheque.

Max and Angelika Jensen arrived finding them all enjoying a bottle of wine. They both looked like newlyweds, but apparently, their son, Carl, wasn't with them because he was in school.

Angelika was what Wilhelm would have called 'sexy' but his father thought her to be a bit of 'a brazen hussy'. She seemed to be openly flirting with his son, flashing her eyes at him, but her husband Max didn't seem to mind much. *A grease monkey, they say,* Martin observed. *Works for his father's garage.* Hans and Lottie, however, felt he could relate better to them.

Lunch was simple—just pâté and salad and Martin forewent further wine. It was going to be a long drive home with valuable livestock on board. He hoped Wilhelm didn't drink too much if encouraged by Angelika, as he might need him to drive part of the way.

Right after lunch, they all helped load Nebel into the trailer. Angelika and Max then left saying they had to collect their son, Carl, from his Kindergarten.

Martin looked at his watch. "We'd better get going now, too, if we're to get back to Berchtesgaden tonight. It takes several hours, but we should make it by ten."

Hans shook hands one more time. "Send my regards to my cousin Sabrina. Perhaps one day we will all meet."

Carefully, Martin drove the trailer out of the Gerber farm and they were on their way. They could hear Nebel bellowing in the trailer before the bull settled down to the rhythm of the road.

* * *

Old Herr Husselman was agreeably impressed when he saw Nebel, and it wasn't long before the bull was introduced to the Husselman herd. That wasn't, however, the only love blossoming in the Husselman meadows in the spring of 2007. Wilhelm met Bernadette.

Bernadette was a young widow left with a five-year-old daughter, Brigitta. Brigitta's father was killed in a car accident during icy road conditions when Brigitta was just a baby. His car had slithered off the road when he was driving back from Traunstein to Berchtesgaden and it had broken the barrier between the road and the river. Unable to get out of his car he was found drowned in the vehicle as it lay upside down in the torrent.

Bernadette worked as a nurse at the Berchtesgaden Hospital. She was assigned to take care of Wilhelm's grandmother, Frau Husselman, when she was hospitalised after a coronary attack. It all happened shortly after the purchase of the bull. Despite 'Intensive Care', the old lady passed away with Martin and Wilhelm at her bedside when her heart just gave up the struggle. Bernadette was there with them.

Wilhelm bought a box of chocolates to give to the nurse, and they met in the hospital café.

"This isn't very much, but I just wanted to give you something for taking care of my gran," he said over coffee. "I know how cantankerous she could be. It's funny actually, she was always that way. My mother never got along with her."

"I probably saw the better side of her," Bernadette said. "I mean, she didn't say much. She was too weak and sedated, but she occasionally smiled and squeezed my hand. Hopefully, I helped her go to heaven."

"Well, I just wanted to thank you."

Bernadette looked straight into Wilhelm's eyes. "She's in a better place now."

Wilhelm reached for her hand. "Would you let me buy you dinner sometime? I'd like to thank you properly."

And so it was that after the funeral, a week later, Bernadette and Wilhelm had dinner together at Acropolis—a Greek restaurant near the Hotel Wittelsbach—where he learned her story, and Bernadette shared a photo of her little girl.

What started in the Greek restaurant, rapidly developed into a spring romance. Sabrina thought Bernadette was 'a sweet girl', and Bernadette's little girl Brigitta thought Leo was 'a super dog' as the animal always let her pet him.

In September, Bernadette and Wilhelm were married in a quiet ceremony at Maria Gern, and Brigitta was the flower girl. Wilhelm adopted Brigitta, and two years later Brigitta had a baby half-sister whom they named Ingrid.

Not long after the marriage of Wilhelm and Bernadette, Leo passed away. The great dog could no longer stand on his back legs and Wilhelm and Bernadette with great effort carried him into the back of their car. On their arrival at the veterinary office, the vet agreed that the kindest thing to do would be to quietly put Leo to sleep. They each lay beside him holding onto his front paws as the vet inserted the needle. It took a moment, as Leo panted, his tongue hanging out. Then his great head just crashed down, landing in Wilhelm's arms. It was over. Tears welled in Wilhelm's eyes.

"Brigitta will be devastated," Bernadette said. "She was so sure that Leo was going to get better."

"She'll get over it, though…it's part of the life cycle of us farming folk. We'll have to tell her as soon as she gets home from school."

Bernadette teared up, too. "Shall I tell her?"

"No, we'll both tell her, then maybe later we'll take her over to the Husselman farm…let her see the first of Nebel's calves. It'll soften the blow."

Following the death of Leo, the rather dark chalet depressed Bernadette. So, after Ingrid was born, Wilhelm and Bernadette moved to the Husselman farmhouse, where Martin and Sabrina had prepared a large apartment for them above the cow barn. Brigitta then threw herself into the farming life. Nebel had now sired many new Hinterwälders and the Husselman herd was revived.

In May 2013, there was much excitement in Berchtesgaden over the opening of a new luxury Hotel and Spa adjacent to the old city centre. During the first two weeks that it was open, the management allowed tours over the complex. Martin and Sabrina thought it would be nice to take them all to have a look. Bernadette was most impressed with the Terrace Restaurant on the rooftop with a small garden and magnificent Alpine views. Wilhelm promised her that he would take her there for dinner, and in early June he did so.

From the terrace, in front of them, the last rays of sun caught the Rossfeld and reflected from the high edifice of Hitler's Kehlsteinhaus—'The Eagle's Nest'. To the right, Watzmann was silhouetted against a darkening sky streaked with dusty rays from the sinking orb. Bernadette and Wilhelm sipped on Schnapps after a wonderful dinner that had been exquisitely served.

"This place will be great for the town," Wilhelm said. "And that spa and rooftop pool…it's all very classy."

"I might try their yoga and pilates classes if you let me," Bernadette said. "I think they have a special opening membership plan."

The evening had been a huge success—a special treat.

Chapter Thirteen
The Merkel Years 2005–2021

The Merkel years opened up great prosperity for Germany. This was in part due to the career that her predecessor chose on his departure from German politics in 2005. As a Rothschild banker, the former chancellor, Gerhard Schröder, set up business with the Russian Federation, working for Russian state-owned energy companies, including Nord Stream, Rosneft and Gazprom. Favourable trading terms with Schröder gave Germany cheap energy to boost its industrial output and, little by little, a supply of Russian energy to power much of the European Union.

During her tenure as chancellor, Merkel was frequently referred to as the *de facto* leader of the European Union, the most powerful woman in the world, one of the leaders of the free world.

In foreign policy, she emphasised international cooperation, both in the context of the European Union and NATO and in strengthening transatlantic economic relations. In 2008, she served as President of the European Council and played a central role in the negotiation of the Treaty of Lisbon ratified in 2009. Prominent changes in Lisbon included the move from unanimity to qualified majority voting in the Council of Ministers and a more powerful European Parliament forming a bicameral legislature alongside the Council of Ministers. The Treaty, however, also made the Union's Charter of Fundamental Rights legally binding, and for the first time gave member states the explicit right to leave the European Union, and established a procedure by which to do so.

By 2016, this became a reality when the British prime minister, David Cameron, offered his country a referendum on whether to stay in or leave the European Union. To his surprise and also to his pro-European parliament, the people of Great Britain, by a very narrow margin, voted to leave. This became most disappointing for Angela Merkel and plausibly shattered her dream of a stronger Europe.

Angela Merkel reached the pinnacle of her power in 2015, when during the German presidency of the G7 she hosted the annual summit at Schloss Elmau. When the secret was out, Martin and Sabrina Husselman, now living with Martin's elderly father at the old Schönau farmhouse, looked at each other in amazement. "Our Elmau!" they both shouted simultaneously.

Sabrina stared at the TV screen. "I can't believe that I was a Helferin there that summer so long ago. If I hadn't met you there at Elmau, I might still be in Switzerland making cheese."

They watched as the great of the world assembled at the restored luxury resort in the Bavarian Alps.

"It's remarkable," Sabrina observed, "including us, the European Union has four of the most influential economic powers in our world with Great Britain, France and Italy. No wonder they now say our chancellor is one of the most powerful people in the world. And the Russian Federation…I mean surely it won't be long before they will be part of our Union."

"Oh, surely not!" Martin said. "They're not part of the G8 anymore. They were kicked out because of their annexation of Crimea last year."

"Only temporarily…I don't really understand all the fuss about that anyway. Crimea has been Russian for centuries. Didn't you learn about the Crimean War in school?"

"Yes…but only about that British nurse…what was her name?"

"Florence Nightingale," she reminded him. "But listen to this…The American president, Barack Obama…he has a private lift at Elmau leading directly from his suite to the spa. We didn't even have a spa in my day…just a rather cold outdoor swimming pool a long walk down from the hotel." She laughed. "I don't know if we would recognise the place if we went back there."

"We wouldn't be able to afford it anyway. I'd say Elmau is now only for the 'Schicki Mickies'."

The TV news continued with a summary of the upcoming conference:

'The G7 summit will focus on the global economy as well as on key issues regarding foreign security and development policy. Additionally, the United Nations conferences to be held in 2015 as well as the post-2015 agenda will be discussed. Other key issues will include protection of the marine environment,

marine governance and resource efficiency...antibiotic resistance like Ebola in Africa and neglected and poverty-related diseases...retail and supply chain standards...and empowering self-employed women and women in vocational training. The leaders of the G7 countries will also discuss energy security, and they will continue the ongoing G7 process in regard to development policy.'

"I still think Russia should be there," Sabrina said. "Europe needs Russia to counterbalance the rising power of China."

Angela Merkel, however, stood firm in opposing the Russian annexation of Crimea in early 2014. She played a part in the Minsk Agreements, trying to stem the civil war in Ukraine in the Donetsk and Luhansk regions. The Minsk Protocol was drawn up by representatives from Ukraine, Russia and the Organisation for Security and Cooperation in Europe. It ensured an immediate ceasefire in the region and the monitoring and verification of the ceasefire by the organisation. There was also to be an immediate release of all hostages and illegally detained persons in the civil war.

Sadly, in the two weeks after the Minsk Protocol was signed, there were frequent violations of the ceasefire by both parties. Talks continued in Minsk, and a follow-up was agreed in September 2014, to ban flights by combat aircraft over the security zone, to withdraw all foreign mercenaries and to create a buffer zone between Ukrainian forces and the Russian-backed separatists. Russia and Ukraine, however, had very different interpretations of these agreements and the sporadic civil war between Ukraine and their pro-Russian separatists grumbled on.

Some sanctions were imposed on Russia after the annexation of Crimea, but the German government had to tread a fine line, still believing that Putin was more use to the European Union than if he was to be against it. Vladimir Putin's Russian intervention in the Syrian civil war in September 2015, after an official request by the Syrian government for military aid against rebel and jihadist groups, including ISIS, also took centre stage. Constructive opposition to the Russian annexation of Crimea evaporated.

The failure of American and British efforts to stabilise Libya, the now raging Syrian civil war and the rise of Isis brought with them a more pressing problem for the European Union—the increasing flood of refugees that in part was responsible for turning that populist referendum vote in Great Britain to 'Leave'.

Refugees from war-torn Libya, Syria, Iraq and Afghanistan, along with others on the bandwagon of financial security popularly called 'economic migrants', once in Europe, crossed through the continent with its 'freedom of movement' policies ending up on Britain's shores. Anti-immigration zest, as well as genuine fears of the new European sovereignty over the sovereignty of the Union's individual member states, swayed the British public.

"How stupid can they be?" Martin Husselman said as he heard the news of the British referendum result.

Bernadette looked at him thoughtfully. "I don't know, maybe they are the sensible ones. They want to protect their borders from all these Middle Eastern immigrants. Look how they're flooding our country because of our open borders."

"But it will weaken us," Martin affirmed. "We need Britain in this Union."

* * *

Sabrina Husselman died peacefully of old age at the Schönau farmhouse early in 2018.

The day before, the old lady had called her granddaughters to her bedroom after feeling a little faint. "I don't think I'm going to live much longer," she said to them. "I want you both to know something before I die. Part of our family was Jewish. While your great-grandmother was alive, I had to hide that from her. She didn't like Jews. Your grandfather, he's not like her, but it did make things a little difficult between us. My grandmother was a Jew. I suspect that she and my grandfather were murdered by Hitler."

Ingrid gasped.

Granny Sabrina continued in her matter-of-fact way, "My father and his sister went to live with Granny Finkelstein's sister and they all fled to Switzerland. I was brought up in Switzerland, but my great-aunt and uncle went on to live in Israel in the 1960s. I used to visit them there when I was a teenager." She squeezed both her granddaughters' hands. "Kiss me," she said. "Never say bad things about the Jews, my dears…Promise me. All we tried to do was survive."

"Don't die, Grandma," Ingrid said. "You're not going to die. Please, don't die."

"No…I just need to rest."

Brigitta took her sister's hand. "We must let Grandma sleep."

Ingrid wiped her eyes.

They never spoke to their grandmother again. A few days later, Sabrina Husselman was committed with a full Roman Catholic ceremony at the Stiftskirche in Berchtesgaden before being buried at the large Christian cemetery of Friedhof Schönau am Königssee looking out to the Rossfelt Massive.

* * *

Young Carl Jensen left the Oberstdorf Mittelschule at sixteen to become apprenticed as a forester. He liked the outdoor life and worked for a logging company felling in the pine forests above Sonthofen on the mountain ranges of the Sonnenköpfe and the Hörnerkette. He enjoyed climbing the tall pines and had no fear of heights. Rapidly, the exercise built up his young muscles.

His grandmother, Lottie Gerber, had told him that his great-grandfather was a climber—not of trees, but of mountains. But she also warned him of the dangers.

"My father fell off our roof clearing snow," she said. "Be careful, Carl. Your work's dangerous. My father Kurt Moeller was an experienced mountaineer and yet he was killed falling from a roof."

After working for the company for a year out of Sonthofen, Carl was told he was to be transferred to a forestry operation in southeast Bavaria, above Berchtesgaden in the Obersalzberg.

"Weren't the Moellers from Berchtesgaden?" he asked Grandma Lottie.

"Yes…they were hoteliers way back before the war. Also, in the Third Reich, your Great-Grandpa Kurt's sister worked for Hitler at his mountain retreat, but the Moellers weren't Nazis. Actually, Kurt's cousins were the opposite…almost commies."

Carl left for Berchtesgaden and the logging project at the Obersalzberg.

He soon realised that Berchtesgaden was indeed where Hitler had his mountain retreat and where his great-great-aunt Hilda had worked as some sort of a domestic. Above ground, there was little in the way of buildings left in the area other than the foundations in the forest of a theatre that the Nazis had built, by report to entertain the local population. A lot of tourists, many American, came up to the Obersalzberg to visit the 'Eagles Nest', and there were always buses parked at what they called The Documentation Centre—a museum providing information on the use of the mountainside retreat by Nazi leaders, especially Adolf Hitler, who regularly spent time in the area from1928 to 1944. Below ground, there were still extensive bunkers that you could tour.

Curious, Carl visited the centre. He was surprised to find much of what was on display showed the horrors of how the Nazis had tried to eliminate the Jews— 'the final solution'. For some reason, it moved him as he had some recollection that Grandpa Hans Gerber had a Jewish cousin, Sabrina Finkelstein Husselman.

In the spring, Carl Jensen's skills at shinning up the pines, led to him joining in the annual 'May Day' celebrations in Berchtesgaden.

* * *

May Day dawned a clear sunny day. After the more formal dancing around the maypole on the green in front of the Edelweiss Hotel, and after beers and refreshments in front of the hotel or across the green at Sophie's Restaurant, it was time for the youths to try their prowess at climbing the maypole to reach rewards hung from the rings at the top. Many of the young dirndl-dressed girls of Berchtesgaden were there to cheer on the lederhosen-clad lads. Among the girls, was seventeen-year-old Brigitta Husselman.

Several slightly inebriated attempts were made to shin up the pole, but so far, none had reached the prized rings at the top.

A good-looking youth spat on his hands and began the climb. He showed professional knowhow as with the ease of a monkey he pulled and grasped his way up. The cheers and jeers of the Fräuleins hushed as in awe the spectators looked upwards. Then there was a resounding round of applause as the youth reached the highest token, holding it up and waving it in the air.

"Who's that?" Brigitta asked her friend Annaliese. "That was amazing!"

Annaliese giggled. "Never seen him before, but he's certainly got muscles."

The young man shinned down the pole with his trophy as easily as he had ascended it. Girls ran out from Sophie's, offering him tall glasses of beer. He quaffed a glass or two to further applause.

"Let's go over," Brigitta said. "I'd like to meet him!"

"No need," Annaliese said, "I think he's coming over here." As the young man approached, Annaliese shouted out, "Muscle man!"

The young climber turned towards them. Their beckoning smiles must have attracted him as he came on over.

"Can we buy you a beer?" Brigitta said as much with her eyes as with her voice.

"No, no…let me buy beers for the two of you." He smiled and extended his hand. "My name's Carl." He ordered three beers from the Edelweiss waitress.

Brigitta blushed, "I'm Brigitta and this is my friend Annaliese. Where are you from? I haven't seen you around here before."

"Oberstdorf, if I ever go back there. I really like it here, though."

"So, where's Oberstdorf?"

"Near the Austrian and Swiss border in the west…almost in Baden-Württemberg," Carl answered.

"Oh…but you think you might stay here?"

He smiled and his eyes sparkled in the ruddy complexion of his face. "Why…would you like me to?"

Brigitta and Annaliese fell into laughter. "I think you should stay in Berchtesgaden," Annaliese said, but Brigitta could see that Carl's eyes were fixed on her.

Brigitta explained to Carl that her family farmed in the Schönau Valley where they had a herd of hinterwälder cattle.

"So do mine!" Carl exclaimed excitedly. "That's really strange…There are not so many herds of them in Bavaria now."

Eventually, Brigitta's family showed up as the May Day celebrations drew to a close. She introduced her parents to Carl—'the winner of the highest token today'. Bernadette invited the young man to lunch at the Schönau farmhouse the next Saturday.

Thus began a summer romance between the fresh-faced teenager, Brigitta Husselman, and the handsome young forester, Carl Jensen.

* * *

Brigitta's father leaned back in his chair at the Schönau farmstead, a finger curled around his nose. "Carl Jensen…from Oberstdorf," he said. "I wonder if he is from the same family from whom we bought Nebel? There can't be too many other hinterwälder herds in Oberstdorf."

"I think their little boy *was* named Carl," Wilhelm answered, "but I can't be sure. We never met Angelika's boy."

Wilhelm Husselman soon realised, when he heard that Carl's father was Max Jensen, that it was from Carl's family that they had bought the bull.

"Nebel's very old now, just out to pasture," Martin Husselman explained when Carl came for Saturday lunch. "We'll show him to you later. He saved our herd…he really did. New blood…it was just what we needed."

Brigitta's eyes lit up. "My cow, Arabella…she was one of his," she said.

Ingrid kicked her under the table.

After lunch, they all went out to the meadows where the grass was now growing fast before the May cutting. The old bull was happily grazing. "That's him," Wilhelm said.

* * *

Carl hadn't taken that much interest in the Oberstdorf farm which was partly why he had become apprenticed to the Sonthofen foresters, but it touched him that this old bull from his family's farm had been able to save Brigitta's family herd. "It's hard to believe," he said with pride, "that he was one of ours."

Carl was more than taken with Brigitta, and obviously, with the approval of her parents, it wasn't long before he invited her out for dinner at a funny little Italian restaurant close to the ducal palace in Berchtesgaden. It was decorated to look rather like a narrow Neapolitan street with laundry hanging out crisscrossed across the ceiling. They served the best carpaccio and Brigitta learned that Carl loved carpaccio, although, in reality, it seemed that Brigitta was more of a 'Schweinebraten mit Knödel' kind of a girl.

Carl joined her family for the haymaking, and Carl and Brigitta often also went foraging for Alpine berries—little wild strawberries that Bernadette made into jam. Finally, in the hope that the lakes would have warmed up a bit, they went swimming on a moonlit night at the Hintersee. It was cold—very cold, but it was so romantic. Little grey clouds scurried across the full moon above them, reflecting in the water as they splashed around. Carl was a strong swimmer, but he never strayed too far from Brigitta in her white bikini that looked luminous in the pale moonlight. He saw that she was shivering with the cold, and his warm arms embraced her and they kissed. It wasn't the first time that they had kissed, but this time it was different, it was passionate, it was serious. Brigitta hung her arms around his neck as he warmed her chilled body.

Things moved fast after that, and Ingrid teased her big sister unmercifully. They still shared a bedroom in the farmhouse.

"So when are you going to marry him?" Ingrid asked. "When you do, I hope I'll be a bridesmaid."

They threw pillows at each other.

"Do you have your 'Handy' on charge tonight; I don't want you to have to share mine?" Brigitta said.

"Why? Are you afraid I will see your sexy photos of Carl?"

Brigitta sighed. "Shut up!" she said and she turned off their bedside lamp.

It was inevitable that one Sunday afternoon, when Carl came around to take Brigitta for a walk in the Obersalzberg forest, they later ended up in bed together. Carl had a little apartment close to the river near the salt mines. They could hear the sound of the running water as they caressed each other.

She loved his embrace, but she was not ready to give herself to him. "Are you Catholic?" she suddenly asked. "We've never talked about that, have we?"

"I'm nothing, really," Carl said. "I suppose my background was Lutheran. My parents were married in a Lutheran church, but we were never active churchgoers…just weddings and funerals if you know what I mean."

"Our mother is very religious," Brigitta said. "She makes us go to mass every week. Ingrid and I even take part…we carry the incense for the priest."

Carl chuckled as he looked at Brigitta. "I might be Jewish," he said. "I had relatives that went to Israel, and others, who might have been murdered in the Third Reich. I was very moved when I was up at The Documentation Centre."

Brigitta expressed surprise. "Don't mention that to Grandpa. His mother…my great-grandmother…she was apparently a bit of a bigot and often said bad things about Jews."

"Was she a Nazi?"

"I don't think so…although she was probably alive in those days."

"Well, I don't really know what I believe," Carl repeated, "nothing really. I think if anything, I just believe in the power of nature. I see the sap oozing from the pines and smell it in the woods. For me, that is the power of God…eternal regeneration."

"So you don't believe in Jesus and the Virgin Mary?"

"I believe that they were real people who probably did a lot of good. Like I said…I'm not very religious."

They dropped the subject and lay in silence together just listening to the sound of the water.

Finally, Brigitta turned to Carl. "So…was your family Jewish?"

He smiled, putting his finger and thumb together. "Just a little bit, maybe."

Carl embraced her. They enveloped each other in the warmth of love, secrets shared.

* * *

In the autumn, The Husselmans were busy preparing for the annual bringing back of the cows from the Königssee alms. Ingrid was excited as this year she was going to be able to join those camping out at the mountain hut before bringing them down to the lake for transportation. Bernadette was busy repairing the floral headdresses that would crown the hinterwälder cows. Annaliese's family also needed an extra cowherd, and Brigitta recommended that Carl could probably help them out. "After all, he was brought up on a farm even if it's not his first choice. He'll be up to it," she assured Annaliese's mother.

The night up on the alm was always exciting. Once they had gathered their cows, they made themselves snug in the old stone hut, heating up a thick soup with dumplings that Bernadette had prepared for them. Ingrid had a new Dirndl that she was wearing for the first time and their father was in his full Lederhosen. In recent years, the annual event had become a tourist spectacle and they wanted to give the visitors what they expected to see—an old Bavarian Alpine tradition.

In the morning, they loaded the cattle onto the large pontoon boat that would take them down the length of Königssee, past the St Bartholomew Monastery with its red onion domes and on to where the moos from the cows echoed off the steep rockface. Ahead of them would be Christlieger Island. Finally, they would come to the lakeside town where Bernadette would be waiting with the crowns. Brigitta's new Dirndl was slightly mud-splattered, but she proudly led Arabella onto the pontoon.

It was a chilly October morning and the lake was shrouded in autumnal mist, but as they slowly passed St Batholomew, a ray of sunlight lit up the domes. When they reached the cliffs, the shafts of sunlight increased, catching the yellow and orange foliage of the trees that clung to the crevices. To the right, they could see that sparkling waterfall where Hitler and Eva Braun had supposedly gone 'skinny-dipping'. By the time they reached Christlieger, the island was bathed in sunshine illuminating the marble statue of John of Nepomuk, patron saint against the dangers of the water. Wilhelm explained to his daughters that the statue was erected a long time ago to commemorate the rescue of four passengers involved in a boating accident on the lake.

Brigitta smiled back at Carl as they approached the slipway. Now, he was going to have to prove that he was a cowherd. There was rivalry after all between the Husselmans and Annaliese's family, and the skills of both families would be on display. Quite a crowd had gathered, and Bernadette was there, holding Arabella's crown in the Husselman colours of gold purple and white.

After all the cows were offloaded from the pontoon and crowned, the journey back through the Schönau Valley and on to Berchtesgaden began. It started as somewhat of a stampede as the cows were anxious now to get home to their winter pastures. Perhaps they could smell them in the air. They knew they were going home. Brigitta laughed when she saw Carl struggling with his beast as it ran into stands outside Frau Forster's Königssee Dirndl Shop. Annnaliese didn't look pleased; for her, today looked like it would be the Husselmans' day.

* * *

It wasn't long after the cows came home that Carl Jensen invited Brigitta to dinner at the prestigious Kempinski Hotel up near where he was working on the Obersalzberg. It was an expensive dinner, but in all fairness, the hotel was not really their sort of a place. Brigitta would have much preferred it if they had just gone to the Hocklenzer where they usually went. But as they were drinking the last of their wine after a rather filling dessert of strawberry crêpes, Carl leaned over and took her hand in his. "Would you marry me?" he said quietly.

Brigitta looked a little startled. "Gosh…Ingrid was right. She's always right. She said you would ask me to marry you."

"Well…what's your answer?"

"Oh, yes of course, but I don't know what Mutter and Vater will say. I mean, I'm only just eighteen. We may have to do the old-fashioned thing and ask them first."

Carl looked a little disappointed at her hesitancy, but then her smile reassured him. Her cheeks flushed and she was glowing. "How soon can we get married?" he said.

"Soon after Christmas? Perhaps early next year when the mountains are glistening in the snow…And you won't mind if we are married in the Roman Catholic Church…maybe at Maria Gern? Ingrid is dying to be a bridesmaid."

"Okay…let's ask your father and mother…perhaps not tonight…they might have gone to bed by the time I get you home, but I will come around tomorrow."

It was a wet, late October day. The rain dripped down from the eaves and balconies of the Husselman farmhouse. The grey clouds obscured the mountain views, and the dampness rotted the last of the geranium blooms struggling in the window boxes. Brigitta was nervous as she waited for Carl to visit. She had almost told Ingrid that she was right, but refrained, fearing that somehow her sister would blurt it out over breakfast. She really didn't know what her father and mother would think. She was only just eighteen and Carl wouldn't be twenty until Valentine's Day. It was legal, but barely. A whimsical smile crossed her face. *Maybe we'll get married on Valentine's Day,* she thought. *That would be romantic.* She heard a car drive up, but it was only the Deutsche Post.

Finally, Carl arrived. He didn't look his best, his hair bedraggled in the rain. "Can we talk?" he said to her father. Wilhelm got them beers from the kitchen.

Carl came straight out with it, "Herr Husselman, I would like to marry your daughter."

Brigitta's mother gasped, but Ingrid was all smiles. "I knew it!" the girl shouted.

Wilhelm put his beer bottle down on the table. "You're both very young," he said and he looked over at his wife.

"Brigitta…how long have you kept this from us?" Bernadette asked, showing little joy.

Brigitta looked at the floor. "Only since last night, Mutter. We really love each other though. Let us get married."

"And I can be her bridesmaid!" Ingrid chirped in.

That brought a slight smile to their mother's face. "But, what do you think Father Johannes will say?"

"It's not illegal, Mutter. We are of age."

"Barely," was all Frau Husselman said. "What do you say, Wilhelm?"

Wilhelm addressed Carl. "You're right, we can't stop you, but you should think very hard about this. How soon are you planning on getting married?"

"After Christmas…sometime in the New Year."

"Valentine's Day…on Carl's twentieth birthday!" Brigitta shouted out.

"Perfect!" Ingrid echoed.

Bernadette shook her head. "It will be in the church?"

"Of course, Mutter. Maybe…at Maria Gern."

Wilhelm picked up his beer bottle again. "Well…we can't stop you and we like you, Carl. So, welcome to the family. But you had better take very good care of our Brigitta."

A broad smile filled the forester's face. He picked up his bottle and clinked it with Wilhelm's.

Brigitta came over and stood beside him and kissed her fiancé.

Ingrid applauded.

"It's a horrible day outside," Bernadette said. "If you're going to be my son-in-law, you had better stay for lunch."

In the afternoon when the rain finally let up, Carl took Brigitta into Berchtesgaden. They stopped at Remme's second-hand shop in Palace Square to see if he had any interesting rings. This 'Alladin's Cave' had treasures of every kind, from furniture and chandeliers to exotic clothing and once-treasured jewellery. There was a perfect ring with a pale blue stone—maybe a sapphire—set in an interesting Art Nouveau style. When Brigitta tried it on, it fit her finger perfectly. Remme assured her that 'it was made for her'. It wasn't expensive, but it was perfect. Carl paid Remme, and Brigitta kept the ring on her finger.

* * *

As they had planned, Carl Jensen and Brigitta Husselman were married on 14 February 2020. Carl's parents Max and Angelika came from Oberstdorf. Lottie Gerber was too old to travel now, but she sent them flowers that were arranged on a little table in front of the gilded wrought-iron screen at Maria Gern. A lot of both Brigitta's old school friends and Ingrid's current ones showed up, along with many of the Schönau farmers. Most were dressed traditionally which was befitting in the glorious neo-baroque church. Bernadette added her touch to the wedding dress that they had found at the bridal shop in Berchtesgaden. Ingrid's white satin bridesmaid's dress was simple but sophisticated, making her look very grown up. Father Johannes performed the ceremony and the organist, Frau Monika Nestle, played, along with a celebrated local flautist. Particularly moving, was their rendering of Cohen's *Halleluja.*

Afterwards, they all went over to the Hotel Maria Gern for refreshments. Across the snowy valley, the mountains glistened in the afternoon sun. Nobody was quite sure where the happy couple was going on their honeymoon, but Ingrid revealed that it was in Austria.

Carl's parents stayed at the Edelweiss, and the next day had the Husselmans over for lunch at Sophie's Restaurant across the green. They finally had a chance to really talk to each other.

"It's funny that our families have come together again," Angelika said to Wilhelm. "I am quite sure now that your mother was my aunt, Sabrina Finkelstein. We can all be traced back to Gerbers from the Lake Constance area in Switzerland. They married into the Finkelsteins who were Jewish refugees during the war. They became cheesemakers in Bishofzell. It became a bit confusing because when they escaped from Germany they were adopted by a family named Drucker."

"It does make sense," Wilhelm said, "my mother was very supportive of Israel, but she wasn't a Jew…at least she never said that she was a Jew. To be fair, I think she was afraid around my grandmother on the Husselman side. Granny Husselman was old-school…not a Nazi, but certainly not flattering when it came to comments about Jews. It was all a bit embarrassing really."

"I don't think they were practising Jews," Angelika said. "My grandmother, Abigail Gerber, was a Lutheran like all of us."

Bernadette looked a little aghast.

"Well, except for Carl," Angelika said. "I suppose he's a practising Roman Catholic now. I really don't mind what they are as long as they're happy."

"It's funny," Wilhelm said, "what we don't know is what really happened to the Finkelsteins before they left Germany."

"Probably best if we don't," Bernadette said. She picked up her wine glass. "To the bride and groom."

They all joined in.